Old Man Jasperson

and other stories

Old Man Jasperson
and other stories

Jim Bates

Bridge House

British Library Cataloguing in Publication Data
A Record of this Publication is available from the British
Library

ISBN 978-1-914199-46-2

This edition published 2023 by Bridge House Publishing
Manchester, England

Cover illustration © Thomas R. Bates

This book is dedicated to the memory of Steven Lester Carr.

Contents

Acknowledgements

Many thanks go out to Gill James and her team at Bridgehouse Publishing and Chapeltown Books.

Introduction

When I first started submitting online, two writer friends of mine, Kathy Sharp and Gail Aldwin, suggested I try CaféLit. Boy, am I ever glad I did!! My first story ever published was by Gill and her team in March 2018. I'll never forget that day. To actually see one of my stories on CaféLit was a thrill beyond belief. Little did I know how much my life would change from that day going forward. Since then, Gill has published over 60 of my stories on CaféLit. In addition, she has published two collections of stories, *Resilience* and *Short Stuff.*

Thank you so much, Gill!

Although most of the stories in this collection have not been in any anthology or collection, they are very near and dear to my heart. I'm very excited to share them with you!

Again, many thanks to Gill James and the good folks at CaféLit, Bridgehouse Publishing, and Chapeltown Books for giving me the opportunity to continue to make my dream of being an author come true and for publishing my work.

You guys are FANTASTIC!

Old Man Jasperson

Ambrose Jasperson looked at himself in the mirror, fluffed out his full beard and pronounced to his wife, Emma, "Alrighty, then. Looks like Santa Claus is all set."

He smiled at his reflection. From his natural beard, curly and white, to his cheeks rosy from a lifetime of dairy farming, to his belly jolly from a lifetime love of anything sweet (cookies in particular), he really did look like Santa Claus. The Santa suit provided by the senior living facility helped, too.

A knock at the door. "Mr. Jasperson. Mr. Jasperson, are you ready? We're waiting for you."

He adjusted the red blanket over his legs, rolled his wheel chair to the door and opened it, doffing his red Santa cap. "Ho, ho, ho. Merry Christmas," he greeted Maggie, one of Riverview's care providers.

Maggie smiled, thinking that it was nice Old Man Jasperson, as he was referred to by the staff, was in a festive mood. She'd only worked at Riverview Senior Living for a few months and didn't know him very well, only that he was quiet and kept to himself in his room at the far end of the hall. She'd also heard that he'd lived there for three years, that he'd had a tragic life, losing his four children over the years to a variety of accidents and misfortunes, and that he'd lost his wife, Emma, to cancer five years ago.

She'd also been told that every year for the past three years he'd volunteered to be Santa Claus on Christmas Eve, and that said a lot, as far as Maggie was concerned. In her mind, Old man Jasperson must have something special going for him.

She smiled. "Ready to go? They've just finished singing Christmas carols."

As attendants went, Ambrose thought Maggie was fine.

Nice. She left him pretty much to himself and that was a good thing. He knew most everyone at Riverview thought he was a bit odd and that was all right with him. If spending time by yourself working on a project and talking to your long departed wife was considered odd, well then so be it. They could get back to him when they were eighty-eight like him, and trying to live out the end of their life in a meaningful way like he was trying to do. Then maybe they'd have something to talk about.

"I'm all set. Let the festivities begin," he said cheerfully. "Ho, ho, ho…" And he rolled out into the hallway but not before waving a cheery good-bye to Emma.

A few hours later, back in his room, Ambrose had changed out of his Santa suit, wheeled his chair to his one window and was looking outside. He lived on the first floor and had an unobstructed view of the parking lot. A few days earlier, a snowstorm had blanketed the world in white and Riverview's maintenance staff had decorated the front of the building with evergreen garlands and wrapped strings of colored lights around all four of the tiny evergreen trees near the entrance. It wasn't much, but he liked how they looked, festive and cheerful. He'd always enjoyed Christmas time, no matter how challenging his and Emma's life had been. He still did. There was a warm and snug feeling associated with this time of year that he loved.

After they became too old to farm, Ambrose and Emma sold their land and dairy herd and moved into a small bungalow in nearby Redwood Falls. There they lived happily for nearly ten years until poor Emma died after a valiant year-long struggle with cancer. Soon after, Ambrose's diabetes got the better of him, confining him to a wheelchair, and he moved into Riverview. That had been three years ago.

Now it was just him. Well, he and Emma. Ambrose had

to admit, it was nice to have her with him. It made his days less lonely.

A knock on the door. Ambrose glanced at the clock. Eight-thirty. This was unexpected. He turned in his chair and asked, "Who is it?"

"It's me, Mr. Jasperson. Maggie."

"Maggie. Hi. What can I do for you?" He was still in a good mood from playing Santa. Plus, Emma was with him, sort of like Mrs. Claus. That helped.

"I wanted to thank you for playing Santa tonight," Maggie said through the door. "You did a great job. I was wondering… We have some leftover Christmas cookies from earlier. Would you like some?"

Cookies? Absolutely. "That'd be wonderful, Maggie. Thank you. Just a second, I'll get the door." He turned to Emma and whispered, beaming, "Christmas cookies!" And watched as she smiled back at him, knowing how much he loved his sweets.

Ambrose wheeled to the door and opened it. As Maggie came in and set the plate of cookies down, she noticed something on the little bedside nightstand. Curious, she pointed. "What have you got there?"

"Oh, that," Ambrose said, suddenly embarrassed and turning red. "It's nothing."

Maggie peered closely. It was a photo album, and it looked like it was stuffed full of old family photographs. "I don't want to pry, but they look interesting."

"You can look at them if you want. Really, though, they're just old pictures." He paused for a moment, fighting off a sudden, encroaching melancholy. After a moment he said, his voice almost a whisper, "My… My wife took them. Emma."

"Oh, my. I love looking at old photographs," Maggie said, enthusiastically, meaning it. It was one of the reasons she liked working at Riverview. She enjoyed being around old folks and hearing the stories they had to tell.

Maggie's enthusiasm perked up Ambrose's' mood considerably. "Well, if that's the case you might like these." He grinned an impish grin, and wheeled next to his bed where he reached under and pulled out not one, or two, but three flat storage containers. "I've got photographs in all of them." He watched Maggie's eyes go wide. "Emma took pictures our whole married life. Do you want to have a look? I'm putting them in order in albums, sort of our family history."

So that's what he's doing in here, Maggie thought to herself. He's organizing his life through old photographs. That's amazing. "If you don't mind, Mr. Jasperson, I'd love to see them."

Ambrose smiled and pointed. "Pull up a chair, then. And, please, call me Ambrose."

Maggie smiled, happy to finally be the first staff person in Riverview Senior Living to start to get to know "Old Man Jasperson" better. "Okay, then. Ambrose it is."

"Great. But first, you might want to go get another plate of cookies. I've got a lot of pictures here."

Maggie, grinned, thinking that she couldn't think of a better way to spend Christmas Eve. "Good idea," she said. "I'll be right back."

After Maggie left, Ambrose selected a cookie off the plate and munched on it as he set about spreading out some of the photographs. He turned to Emma and said, "You don't mind sharing our photos, do you Em?" He pointed toward the door. "She seems nice." He listened for a moment in the silence of the room and then smiled. "So you don't mind? Good. I didn't think so."

He then happened to glance out the window and saw that snow was beginning to fall. He was quiet for a moment watching the flakes drift past the floodlights outside, carrying with them for him a lifetime of memories of past Christmases, memories that made him feel warm inside.

He turned his head as if listening and said, "What's that? Why, yes it is Em. It really is a pretty scene out there. Like being back on the farm." The room was quiet while he listened some more. Finally, he spoke. "I agree. Merry Christmas to you, too, Sweetheart. It's been one of our best Christmases ever." He paused once more, nodding his head along with what his wife was saying. "That's right, Em, I agree. Every Christmas is special, just as long as we're together."

They Say It Gets Better

The name tag worn by the guy at the guard desk read *Dan*. His job was to check the ID badges of the employees as they entered the huge office building through the revolving doors from the parking ramp. All day long during his eight-hour shift he eye-balled everyone who passed by, checking to see if the photo on the badge matched the person wearing it. He was maybe fifty years old and his hair was buzz cut so close that his scalp shone through. His eyes were steel gray and they never seemed to stop moving. He missed nothing. He had a weightlifter's build and his blue uniform strained against his hardened muscles. His gun belt was thick and black and held a Smith and Wesson that seemed too big for its holster. He also carried mace, pepper spray and hand-cuffs. He looked ready for anything.

Dan never smiled. He rarely spoke and he seemed like the kind of person you just wanted to avoid at all possible costs. So when tall, thin, haggard-looking Jeremy Larson tried to walk past without his badge and Dan stopped him, who knew what was going to happen?

"Wait a minute, there, buddy," Dan commanded. "What do you think you're doing?"

Jeremy was a young man, maybe thirty, but looked at least ten years older. He paused, confused, acting like he had no idea where he was. "Wha… wha… what?" he stammered. The question hung on the edge of his lips, barely having eked out.

"Your ID, pal. Where is it?"

Jeremy looked down at his shirt pocket where his badge was normally clipped. "Oh, geez. Sorry. I must have forgotten it"

"You can't go in, then. You know the procedure. Rules are rules."

Jeremy looked around, visibly distraught. It came to him right then that he had no idea where he was. He took in his surroundings for a moment before finally recognizing their familiarity. Oh, yeah. He was at work. The problem was, he had no idea how he got there. He must have used his car but had no recollection of driving in from where he lived in Long Lake, twenty-two miles to the west. This was not good. The inability to recall his actions suddenly frightened him. What a mess his life was. His eyes welled up. Tears formed. His briefcase slipped from his hand and thudded to the carpet as he put his head on the counter and started to cry.

What the hell? Dan was taken aback. Crap. Of all the things he was prepared for, this wasn't one of them. Criminal activity? Sure. A gun-wielding nut job? Absolutely. A burned-out, broken-down man sobbing on his guard desk? No. That just wasn't supposed to happen. This was a highly regarded office building filled with clean and polished white-collar workers, for Christ's sake. Professional people. Someone losing their composure and breaking down in tears in the middle of the crowd hurrying past the security desk? Well, that just didn't happen.

Dan took an instant to size up the situation. While he did, the steady stream of well-dressed men and women continued to rush by with only a few curious enough to take the time to glance at the scene unfolding. They, like everyone else, though, may have slowed but ultimately kept on walking, embarrassed for the weeping man. It was clear that no matter how concerned people may have been, no one wanted to do anything to help. Later on, Dan would be at a loss to explain why he did what he did. The best answer he could come up with was, "Well, there was just something about the poor guy. He seemed like he needed help and I was there, so I did what I thought was the right thing to do." Whatever the case, what happened was good for Jeremy. Maybe, even, in the long run, for Dan as well.

Dan jumped into action. He immediately called his boss. "Ed, send someone down to fill in for me. Anyone. Right now."

Then he hurried to where Jeremy had now sunk the floor. He reached down and helped the broken man to his feet, picked up his briefcase and carefully moved him to a quiet corner off to the side of the flow of human traffic, all the while his eyes never missed a face or a badge passing by. That's where he stayed until a few minutes later when another member of the security team arrived.

"Take over for me," Dan said when she showed up. "I'm going to take this guy for some coffee."

She gave him a curt nod, all business. "Got it." Then she took over and began watching badges and faces.

As they started walking, Dan figured it would be good to give the guy some time to collect himself so he didn't say anything. With each step down the hallway, though, the security guard's gruff demeanor began to change and become more compassionate. He was taking seriously the young man's breakdown and trying to figure out the best way to handle the situation. Would it be best to bide his time before he said anything? At least until he had a handle on the situation. But when would that ever be? The guy was clearly in bad shape. Maybe he should do something now. But what if he did or said the wrong thing? Then what?

Finally, after a couple of minutes of indecision, he said to himself, *To hell with it. I'll just do what I think is the best thing to do.*

He put his arm around the young man's shoulder, leaned into him and asked, simply, "Can you tell me what your name is?"

"Jeremy. Jeremy Stendahl."

"Nice to meet you, Jeremy. My name's Dan." He pointed to his badge. Jeremy looked at it.

"Yeah, sorry about that. I don't know where mine is. Must have lost it." Tears suddenly welled up in his eyes.

Dan was quick to offer reassurance. "Hey, hey, man. That's all right. Don't worry about it. The badge is no big deal. We'll get it taken care of." Relief passed across Jeremy's face and the tears disappeared. With the ice broken, they continued walking. Dan asked, "You were in pretty bad shape back there. What was the matter? Can you tell me what's going on?"

Jeremy was still shaken and finding it hard to speak. But there was something comforting about the muscular security guard walking next to him; something soothing. By the time they'd neared the end of the hall he'd calmed down enough to be able to softly articulate, "Well, this is what it is: my wife passed away a month ago. I thought I was ready to go back to work. I talked to my boss." He arbitrarily pointed up above where they were standing. "I work up on the third floor in the engineering department. Programming. Anyway, my boss Sara Schneider said I could come back if I was ready. I thought I was, but," he shrugged his thin shoulders, "I guess not." He glanced at Dan and cracked a weak, embarrassed smile, resignation written all over his face. Then more tears began forming. "I'm so sorry…"

All the while Dan walked beside Jeremy he kept his arm around the young man's shoulder. It seemed like the right thing to do; to stay close to the poor guy. All around them people hurried by, only a few giving a passing glance to the odd-looking couple slowly making their way down the crowded hallway. As they talked, Dad listened carefully to what Jeremy was saying. At the mention of the loss of his wife, his eyes softened. He slowed his steps and ducked his head close to Jeremy's ear. His voice just above a whisper he said, "Hey, man, I understand. I get it. I really do." He inhaled and then let out a long breath before going on, "I lost my wife ten years ago. It hurt back then. It still hurts now. It's still painful."

Jeremy stopped walking and wiped his eyes. He turned and said, rather formally, "Oh, man. I didn't know. I'm so sorry for your loss." Of course, he wouldn't have known. Dan hadn't told him. He hardly told anybody. The stoic guard acknowledged the comment with a quick nod but said nothing. There wasn't anything to add.

Jeremy paused for a moment. The last thing he expected was to find that they had something in common. In a way, it was rather comforting. He said, "For me, I just don't know if I can go on, if I can take it anymore." Suddenly, his body went rigid and he clutched his fists. His entire demeanor changed. He became almost frantic. He grabbed Dan by both shoulders and looked him straight in the eyes. "Tell me," he said, his voice pleading, imploring Dan to give him an answer. "Tell me. I've got to know. Does it ever get better? Does the pain every go away?"

Dan looked at Jeremy, taking his time with what he wanted to say. He felt an affinity for the young man, he really did. He wanted to give him a sense of hope. To help him and somehow boost his spirits. He wanted to say something that would relieve his pain and take away his anguish. He didn't like seeing the poor guy reduced to such despair. Finally, he said, "It does get better, Jeremy. It does. Eventually. "He saw a measure of relief appear in his eyes and was quick to add, "But I won't lie to you. It's hard. Especially those first months, like you're now finding out. But you know what? If you're lucky, you eventually learn to live with it. It does get better with time."

Jeremy grimaced at Dan's words. "You know, that's what people tell me. But I don't know if I believe them. I loved her so much."

They started walking again, each lost in their own private thoughts. After a minute or two Dan slowed his pace and turned to Jeremy so they were facing each other again. He put his hand on his shoulder, tightened his grip and said, "You'll find a way, man. You have to." He paused, then added, "For me, it helped when I thought about what it was my wife would have wanted me to do. She'd have wanted me to go back to work. You know, get out in the world and keep living. She for sure wouldn't have wanted me to hide out at home, feeling sorry for myself."

Tears formed again and Jeremy did his best to snuffle them back. "Really?"

"Yeah. It helped me a lot to think like that. To think about what she'd want me to do."

They turned together and continued walking. To Dan, Jeremy appeared comforted by his words. By the time they reached the break room, he seemed more in control of himself. Dan found an out-of-the-way table and helped the young man to sit down.

As he made himself comfortable Jeremy said, "Thanks, Dan. Thanks a lot for talking to me; for taking some time with me. I know I sound like a basket case, but I can't help it." He shrugged his shoulders in resignation. "I don't have a lot of friends. It feels good to get some things off my chest."

Dan stood by and listened. Even in Jeremy's pain, he had the feeling the young man was going to rally. Maybe not today or tomorrow, but eventually. He was beginning to talk about how he was feeling and that was good. Someday he'd begin to heal. One thing was certain: Jeremy was stronger than he first appeared. In fact, the longer Dan was with him, the more he had the feeling that Jeremy was going not only going to be okay, but he was going to thrive. The guy seemed like a survivor.

They were both quiet for a minute, thinking. Jeremy broke the silence by adding, "Anyway, thanks, for listening, Dan. I really appreciate talking to you. Thanks for your patience."

"Don't mention it." Dan pulled out a chair and sat close enough so their voices wouldn't be heard. "It's hard, I know it is. Believe me, you just have to have a little faith that it can work out. Eventually, it will."

Jeremy smiled with a sense of relief. "That's what I needed to hear, because, you know what? It's been hell so far."

"I know, man. I hear you. Just hang in there. You'll get through it."

They chatted for a while. Later on, Dan went for some coffee. He also called his boss and told him that he'd be awhile getting back to work and that he had an emergency to deal with. His boss told him not to take too long, and Dan told him he'd get there when he could.

When he brought the coffee back and sat down, the two continued to talk. It was good to be with the young man. He saw a guy who was starting to come to grips with himself and his situation; this life of his right now and how he was going to have to learn how to cope with the death of his wife. In Dan's mind, he knew It wasn't going to be easy, in fact Jeremy had a long road ahead, but at least it was a start. He was happy for him about that. There was something about the young guy. Dan found himself liking him and he wanted things to get better for him. He could see them talking more in the future.

Well, maybe.

The thing was, all the time they were sitting together, and all the talking they did, Dan never let on the truth about the depth of the sadness he still felt for his wife; the numbing emptiness he still lived with every day. In fact it had been ten years, two months and seventeen days since his beloved Amy had passed away. The pain was still there. The loss was still intense. The love not diminished. Sure, he was out in the world. He was working, and doing the things he should be doing. The things Amy would have wanted him to do. The things he told Jeremy he should do. And maybe it would work for him, for the likable young man. Dan sure hoped so. For himself, though, it all came down to this: for all those years that had passed since Amy's death, he was still waiting. He was still trying to heal. And, despite what he had told Jeremy, the truth of the matter was that for him, it really wasn't getting any better. Not even close. It wasn't getting any better at all.

His thoughts were interrupted by Jeremy. "Say, Dan, I don't know. I was wondering. It's been good talking to you. Nice, actually. I don't have a lot of friends. No close ones, anyway. Anyhow, I don't know. I was wondering if you'd like to go for coffee sometime. You know, just to hang out or something?"

Dan dragged his thoughts back to the present. Back to the here and now. Back to Jeremy and the pain he was feeling and now starting to cope with. What was it he had said? Did he actually say, "Maybe hang out?" Dan smiled to himself. He was not what anyone would remotely call a "Hanging out" kind of person. But he liked Jeremy. He seemed like an alright guy. An image of Amy flashed in his brain. Was she smiling? Yeah, he thought, maybe she was.

Hell. It'd been over ten years. Maybe it was time for him to do something to try to move on with his life. Maybe now was the time to try something different. In fact, when you got right down to it, maybe he should pay attention to Amy's smile.

Why not? What did he have to lose?

With only the slightest hesitation, Dan smiled and said, "Sure, thing, Jeremy. I'd like to do that. It might be fun."

Crazy Old Wilbur

The two old friends, Becky Johnson and Maggie Jones, were among last ones to stop by Wilbur Smith's estate sale. Dead now for two weeks everyone in the small town of Long Lake had wondered what was to become of the house, or Crazy Old Wilbur's place, as the small stucco home on Lakeview Avenue was referred to.

Wilbur's wife had died twenty years earlier and she'd been sixty-five. Wilbur, everyone guessed, had been around the same age as she was back then, putting him at eighty-five or so now, this year of his own demise. Anyway, he'd been retired when Edith Smith had passed, that was for certain. What he'd been doing in all those years as a widower was anybody's guess. Becky and Maggie had their opinions, reinforced by what they'd seen wandering through Crazy Old Wilbur's place that bright spring afternoon. The day of the estate sale. The day when everything the old man owned was on display for all to see.

"No children, I guess," Becky said to Maggie, pawing through a table full of old men's and women's clothes.

"I heard that they had kids, but they were all dead," Maggie said, picking up and quickly discarding an old bra of Edith's. "Jesus, this thing has to be fifty years old. Didn't that crazy old coot ever get rid of anything?" She took out a handkerchief and diligently wiped off her hands.

Becky looked around, hands on hips, surveying the tiny living room jammed with boxes of old clothes and tables full of every kind of piece of junk one could imagine being accumulated over one's lifetime: kitchenware, old lamps, furniture, magazines, newspapers, etcetera, etcetera. And then there were the tools; boxes and boxes of tools, mostly gardening-related. Wilbur had been a gardener, that was for sure, and he had the tools to prove it: trowels, hoes, hand-held claw-shaped things that looked dangerous to the uninformed; all kinds of gardening paraphernalia: hoses, shovels, pitch forks, wheel barrels. Tons of stuff, really.

The two friends picked through the boxes, more curious than anything, before finally deciding that no, not today, thank you very much. They didn't need any of Crazy Old Wilbur's junk. Not one little bit. In fact, what they really wanted to do was to spend a solid five minutes with some soap and warm water getting cleaned up.

"Let's get out of here," Maggie said.

"Let's," Becky responded. "Why don't you come over to my place? After we wash up we can have some tea. Maybe a nice cup of chamomile?"

"Sounds wonderful," Maggie said and checked her watch. "It's nearly five. They'll be closing soon, anyway."

The two old friends made their way through Wilbur's lifetime of debris and went out the front door. It was early May and the sun was low behind the back of the house, bathing the front yard in golden late afternoon light. It was a yard planted from boarder to boarder and meticulously cared for. Right up until his passing, Wilbur had continued to maintain and improve upon the gardens he and Edith had begun planting when they had first moved into the little cottage-style home on Lakeview Avenue over fifty years earlier, back in the mid-sixties. Even though Wilbur and Edith were reticent by nature, gardening was their passion. Throughout the years they had dug up the lawn and planted flower and vegetable gardens in both the front and back yards. They were gardens that neighbors had not only enjoyed the sights of but even begun to depend upon, looking forward every year to new displays of gladiolas and hollyhocks and whatever else the quiet couple decided to plant; the same gardens that Wilbur continued to nurture and maintain even after Edith's passing, the old man carrying on their floral tradition despite the death of his wife.

On this day, bright tulips of yellow and orange and mauve and red were blooming in profusion. Mixed in were white narcissus, yellow daffodils and even some tiny blue cilia. Maggie and Becky paused on the front steps to take in the colorful scene.

"What's going to happen with the gardens?" Becky asked.

"I heard someone bought the house and they're going to tear it down. Bulldozer it to the ground and build one of those big new ones. I'm assuming the gardens will go, too. I guess it's supposed to make everything easier."

"A brand new house?" Becky looked up and down the street: a quiet, tree-lined block of predominately one-story bungalows built a hundred years earlier. "It'll look stupid here, won't it? A big, huge house. It'll look out of place."

"The price of progress, I guess," Maggie said. "Time marches on."

"Phooey," Becky spit out derisively. "Maybe it marches on, but that doesn't mean that it has to go in the wrong direction."

Just then Jacob Fry, the man in charge of the sale, stepped outside for a cigarette. He lit up, blew a stream of smoke away from Maggie and Becky, and said, "Say, ladies, I couldn't help but overhear you talking about Crazy Old Wilbur's house and garden."

The two friends both made it a point of waving Jacob's cigarette smoke away. Becky said, "Yes, it'll be sad to lose these lovely gardens. They're so pretty."

Jacob looked at her with interest. "Who said anything about losing the gardens?"

"Well, that's the rumor, isn't it?" Maggie said.

Jacob laughed. "It might be the rumor, but it's a rumor

that's wrong. Wilbur Smith loved these gardens. He'd never let anything happen to them. In fact," he leaned close, an air of the conspirator about him, "I guess I can tell you." He winked. "You can keep secret, right?" The two old friends nodded and Jacob continued, knowing full well that what he was about to say would be all around town by the next day, if not sooner. He didn't care, in fact, he was counting on it. "Wilbur left his land to the city for green space."

"What?" Maggie and Becky managed to sputter at the same time. They were both incredulous. "Green space? Crazy Old Wilbur? What the…?"

Jacob held up a hand to interrupt the two friends and their sputtering. "Yeah. Although he didn't call it green space. He said, 'I want the city to have it. I want people to enjoy the gardens just like Edith and I have. It'd mean a lot to the both of us.' At least that's the way I heard it from Sam Rickenbacher on the city council."

"Well, I'll be…" Becky started to say.

"…damned," Maggie finished her friend's thought.

"Yeah," Jacob said. "It was a wonderful gesture on his part. At least I think so, anyway."

Then he stopped talking while he smoked, taking his time while looking out over the pretty front yard, bursting forth in a profusion of springtime color. Becky and Maggie joined him, all three quietly enjoying the peace and serenity of Wilbur and Edith's gardens. They even saw an early arriving bluebird.

When Jacob was finished with his cigarette, he bent down and ground it out in some soil, and stuck the butt in his coat pocket. Maggie and Becky watched and shook their heads, in complete and shared agreement regarding the filthiness of Jacob's habit. He stood up, looked at the kindly old ladies and said, "He did a good thing, Crazy Old Wilbur did. A real good thing." He smiled and went inside to close down the estate sale.

Captivated by the magic of the beauty of the front yard, the two friends stayed on the front steps for a while before leaving. It had been a long day and they were both looking forward to that refreshing cup of tea Becky had offered earlier. As they walked past a particularly colorful clump of daffodils, they both remarked how happy they were that the gardens were not going to be destroyed but would remain into the future for all to enjoy.

A few hours later, the sun had set low in the west, casting long shadows over the gardens – gardens that now and forever would be referred to as the Long Lake Gardens and Green Space. Nobody figured the old couple would mind the name at all. Not one little bit. Not as long as the flowers Wilbur and Edith had planted continued to bloom.

Besides, that's the way the old couple wanted it.

The last words Edith, or Edie, as Wilbur had affectionately called his wife – his favorite name for her for the fifty-odd years they'd known each other, starting in grade school and continuing on for all of their married years – the last words she ever spoke to him were, "Take care of the gardens, Will. Please take care of our flowers." Then she was silent for a long moment before softly adding, "Please..." It was the last word that escaped her lips with the last breath she ever took. Will, as Edie had affectionately called him all those years, held his dear wife close for one last time. For many minutes, actually. When he finally stood he looked around the room and wondered how he was going to spend the rest of his life without her. A life he'd be the first to admit, if anyone asked (and no one did), was so much more empty now without the love of his life in it. The love of his beloved Edie.

So, years later, when the same cancer took over his

body that had taken over Edie's, Will didn't protest. He didn't seek treatment, and he didn't try to get better. He reasoned it this way: What was the point? He'd lived long enough. It was time to move on. It was time to be with Edie.

He knew what he needed to do. He'd figured it out long ago. He went ahead and contacted the Long Lake City Counsel and told them of his plan. After a few weeks of back-and-forth meetings, Wilber's plan was approved in a closed-door session. When he heard the news, he sighed in relief. "Now I can let go," he thought to himself. "Now I can join Edie. Now I won't be alone anymore." Two days later he died at home in his sleep.

Maggie and Becky and their friends and neighbors walk past Wilbur and Edith's gardens every day. It's mid-July, the little stucco house is long gone and the spring flowers have long ago faded Now it is glorious summer and the summertime flowers are in bloom: purple and white phlox, terra-cotta coneflower, blue bachelor buttons, yellow sunflowers and a myriad of other plants and colors. "It's a riot of color," neighbors say proudly to anyone who asks. "It's the best garden in the city, if not the entire county," they are quick to add. Whether or not that statement is true or not, it doesn't matter, because, for Crazy Old Wilbur's neighbors, they are as proud of the notoriety of the gardens as if they were their own. Which, in a way, they are.

Though Wilbur has been gone from the world for three months, his and Edith's gardens flourish. The city has provided jobs for kids from the local grade school and middle school and high school, just like Wilbur had requested. Being young, some of the kids (but not many) need proper supervision, and Jacob Fry is just the person to do that. He's firm, but kind. The kids like him. So, yes, the gardens are profiting from the meticulous care the school-aged children are giving them. Everyone agrees they've never looked better.

Do Wilbur and Edith watch over the city's new green space? Does the reclusive couple know how beautiful their flower gardens continue to look? Maggie and Becky often wonder. They've taken to walking to the Long Lake Gardens and Green Space every day to sit and relax on one of the teak wood benches scattered here and there. Some mornings they even bring along their tea and sip a refreshing cup of chamomile. It's a perfect way to begin the day, nestled among the pretty flowers, twittering song birds and busy bees and butterflies. Of course, they'll never have an answer as to whether or not Wilbur and Edith are watching over the new green space, and they really don't care. What the two friends do know, however, is this: really, when it came right down to it, maybe Crazy Old Wilbur really wasn't so crazy after all.

To Hold a Hand

"See you later." I waved. "Hope it goes well."

My brother waved back and made his way to where the eye technician was waiting. His look belied his true feelings. I knew how nervous he was. His eyes were pretty bad, scarred years ago from a rare form of glaucoma. There'd be a lot of tests over the next two hours and the end result would be this: Would he be able to continue to drive or not?

A moment later he had disappeared into the inner catacombs of the Minnesota Eye Care Clinic. Now it was just Beth and I.

"Where's Tim?" Beth asked a minute after he'd left us. "Where'd Tim go?"

"It's all right, Beth. He just went for his eye exam. Remember. We talked about this."

"Oh. Okay."

Shit. I shouldn't have said, "Remember." I felt like an idiot. Beth is in her seventh year of dealing with Alzheimer's. She's still able to live at home and Tim does an admirable job of caring for her, but still… I brought the two of them here last year for the same tests and the entire time Tim was away from us Beth asked every five minutes, "Where's Tim? Where's Tim? Where's Tim?" I reassured her each and every time that "He's just getting some tests done. He'll be back soon." But, you know how it is with memory loss. You forget.

I was ready for the same scenario this year. After Tim left us, I made sure Beth was settled. "Do you want something to drink? Some water?" A blank look and then a shake of the head. No. "Are you comfortable? A blank look, then a shake of the head. No. "You're okay then? A nod yes. Okay, good.

Beth was wearing all black today. Black slacks and a black turtle neck. Our Minnesota winter was winding down, but it was still cold out, so she had her black winter coat. Black is and probably always will be her favorite color. Around her neck, she wore a black polished piece of basalt in the shape of a heart on a black cord, a gift years ago to her from my brother, worn today to, as Tim told me earlier, "To make her look pretty."

I opened my magazine, a publication put out by the Minnesota Department of Natural Resources. The lead article was about an artist who did plein air painting of northern Minnesota, specifically of the boundary waters and lake superior. They were well done, in my estimation, and I showed them to Beth. She, at one time, was known regionally for her elegantly exact paintings of flowers. She called her work photorealism and it was not only beautiful but highly sought after. Over the course of her life, she'd won many awards and her work is still featured in galleries in the upper Midwest. She hasn't painted in over ten years, though, not since to onset of her disease.

"Beth," I said to get her attention. She turned to me and I pointed to a scene of waves crashing against a rocky shoreline on Lake Superior. "What do you think about this painting? Do you like it?"

She looked at the colorful watercolor: the shades of blue for sky and water, the tones of brown for the rocks, and the white of a nearby birch clump with dots of green for its leaves. I gave her time, wondering what her reaction would be. Finally, she looked at me and silently shook her shoulder, indicating, I guess, she had no opinion.

"Do you remember that you used to paint? I asked. "Both you and Tim did."

She gave me a long look. Would she remember? It would be so great if she did. She and my brother had produced nearly seven-hundred and fifty paintings each over their lifetimes. More than enough, to my way of thinking, to remember.

"I don't remember," she said and sat back.

"Too bad," I said sympathetically. I thought for a moment, not wanting to give up on helping her to retrieve a portion of her memory, tiny and fleeting though it may have been. I leaned over and said, "They were really good." I'm not sure if she heard me. Probably not. She'd closed her eyes and it looked like she'd dozed off.

I spent the first hour reading, checking my phone and making sure Beth was doing all right. She was. She dozed a bit and was awake a lot. I was happy that she was comfortable and not freaked out that Tim was not with us. Once when I asked how she was doing she said, "I'm fine. I like watching the people." I didn't blame her. This was a big outing for her. Usually, she and my brother stayed home, spent their day together and their only break in the day was an occasional walk in their neighborhood. Outings were becoming fewer and farther between, what with his failing eyesight and her increasing memory loss. Getting out like this was good for her. She hadn't even once asked where Tim was.

Into the second hour, I was reading and kind of dozing off a little myself, to be honest, when I felt a stir to my right. It was Beth. She was awake. I looked at her and smiled and she smiled back. I went back to reading. Suddenly, softly, I felt her move again and in a moment her hand slipped over the arms of each of our chairs and into mine. Her left hand into my right hand. She gently interwove her fingers into mine, and, with her right hand, she leaned over and covered them both. Then she patted them. She and my brother had been together for over forty-one years and in all that time, I doubt she and I had ever even touched, and certainly never held hands. Even to shake "Hello," in a greeting. We are not what you call a physically demonstrative family.

I was shocked, yet touched. What would cause her to do something like that? I turned to her and smiled. "Are you doing okay?"

She smiled back. "Yes, I am." She was silent for a moment and then added, "Thank you for being here."

Well, I never… What can you say to something like that? Well, obviously, "You're welcome," so that's what I said. She didn't say anything in return, only smiled back. We were both quiet. Then I had a thought. I went ahead and seized the moment and asked her something I'd been wondering about for the last few years, "Beth, I have a question for you. Do you know who I am?"

She gave me a long look, still holding my hand, and said, "I don't remember."

"Do you know who Tim is?"

"Oh, yes," she smiled, happily. "I know Tim."

"I'm Tim's brother," I told her. She stared at me. Another blank look. "Like Dennis," I said. "You know, your bother."

"Dennis?"

"Never mind," I decided not to push and make her uncomfortable with not being able to remember who her brother was. I shifted gears and asked, "Are you doing okay? Should we just sit here?"

"Yes."

So we sat together. I went back to my magazine and read. Beth continued to hold my hand. It was a good feeling.

Fifteen minutes later, when Tim came back and saw us he smiled. "I guess you guys are doing okay. He pointed to our hands, still interlocked. "Beth likes to do that sometimes. It gives her a sense of security. I'm glad you were there for her."

He sat down on the other side of Beth and she released my hand and took his. We talked for a while before leaving. We went out to lunch and then I dropped them at their home and I went on my way.

I don't know if I'll ever forget that morning with Beth and being with her in the waiting room, being there when she needed someone to give her comfort and a sense of security. Being there to help fill in for my brother. Being there as a friend. I was glad to do it, glad I was there.

Oh, Tim passed his tests. He can still drive but has to go back again next year to be checked out. He wants to know if I can drive him and Beth. I told him I'd be happy to.

Friends

Dave was sprawled on the couch watching the evening news when an incoming text beeped. He glanced at it and sighed. "Shit, JT, what the hell?" He set his phone down without looking at the message. "Man, just give me a moment to myself," he was thinking. "Just let me chill and unwind a bit."

He'd been home for half an hour, had showered, put on some clean clothes and fixed a plate of fruit: a sliced-up Honeycrisp apple, a hand full of red seedless grapes and a little chunk of Havarti cheese. All he wanted was to chill a little; hang out and relax. He was beat. He had just finished a ten-hour shift as what his boss called a sous chef at a local restaurant. Right. Dave grimaced when he thought about his job because he was under no illusions whatsoever about the work he did; what he did was food prep and that was that. Pure and simple. Any idiot could do it. The fact that The Egg and I was a locally sourced, natural foods eatery that regularly made the top ten list for places to eat in the Twin Cities didn't hide that fact, not one little bit. At least to Dave, anyway.

But he didn't mind. He liked the work. Liked that he made enough money for him and JT to rent the one-bedroom apartment in the hundred-year-old brown stone on Emerson Avenue in an older neighborhood of Minneapolis. Liked that he was close enough so he could walk to work in ten minutes and not have to drive his old Ford Fiesta. Liked that he could help pay the bills. (JT made good wages working for Gibertson's Environmental Services, cleaning high-rise office buildings in downtown Minneapolis late at night.) He liked that he could even save some money so maybe he could go to college one day; if he ever decided he wanted to.

But for now… now he had to deal with JT. He fired up his water pipe and took a hit of Raspberry Crush, pulling the smoke down deep into his lungs and savoring it as he reached for his phone. "Let's see what the guy's up to."

He read the text. It was short and sweet. Well, not all that sweet. What it said was a cryptic "Come get me."

What the hell was going on now? Dave knew JT had had the day and the night off. He knew his friend was going to ride his fat tire bike somewhere. But it was the middle of winter and cold out for Christ's sake. How far could he have gone?

Dave looked out the window. Their apartment was on the third floor of the three-story building. It was in the middle of the block, right across from a street light. Through the bright illumination, he could make out the snow flurries that had begun to fall earlier in the day. It was beginning to snow harder, now, showing no sign of letting up.

Damn.

"What's up?" he texted back.

"At RR. Need ride."

Well, for double Pete's sake. RR was the Red Rooster, a bar in Long Lake. It was the bar Dave and JT would sometimes stop at when they rode their bicycles from Minneapolis to the little town, twenty miles to the west. It was an area of woods and fields in western Hennepin County known for its well-kept bike trails. They enjoyed going fat tire riding on those trails. Liked it a lot. But that was during the summer (or spring or fall, for that matter), not in the middle of February. Not in the middle of winter. Not with a foot of snow on the ground and more on the way. What the hell had JT been thinking?

Well, Dave had a guess. JT had developed a thing for the bartender out there. A serious infatuation. At least he had last Christmas when the weather had been mild and they'd both ridden out to check on the trails. On the way home they'd stopped at the Rooster. The bartender was a handsome guy named Jeff and JT had immediately been drawn to him. In fact, he'd stayed drawn to him even though he'd never once been back to the bar to see him. JT liked to imagine the best when it came to relationships, instead of taking steps to show the person how he felt – imagine being the operative word here. He liked to pretend that whomever he'd fallen for was going to reciprocate his feelings. The way Dave saw it, it was easier for JT to just play the game in his head rather than act on his feelings. Except for now. Now, apparently, his friend had decided to follow his heart and take things a step further. Yep, the more Dave thought about it, the more he figured that, yeah, that's exactly what JT had done.

"Jeff?" Dave texted back.

"No. Jeff's gone. Marybeth."

Dave sighed. Jesus. When it came to infatuations, JT was an equal-opportunity kind of guy. A good-looking man or a good-looking woman, it didn't matter. If there was a spark that JT felt, that's all it would take. Next stop, Love City.

Dave and JT had been friends for almost their entire lives, having met back in grade school in Miss Whipholt's third-grade class. Back then parents and teachers called the two boys introverted and socially awkward. Labels notwithstanding, Dave and JT only knew they preferred to not be around a lot of other people. They bonded over a love of bicycles and bike riding. Over time, their small coaster brake Huffys evolved to trek dirt bikes, diamond back mountain bikes and Schwinn fifteen-speed racers, until finally, now, to each of them owning a treasured Raleigh Pardner fat tire bicycle. Riding bikes was a pleasant, solitary activity, something they could do alone or together. As the years passed, they did it together, more often than not.

Now in their mid-twenties, they were still friends, close friends, best of friends. Close enough that Dave texted back "What a bunch of BS."

Apparently unperturbed by Dave's response, JT responded with a smiley face. Then, after a short pause, another text pleading "Come get me?" and another smiley face.

Jesus.

Dave could see it now. JT had ridden his bike out to the Red Rooster on his day off, thinking he'd be able to make it with Jeff. Jeff had been gone. Who knows, quit maybe; maybe even hiding in the back room, but gone nevertheless. So, JT strikes up a conversation with Marybeth, a new bartender, and one thing leads to another. It gets to be make-it-or-break-it time and MB informs JT that she's not interested. Maybe she has a boyfriend. Maybe a girlfriend. Whatever… The point is, she's not interested. JT starts drinking and time goes by. It starts snowing. He's getting drunk. Suddenly he realizes he can barely stand, let along ride a bike all the way back to Minneapolis. So what's he do? He sends a text to his pal. His good buddy. Good old Dave.

Dave sat back on the couch and glanced at the television. Colbert was just coming on. He watched for a minute or so and laughed once or twice at some jokes made at the expense of the current president. Colbert was really pretty funny sometimes.

Beep. Another text. "U coming?"

Dave lit up the pipe and took another hit. He looked around the living room, the main room of the apartment. It might not have a lot of furniture but that was all right. He slept on the couch he was now sitting on. JT had the bedroom. There was also a small bathroom and a tiny, galley kitchen. It wasn't the biggest space in the world, but the price was right and it worked for them. And it was clean. They both made sure of that. No one said that just because you were a guy in your twenty's you had to be a slob. Both he and JT liked to keep their place neat and tidy and looking good. And it was.

On the table across from him was the television. Next to it was a red lava lamp with a gold base they'd bought together over three years earlier when they'd first moved in; a kind of housewarming gift to themselves. Dave watched the red mass bubble away for a few seconds and then got to his feet. He turned off Colbert, picked up his plate, went to the kitchen and washed it. Then he took out a stick of sandalwood incense, put it in its holder and set it carefully in the base of the aluminum kitchen sink. It'd be safe there. Then he lit it. JT would like the aroma when he came in.

He picked up his phone and texted "On my way. B there in 45."

He put on his boots, winter jacket and wood cap before grabbing his car keys. He locked the apartment and made his way downstairs to the parking lot where his old Ford Fiesta was parked. He started the engine and turned on the heater. While the car warmed up he took his brush and stepped outside to clean off the snow. It felt like the temperature was around ten degrees. What the hell had JT been thinking, riding out to Long Lake today? Twenty miles in the winter. Man… Dave shook his head, fighting back a grin. What a crazy guy.

When the snow was removed, he got back inside. The warmth from the heater felt good. Some of the snow on the sleeve of his jacket started to melt. He put the car in reverse and backed up. It usually took about thirty minutes to drive out to Long Lake, but what with the snow and all on a night like tonight it'd definitely take longer. That was okay. It'd be good to see JT. He'd been kind of missing the guy.

Just before he pulled out of the lot his phone beeped. Dave stopped and checked it. JT had sent a message: a smiley face and a thumbs-up emoji.

Dave texted a smiley face back.

Then he put the car in gear and headed out into the snowy winter's night. Yeah, it'd be good to see JT. It'd be nice to see his friend.

The Rabbit

"I'm going to the compost bin. I'll be right back," Blake Jorgenson said to his wife.

"Okay. I'm almost done with the tea. We can have a cup on the back patio if you want. It's a beautiful morning."

He grinned. "Sounds good."

Blake stepped out the back door with his pail of breakfast scraps: eggs shells, coffee grounds and a banana peel. He stopped and took a moment to breathe in the scent of a nearby climbing yellow rose bush. *Ah, roses so sweet!* he thought poetically to himself. *Wasn't life grand?*

He was feeling wonderful. A warbler chattering away in a nearby clump of honeysuckle seemed to echo his jaunty mood. Morning dew sparkled on the lawn and the sky was glorious robin's egg blue. It was the last week in June and the sun was shining, the temperature a pleasant sixty-five degrees. It was going to be a perfect day.

Blake was an avid gardener; it was not only his hobby but his passion. He planned to spend the morning working in the front yard, weeding and hoeing the many gardens he'd planted there over the years. It was the sunniest spot on his property and that's where all the sun-loving flowers were planted: delphinium, garden phlox, coneflower, sunflowers, daises and black-eyed Susan's to name but a few. When he was finished in the front, he'd move to the backyard, where he was now, to the shady gardens and do the same with the hostas, ferns, wild ginger, Solomon's seal and foxglove. He prided himself on the gardens he and Alicia maintained. They'd won a disappointing second place in the Long Lake garden contest last year and he was ready to do battle.

"Not this year," he'd told his wife a few months earlier at the beginning of the season. "No siree. This year we're going to kick some ass. We're going to win!"

He hadn't noticed when Alicia turned away, rolling her eyes at him. Sure, she liked to putter around with the flowers, but that was all. She could have cared less about the garden contest and didn't care one whit about winning. And she certainly wasn't like her competitive husband, who had waited and dreamed and plotted all winter long for the chance to wipe last year's second-place debacle from the books.

Blake happily sauntered from the back door to the far side of the garage where the compost bin was located. Suddenly a movement to his right caught his attention. Thinking it might be a robin searching for a worm he glanced out into the yard. It took a moment to locate the movement and when he did his blood pressure suddenly sky-rocketed, his good mood vanishing in an instant. "Shit!" He dropped his pail and ran back to the house yelling. "God damn it, anyway!"

Alicia hurried to meet him as he burst through the backdoor. "What's the matter? Is it your heart? What's wrong?"

"I'm fine, but I'm not okay. I've got to call Toby."

"Why?"

"That damn rabbit is back. I can't friggin' believe it."

"Why call Toby?" Toby McCourt was Blake's best friend.

"He's got a trap. I'm going to catch the blasted thing and when I do, that'll be all she wrote for mister bunny rabbit. Mark my words. That thing is toast."

Alicia sighed a heavy sigh, thinking, *Good grief, here we go again.*

Toby's trap was called a "Havaheart." It was a rectangular wire mesh box-like contraption that an animal was enticed into with food. Once inside, a trip-lever shut the door so the animal couldn't get out. The idea was that the trapper could then take the animal far away and let it go to run wild and free in some woods or fields somewhere; anywhere but where they could do damage and destruction to humans. Toby used his to trap squirrels. He was a gentle and compassionate man who drove twenty miles away to the other side of the Minnesota River down near Jordan where he set the unharmed animal free. Blake wasn't sure he'd be that kind and considerate with the rabbit.

"I might just drop the whole thing in the middle of Long Lake and be done with it," he told Alicia when he returned home from Toby's, hauling the bulky Havaheart, "I've had it with the damn thing."

The "Damn Thing," the rabbit, had been the scourge of Blake's for a couple of years right up until last year when it had mysteriously disappeared. "Yea!" Blake had said earlier that spring as he prepared his prized gardens for the garden show judging (only to be awarded the gut-wrenching second plate silver metal. It still grated on his nerves.) "Maybe a fox got it or something. Hopefully, the stupid thing is dead. Goodbye, and good riddance is what I say."

But, now, a year later, apparently it was not dead. Now it was back, hopping around in his yard, and it had Blake's blood pressure up in the danger zone.

"Blake, sweetheart, you've got to calm down," Alicia told him, as he stalked his property searching for the perfect place to set the trap. "You'll give yourself a heart attack."

Blake was a recently retired product development specialist for Heartland Incorporated, an electronics control manufacturing company. He'd worked there for nearly forty years, as long as he and Alicia had been married. He'd been a dedicated employee and was a devoted husband. He was also fiercely competitive, and he wasn't going to let a measly cottontail rabbit ruin his chances of winning first place at the garden show this year. In his words, "No friggin' way." He'd already picked out a nice spot on the fireplace mantel to be home for the shining golden trophy, much to Alicia's chagrin.

After an hour's contemplation, and trying various locations, he finally decided to place the trap in the front yard, in the middle of his favorite flower bed. He baited it with fresh romaine lettuce, sliced radishes and succulent baby carrots. The mixture looked so delectable that Blake fought back an urge to eat some. "Nope, save it for the rabbit," he muttered to himself. "I can't wait to get the damned thing."

With the trap and bait in place, he impatiently waited. One day went by. A second day passed. A third. Nothing. At the end of the fourth day, with still no rabbit, Blake was starting to calm down somewhat and to think, *Maybe the blasted thing has moved on to another neighborhood to terrorize another gardener.* Or, now that he was thinking about it, *Maybe something even better has happened. Maybe it got hit by a car and is dead.* To that end Blake got in his brand new Ford Focus and took a drive around the neighborhood looking up and down the streets to see if he could find evidence of the smashed remains of the rabbit's demise. He found nothing.

But that was fine with Blake. At least the rabbit wasn't in his yard or his flower beds, or anywhere nearby. Apparently. He allowed himself some cautious optimism. His bachelor buttons had just popped up in his front yard garden and were growing with enthusiasm. They'd be the final colors of blue and pink and white to fill in amongst the deep violet delphinium, the terra cotta coneflowers, the yellow sunflowers and the deep fuchsia and reds of his phlox. The judging was next week. He and, more importantly, his garden, was ready. "First place, here we come," he told Alicia. "No doubt in my mind." To which his poor wife sighed and, again, rolled her eyes.

The next morning he took the breakfast scraps to the compost bin. On a whim, he decided to take a little stroll to the front yard to check on the trap. He walked on yesterday's freshly cut grass along the side of his house, reveling in the beauty of the natural world and the fact that, with the rabbit seemingly nowhere to be found, all was right with it. He turned the corner to the front yard and let his eye run over the riot of color, the beautiful combination of flowers of all types and varieties. He'd definitely win first place this year. Easily. Then he happened to glance at the Havaheart, tucked carefully among the bachelor buttons. At first, he didn't believe what he saw. He had to blink twice to make sure it was real. Unfortunately, it was. There, sitting calmly and unafraid on top of the trap was the rabbit. His nemesis. Blake stared, his blood racing to his brain, his heart pounding. He put his hand to his chest to ease the pain. It subsided, fortunately, but he was frozen in place, a combination of anger and numbness stopping him in his tracks.

The rabbit, a doe, a big female, sat staring back at him. She calmly munched on the new growth of the bachelor buttons growing right up beside her. She was taking her time, all the while watching the man clutch his chest, speechless and consumed by rage. Munching, munching, munching, she was, enjoying every bite, in no hurry at all.

When she was finished, she lightly jumped to the ground and leisurely hopped away, turning every now and then, keeping an eye on the crazy man standing nearby with his eyes bugging out, silently moving his mouth, speechless. Then she spied a delectable delphinium. She stopped next to it, daintily bit it off at the stem and started eating, savoring every bite, watching as the female who lived with the man ran out to help him. She put her arm around his shoulder and slowly they made their toward their home.

When they had gone inside, she hopped past more of the man's succulent gardens, so full of good food. For now, though, she ignored them. She was heading for the yard next door. At the back of the garage, she'd dug a borrow for her nine babies. They'd only been born last week. She was still feeding them her rich mother's milk. Soon they'd be old enough to go out on their own. Then she would teach them the ways of the world and how to survive: where the safe places to hide were and where to find food, like this particular garden, this lovely banquet of healthy food, so abundant and tasty.

But that was still a few weeks away. Until then she'd be busy, feeding mostly, both herself and her babies. She was glad there were so many flowers nearby. The man's garden held the best food in the area; in fact, the best food she'd ever eaten. She was sure her babies would grow strong and healthy from it. Her milk was good. The garden was big. The food source was almost unending. There was no doubt about it, she would definitely be back, if not this afternoon, then tonight. After all, she had a growing family to care for. She had a lot more eating to do.

Mellowing Out

Alicia Jorgenson set the cup down and said, "Here you go, Blake. A nice cup of chamomile tea for you."

Blake held up a hand, smiled his thanks, and said in a low voice, "Come and join me. This will be done in just a minute." Then he closed his eyes and went back to his relaxation tape, earbuds firmly in place, listening to the melodic strains of *Trickling Forest Stream.*

Alicia went to the kitchen, made herself a cup, came back to the den, and sat down. She wasn't sure what to think about her husband, recovering from the mild heart attack he'd suffered earlier in the summer. A heart attack six weeks ago brought on by his obsession with his garden and with ridding it of the female rabbit and her babies that had taken over. He'd wanted to win first place in the garden contest this year after settling for second place last year. Well, this year he'd placed third.

Alicia remembered the outcome of the judging very well. At the time, Blake had been into his third week of recovery. When the announcement was made, Alicia had expected him to explode and rant and rave and go completely nuts and out of his mind. It would have been par for the course given his competitive nature. But he hadn't even gritted his teeth or sworn an oath of revenge. Instead, he'd shrugged his shoulders and grinned. "Well, at least it's something," meaning the third-place award, a simple plaque, not the shining gold trophy he'd envisioned. It was so out of character for her high-strung husband, that she'd had to look twice to see if the tall, slightly overweight man she'd been married to for over forty years really was, in fact, the same man. He definitely was. *Maybe*, Alicia thought to herself, as she went back to sipping her tea in companionable silence while Blake finished listening to the trickling stream, *maybe he really was starting to change.*

At just that moment, Becky Johnson and Maggie Jones, two old friends who had outlived each of their respective husbands by over twenty years, were walking past Blake's house.

"Look at how lovely the pink geraniums are looking in those hanging baskets," Becky remarked.

"Humph. That Blake. He's such a jerk," Maggie rejoined. "Thinks he knows everything about gardening."

"Well, his flower beds do look awfully nice."

"He's just so full of himself. He doesn't even bother to help out at the community garden. He's a jerk in my book."

The garden Maggie was talking about was the recently established Orchard Lake Community Garden, a lovely planting space donated to the city by Wilber Smith and his wife Edith after they had passed away. The two friends volunteered their time, both being avid gardeners themselves, usually for a few hours most mornings before the summer days became too hot.

Becky grinned at her friend. Deep down she agreed with her assessment of their arrogant neighbor, but she enjoyed winding Becky up occasionally. It helped keep their friendship interesting. It was easy to do, too, since Maggie had opinions on nearly everything and everybody under the sun, Blake Jorgenson being near the top of the list. Not that either of them was happy he'd suffered his heart attack. They weren't those kinds of people, not at all. But they both secretly agreed that Blake really was, in their opinion, a little too big for his britches. Plus, the fact that the heart attack, which had been brought on when he'd freaked out over what he referred to as "That Damn Rabbit," well, you had to admit, in the right context, it was kind of funny.

That being said, Becky pointed and grinned. There was the aforementioned rabbit, calm and unafraid, nibbling contentedly on one of Blake's orange nasturtiums. She was about to shoo it away when Maggie put her hand on her friend's arm to stop her. Becky just grinned. "Okay. He does sort of deserve it, doesn't he?"

The two smiled at each other and continued walking on, arm in arm, happily enjoying the tranquility of a quiet August morning, ambling down the street and away from both Blake's garden and the healthy-looking rabbit, who, having finished with the nasturtiums was now moving on to some delectable looking bachelor buttons.

Back inside, Blake's tape had ended. He happened to glance outside and spied the two elderly ladies. "Look at those two old bitties," he said to Alicia. "God, they're so high and mighty." He took a gulp of his supposedly relaxing tea, choked on it a little, and coughed.

Alicia patted him on the back. "Blake, calm down. You know what your doctor said."

"I know, 'You've got to try and learn how to relax and mellow out.' " he said, in a sing-song voice, mimicking the words of Dr. Rose, a doctor chosen by Blake as much for his last name as anything else. "I'm trying."

Alicia took a sip of her tea. "I know you are dear, but you really do need to try harder. Especially when it comes to your gardening. It's supposed to be fun, you know. Relaxing. A hobby."

Blake gazed at his wife with affection. Of course, she was right. He wasn't a dummy. He knew that for the sake of his health, he needed to learn how to relax. But it was hard. If it wasn't for that "Damn Rabbit" (as he referred to the beast), he'd have won first place in the garden show this year. A big, shining, gold trophy for the mantel above his fireplace instead of that stupid wooden plaque. Everyone said so. But, no, Mrs. Bunny Rabbit had chosen this summer to not only return to the neighborhood but to have about a million babies, all of which she brought to feed on his prized flowers. Damn it, life just wasn't fair.

He felt himself getting worked up all over again. Alicia was right. He really did need to learn to calm down. To mellow out, as the doctor had said.

He took a deep breath and exhaled. "I know, dear," he said, sighing. But deep down in his heart, he had a feeling he was only kidding himself. He really did hate that rabbit.

Alicia stood up. "Well, that's good. Now, I've got some errands to run. I'll be stopping at the grocery store. Need anything?"

How about a shotgun for that Damn Rabbit, Blake thought to himself, but, instead, said, "No. I'm good." He paused and added, smiling, halfway joking, halfway not, "Maybe something a little stronger than this tea?" He grinned and mimicked a drinking motion.

"Blake," Alicia admonished him, "you know what the doctor said."

"I know. No booze. No red meat. No nothing fun. I get it. Tea and saltines." He sighed again, starting to feel just ever so slightly sorry for himself.

"It's not that bad. All of us just want you to get better." She bent to give him a kiss on the forehead. "I'll see you in a little while." She patted him on the arm. "Goodbye, dear."

Blake waved her goodbye and returned to his iPod and his relaxation music. He scrolled down the playlist until he found, *Soft Springtime Rain,* and set it playing. He sat back and closed his eyes, dreaming of better days. Better days when that rabbit was finally gone. They couldn't come soon enough as far as he was concerned. It was frustrating. All the time he put into his garden had gone to waste. Third place. What a disappointment. Alicia didn't care about the award, she just liked to garden. Maybe he should be more like her. Food for thought. On the other hand, maybe he really should get a gun and blow that rabbit to kingdom come. He thought about it for a minute, picturing a disgusting, bloody scene. Naw. He could never harm any animal, even the rabbit, much as he despised it. Maybe he really should learn how to relax. Yeah, that would be the best thing to do. He signed once again, leaned back in his chair, and drifted off to sleep, the sound of soft summer rain gently caressing his ears.

Blake didn't see it, and it was probably a good thing, too, that out in the garden the female rabbit Maggie and Becky had seen was still there. Only now her four babies had joined her. They moved as a group through the flowers, happily feeding on newly sprouted bachelor buttons and whatever other delectable treat they could find. They were so many choices.

After a few minutes, before they became too full, the big female gathered her young ones to her and led them away. She had learned over time to never completely eat all the food in a given location. She always left some for another day, and that's what she did now.

She began making her way to a field of clover across the street and the next block over, down by the railroad tracks. The clover was sweet and tasty, a nice change from the flowers in the man's garden. In fact, the more she thought about it, maybe she'd just leave his garden alone for the rest of the season. There was whole summer's supply of clover, fresh for the taking in the field. She could always come back to the man's garden. Anytime. If not this year, for sure next year.

As she hopped along leading her babies she made her decision. She wouldn't return for the rest of the season. But next year she'd be back. Maybe with a new batch of babies too. Why not? It made perfect sense. She liked almost all the flowers in the man's garden. The food was good for her babies, a welcome change from the clover in the field. Besides, in a way, she felt she owed it to the man. Especially since he had so thoughtfully planted such a lovely garden with all those delectable flowers. It was almost like he had done it just for her.

At any rate, she was finished with his garden for this year, but next year? Next year she'd be back for sure. She was already looking forward to it.

The Last Garden Contest

"And the winner is…"

Blake Jorgenson held his breath. This was it. This was his chance. Was this the year he'd win first place in the Long Lake Garden Contest? He closed his eyes and thought back over the past two years. The memories weren't pretty: two years ago, second place; last year, third place. This year, could he hope, could he even begin to imagine that he'd win? "Yes," he thought to himself, "yes, he could."

Next to him Alicia, his wife of over forty years held his hand and said a silent prayer, *Please, please*, she thought to herself. *Please let this be his year. Please let him win.*

Last year her husband had suffered a mild heart attack brought on by doing battle with a female rabbit who'd been spending much of the summer eating his prized flowers, especially his pretty blue and white and pink straw flowers, often referred to as bachelor buttons. He'd placed third, which to her highly competitive husband was unacceptable. A slap in the face really. And that wooden third-place plaque he'd been awarded? Not even worth mentioning. This year Blake still had his heart set on winning first place and the big, shining, gold trophy that he'd already cleared a space for on the fireplace mantle in their living room.

Alicia sighed, something, it seemed, she was doing way more often than she used to the last few years. She really could do without having a trophy in the living room for the whole world to see. There was no doubt in her mind about that. None at all.

Blake felt the calming touch of Alicia's hand in his, and he appreciated it, he really did. But he was here to win, not be gently encouraged by his wife. Or his friend, Toby, for that matter, who was standing with him too. Toby McCourt, his best buddy, the guy who'd loaned him the Haveaheart trap last year that he used to try to catch the pesky rabbit, the one he often referred to as That Damn Rabbit.

Blake still bristled sometimes when he thought about it. The trap had proven useless; the rabbit was too smart or too uninterested, or too something, to be enticed into it. Yes, Mrs. Bunny Rabbit apparently was not the least bit interested in partaking of the delectable salad mixture he'd baited the trap with: romaine lettuce, baby carrots and sliced radishes. No. All she wanted were to eat his beloved nasturtiums, bachelor buttons, delphiniums and any other flowers she could sink her rabbity teeth into. It was horrible. Then, to add insult to injury, she started bringing her babies into his yard! Blake sighed at the upsetting memory. It had been a long summer last year, a long, long summer indeed.

But this was a new year, and he felt he'd spent the intervening months wisely. He'd changed his diet, listened to his relaxation tapes and tried to learn how to calm down. Plus, and this was more to the point, he'd made a plan. Over the winter, he'd studied the behavioral habits of rabbits, specifically cottontails. He found out that among their favorite food was red clover and creeping charlie, plants considered by most, Blake included, to be weeds. They also liked watercress, collard greens, and swiss chard. *Well*, thought Blake to himself, *why not plant all of that for the rabbit to eat? If I grow what they like to eat, maybe the damned thing will stay away from my flowers.*

And early this spring that's exactly what he did. He dug out and planted a new garden, one especially for the rabbit. It was a five by ten-foot space, rich with sweet clover, creeping Charlie, watercress, collard greens, and swiss chard. The plants had flourished (Blake really did have a green thumb) and the female rabbit fed exclusively there, in her garden, eating what she was supposed to eat. Blake was ecstatic at his success. He even got into the habit of spending a few minutes each day watching her, first, early in the season when she was all by herself, then later during the summer when she brought her seven babies. It was kind of cute, really, Blake thought to himself, when he wasn't thinking about all the damage she'd done in years past.

Feedback on the microphone drew his attention back to the present. The past was, as they say, past. This was now. It was a new Blake with a new, rabbit-friendly garden, and now it was time to find out who the winner of this year's garden contest was going to be.

Everyone turned their attention to the small stage set outdoors down by Lakeside Park. Gwendolyn Pickle, Long Lake City Council President, stepped to the mic and said in a voice loud and clear, "And the winner this year, for not only having a beautiful garden but one that also is home to some of the critters and wildlife in the neighborhood. The winner is Blake Jorgenson."

"Finally," thought Blake. "It's about damn time."

Then he accepted the congratulations from his wife and Toby and about a hundred other people, none of whom he knew. But that was okay. He'd won. That was the main thing.

Later that evening, Blake and Alicia were strolling through the front yard, looking at the pretty flowers and waving at passers-by who were stopping by to congratulate them. Then, just as the sun was dipping below the horizon, they took a moment to sit in a pair of white Adirondack chairs, strategically placed to give the viewer a sweeping view of the front yard and all the lovely gardens. After a few minutes, Alicia said, "It's such a wonderful evening. How about if I go inside and bring us out some nice iced tea? Would you like that?"

Blake smiled at his wife. "Yes, I would, dear. Thank you."

He watched as she went inside and then turned his attention to his yard and his gardens. My how pretty everything looked, he thought to himself. The last year had been very trying, what with his heart attack and all. But he'd preserved, and now he'd won the first-place trophy. It was already proudly displayed inside on the fireplace mantel. His garden was the best in the city. Good for him.

Blake felt wonderfully calm and at peace. All was right with his world. He sat silently as the twilight deepened, listening to the last song of a robin and the final cooing of a mourning dove. Over the past year, he'd listened to many different types of relaxation tapes on his road to recovery, but there was something to be said about being in his own yard at sunset. It was better than any damn relaxation tape. He was in the natural world and it was real and it was right here, all around him. He felt himself mellowing out even more. After a few moments, he nodded off to sleep.

A few minutes later, Alicia came out with their tea and found her husband dozing peacefully in his chair. She smiled and set his glass aside and then sat down to savor a sip of her own tea while she enjoyed the serenity of the quiet evening. Out of the corner of her eye she caught a movement. She looked closely and saw her husband's nemesis, the big female rabbit, confidently hoping across the yard, carefully skirting the flower gardens, making her way to the sweet clover and watercress and creeping charlie – her garden. She had three young ones with her. Alicia watched as the mother and her young made a meal in the garden Blake had planted especially for them. She wondered if she should wake him so he could watch with her. No. Better let him rest. It'd been a long year. She closed her eyes and rested with him.

In amongst the creeping charlie and clover the female and her young fed hungrily. The man had been nice to plant a garden for them. She had done her part and stayed out of his precious flowers. It'd been a nice year for her: abundant food, a nice litter of babies, and, most importantly, no metal trap. She was happy.

When they were finished feeding, the female led her young ones away, back to their burrow on the far side of the garage next door. On the way, she couldn't help herself, she stopped and nibbled some of the man's bachelor buttons. Oh, did they ever taste good! She'd almost forgotten how tasty they were. She encouraged her babies to have some. They all agreed it was a welcome change from their rather bland diet in "their garden". Then she led her little family away. Maybe tomorrow they'd come back for some more of the man's flowers. As she hopped away, she thought about it for a few moments and then decided that why not? She'd been a good little bunny rabbit all summer. She deserved a treat. Yes, that's what she'd do. Tomorrow she'd come back for more of the man's flowers. There were a lot of them for the taking. After all, there was only so much sweet clover and creeping Charlie a hungry rabbit family could eat. Especially with a garden full of so many other tasty flowers to choose from.

Autumn Leaves

We waited off to the side for our order, all three of us quiet, unused to this. Sure, we'd eaten at McDonald's before but not under circumstances like these – me taking Sammy and Elise out after school because I couldn't take them back to what used to be our home. Lynn and I had been separated for six weeks and it was still weird, mostly with the kids. Well, especially with the kids. Lynn and I, we'd grown apart and just weren't good for each other anymore. The separation made sense for us, but this estrangement from my children was pretty bad. I only saw them a couple of times a week after school plus every other weekend. I guess I just hadn't anticipated how emotionally traumatic it would really be; both for them and for me.

"So school's going okay?" I asked Sammy.

"Yeah, it's good, Dad."

"How about with you sweetheart? Have you made any new friends this year?"

A heavy sigh from my precocious seven-year-old and then, "Yeah, Daddy. Remember? Brianna and Emma. I told you already."

Oh. Sure. Right. She had.

Shit, I hated this. We used to be comfortable with each other. Conversation? Never a problem. Ten-year-old Sammy would go on and on about his favorite class, science, the experiments they were conducting, and what he was learning. Elise would tell me about her friends and who liked who and who was being mean to who. It was our own unique kind of communication, and it had been nice. Comfortable. We'd been close to each other. Now this, this drifting apart. How could things change so dramatically in just six lousy weeks? The reality was right in front of me. What had I expected?

Our order came up, and Sammy helped me carry the trays back to the play area where we normally sat. While we ate the kids watched the other children playing and slowly the mood began to lighten, all of us being in a familiar setting. When they finished, Sammy said, "Dad, can we go play with the other kids?"

"Please, Daddy," Elise chimed in. "Pretty please."

Happy to see my children excited about something, I readily agreed. "Sure. You guys go for it." I smiled and checked my watch. "Fifteen minutes, okay?"

"Okay," they said in unison, and off they went.

I watched them playing, first with each other and then with the other kids. It was gratifying to see them acting like they normally did and having a good time. Someone told me once that children had a built-in capacity to be survivors and apparently the statement was true. I just needed to give my kids time to adjust, the credit to be able to do so, and to be there to help them along when necessary. I could do that. As hard as the estrangement was for me, I was committed to helping Sammy and Elise get through it with as little emotional damage as possible. My own personal survival? I guess I'd just have to wait and see.

Later on the way home, we drove by a forested park. We were at a stoplight when I noticed both Sammy and Elise gazing out the window. It was late October and most of the leaves had fallen from the trees. The ground with thick with them.

Sammy turned to me. "Dad, remember when we used to help you rake the yard?"

"Yeah," Elise said. "We'd make those big leaf piles and jump in them?"

"That was really fun," Sammy said, wistfully. Then he went back to looking at the park.

"Yeah," Elise added, gazing longingly out the window, uncharacteristically subdued.

I was drawn to looking out the window, too, traveling back nostalgically into the past, reliving those old memories. Playing in the leaves had been fun. A lot of fun.

What the hell? When the light changed, I made a snap decision and turned left into the parking lot, squealing the tires a little.

Sammy looked quickly at me. "What are you doing, Dad?"

I was supposed to be taking them home but, instead, was suddenly motivated by seeing my kids reminiscing happily about a past memory. "I thought we could check out the leaves. You know, play in them."

The energy level in the car soared through the roof. It took only a moment before both the kids yelled, "Yea!"

We played in the leaves for nearly an hour, until just before sundown. We made piles and jumped into them and had leaf fights and threw armfuls of them at each other and ran around like there was no tomorrow. The three of us hadn't laughed so hard in weeks; since before I'd moved out.

At one point I called Lynn and told her I'd be a little late getting the kids back. She said that that was fine and asked what we were doing. I told her we were playing in a park.

"Well, that's good, Philip. The kids always liked doing stuff like that with you."

Later, I dropped Sammy and Elise off with a big hug for each of them and a promise to see them in two days. Then I drove to my apartment building and took my backpack to my single-room efficiency. I took out my laptop, lifted the lid, and went to boot it up. That's when I saw it. Set on the keyboard was a single beautiful leaf – a burnished red and orange maple leaf – left by my kids. There was a note, too, written, I could tell, by Sammy, and signed by both he and Elise. It read *We love you, Dad.*

I have to say that I got a little teary-eyed. I walked to the window and looked outside. In the fading twilight, I could see clouds racing across the sky and leaves swirling along the ground. I'd be with Sammy and Elise in two days and I was already looking forward to it. Maybe we'd go back to that park and fool around in whatever leaves were left. My guess was that the kids would like that. I would, too. Yeah, that was a good idea.

I wiped my eyes and returned to my desk where I carefully laid out the leaf and the note. Their thoughtfulness was overwhelming. The future might be uncertain, but there was one thing I knew for sure – tomorrow, as soon as it opened, I'd go to the store and get a frame and put both the leaf and the note in it. Then I'd hang it on the wall just to remind myself that one way or the other the kids and I would get through this. It was written in the leaves. We belonged to each other.

Silent Night

Ralph Kaczynski had been a salvation army bell ringer for seventeen years and it was by far and away the coldest and the snowiest winter he could ever recall. In spite of wearing long underwear, jeans, two sweaters, three pair of socks, heavy boots and a thick, insulated snowmobile suit, he was still cold. It didn't help that standing outside the huge big box store was a lesson in both the good and the bad in humanity. Mostly the bad. People hurrying and yelling at each other, shoving and pushing… Man, talk about a lack of good will toward mankind. He stole a quick glance at his wristwatch. Nine forty-five. Only fifteen minutes to go until the store closed. Then Christmas Eve tomorrow, and then he was done until next year. Thank god. It'd take him until July to thaw out.

Suddenly, out of the corner of his eye, he saw a commotion near the exit. A young woman was arguing with one of the security guards. He recognized her. She and her daughter had been frequent visitors since Thanksgiving, and he'd occasionally wondered what they'd been doing, spending so much time in the store like they did. They rarely left with any packages, anything he could see anyway. Hmm. Shop lifters, maybe? There'd been a rash of them this season.

Suddenly the little girl, she must have been six years old or so, stepped away from her mother. She looked Ralph right in the eye, smiled a friendly smile and skipped across the slushy sidewalk toward him, going too fast in his estimation. "Watch out," he called out above the noisy throng of shoppers. "It's slippery."

She tried to slow down but slipped and fell hard anyway. "Oww," she said quietly as she slid along the sidewalk right up next to the less than merry bell-ringer.

Ralph's heart immediately went out to the little girl. With her pink stocking cap and unicorn-themed snow jacket, she reminded him of his daughter when she was that age. He bent down. "Here, honey, let me help you." Her mother was still preoccupied with the security guard. "Are you okay?"

"I'm okay, mister," she said, wiping the slush off her tights. "It doesn't hurt too bad."

He lifted the little girl to her feet and made sure she was uninjured. He glanced back just as the security guard waved the mother away. She hurried over, saying to Ralph, "Thank you so much, sir." Then she knelt down next to her daughter. "Are you okay, Lisa? I told you to be more careful."

The little girl's tights were torn at the knee, but she only had a small scrap, a tiny amount of blood. "I'm okay, Mommy, really. This nice man helped me."

Ralph was suddenly embarrassed. "It was nothing. She's a tough little girl."

What was he talking about? He didn't know anything about her, but the little girl, this Lisa, had a way about her, a presence almost. He had to ask, just to be polite, because, after all, it was the holiday season, "Do you want anything special for Christmas, honey? A doll or something?" The little girl shocked him. "No. Not really."

"Are you sure? Nothing at all?"

The little girl thought hard for a moment and then said, "Well, what I'd really like is to sing a Christmas carol."

"A Christmas carol?"

"Yes, please. Right here." Ralph couldn't believe how polite the little girl was.

"She didn't get to sing in the school concert this year," her mother added. "I had to work so I kept her with me." There was something about the two of them that Ralph found endearing.

He put his bell aside and said, "You know. I'm not sure if it's against regulations or not, but to heck with it. You go right ahead, young lady. Sing any song you want."

Lisa beamed a bright smile and took a moment to compose herself. Then she stood up straight and tall and started singing *Silent Night*. Her voice was quiet at first and the song hardly recognizable, but by the time she had gotten to "Sleep in heavenly peace," she had found her confidence and passion, and her voice rang out loud and clear into the cold night air. Soon, a small crowd formed around the little singer, some even humming or singing along themselves. Ralph stood off to the side with Lisa's mother, watching, enjoying a bit of Christmas magic right there on the sidewalk of a big box store.

When she was done with her song, the crowd applauded and asked for more. With a nod from Ralph, she sang, *Joy To The World*, and even the bell ringer, old curmudgeon that he was, felt a tear form in his eye.

While her daughter sang, her mother, went through her mental checklist. Get Lisa into bed, snug and secure. Make sure the doors were locked. Make sure their extra blankets were handy because it was going to be cold tonight. Get to work tomorrow by nine in the morning for a full six-hour day. Then back to the parking lot for the night, Christmas Eve.

Meg considered herself lucky because she had a car to call home and a place for her and Lisa to sleep. Others weren't so fortunate. But it almost had all gone down the drain when that security guard had gotten in her face, telling her she had to move on and couldn't park there overnight. She had to remind him that she could, that the owners of the store had agreed to let ten cars park there for the winter and she was one of them, one of the homeless finding a place to live in the big box store parking lot.

Finally, he'd agreed, saying, threatening, "Well, you better watch yourself. No drugs or alcohol or anything like that."

No problem. Meg told him. "Look, it's just me and my daughter. You've got nothing to worry about."

He didn't either. Lance, her former boyfriend and Lisa's father, had no idea where they were and that was the way she wanted it. He was a drunk and was physically abusive to her, and she needed to stay away from him for the sake of herself and Lisa.

When Lisa was done singing, she ran over. "Mommy, Mommy, did you like them? Did you like my songs?"

Meg smiled. "I did very much, sweetheart. You did really good." She turned to Ralph. "Thank you so much."

He suddenly had a thought. "You know, tomorrow's Christmas Eve. I'll be here from four until six when we close. Maybe Lisa would like to come and sing. I'd like it, and I think the crowds would, too."

Meg thought for a moment. Why not? "What do you think, Lisa? Would you like to sing some more tomorrow?"

"I would, Mommy, I really would."

"Well, you heard her. I guess we'll be back."

Ralph smiled. "Good. Great. See you then."

"Okay. Right. See you tomorrow." The three of them all waved good-bye.

The snow was starting to fall as Meg and Lisa made their way to the far corner of the parking lot to their car. They got in the backseat and spent a few minutes wrapping themselves in blankets for the night, then curled up together for warmth.

Just before she fell asleep, Lisa spoke. "Mommy?"

"What sweetheart?"

"Am I really going to be able to sing tomorrow?"

"Yes, you can. If you want to."

"Oh, I do. I do."

"Well, then you can."

"Thank you, Mommy."

"Don't thank me, thank the nice man. Ralph."

"I will tomorrow. Okay?"

"Okay. Now, good night."

"Good night. And Mommy?"

"What, sweetie?"

"If I can sing tomorrow, it's going to make it my best Christmas ever."

Meg snuggled in close to her daughter. It was so peaceful and quiet that she could hear the snowflakes settling on the roof of the car. A silent night. They were safe from Lance. They had a roof over their heads and she had a job. Most importantly, she and Lisa were together. Things could be a lot worse. "Mine, too," she said, hugging her little girl tight. "My best Christmas ever."

Footprints in the Snow

Out for a winter walk, I came upon some footprints in the snow. *Whose were they*? I paused for a moment, thinking, but came up with no answer, so I impulsively decided to follow them. As I walked, I began remembering how much I enjoyed this, walking outside like I was, not up and down those long hallways in the mall like I'd been doing lately. You see, I've been having a little trouble remembering where I am over the past year, so my wife has taken to driving me to Ridgedale where she and I walk with an oldsters' group. It's been okay, and I liked walking with Kath, but it's nothing to write home about. However, let me tell you, back in the day, back when my memory was clear, I used to do it a lot, this walking outside. I liked it then and I was liking it now, even though I didn't know where I was.

Having the fresh invigorating air with the cold bite of winter on my cheeks not only felt wonderful, it made me feel young again. Out of the blue, old-time memories came flooding back: My younger brother Tim and I in our youth, walking in the winter woods outside of town with our field guides in our backpacks, teaching ourselves how to identify birds; young Kath and I before we were married, shuffling along a snowy, moonlit trail in a wooded park in January, talking quietly, planning our future and stealing warm kisses behind a convenient oak tree; my daughter Janet and I strolling along a snowy river path near the college she attended as she told me of her dreams for her future; my grandson…

Suddenly I heard Zak's voice calling, shaking me out of my reverie, "Grandpa, Grandpa, you need to come inside. Grandma Kath says it's time for dinner and great uncle Tim's starving." I looked over and saw him grinning. We all knew how much my brother liked to eat.

"I'm coming," I said, pulling my mind back to the present and making my way through the snow to the back door of the home Kath and I have lived in for over fifty years. So that's where I was. Our backyard was a tiny open area, and the edges of the property were thick with evergreen trees. In a way, it was kind of like being in a wooded clearing in northern Minnesota. I'd have to try to remember that.

"What were you doing out there, Grandpa?" Zak asked as I came up to him, stomping snow from my boots. He was eleven and in middle school, and this winter he was busy with hockey, his friends, and class work, in that order. I didn't see him as much as I used to, or liked to, for that matter.

"Reminiscing," I told him. He didn't need to know that I'd had absolutely no idea where I'd just been except lost in fond memories, reliving the past. I recovered valiantly and said, "Thinking about walks we used to take."

"Like when you took me out that one winter night and showed me the constellations? I remember we saw Cassiopeia and Orion."

"Yeah, exactly," I said, mentally shifting gears back to the present (rather smoothly, I thought.) "Back when you were young and just a kid, like four or five." I reached out to jokingly muss up his hair as he ducked away, laughing.

I stepped into the back entryway, closed the door against the cold and began taking off my winter jacket, scarf, boots and hat. I used to babysit him one day a week before he started grade school. Those were good times back then, special times, especially now that he was getting older and busy with other activities. I glanced up and saw Zak looking past me to the backyard, quietly thinking. The hoe was filled with the aromatic scent of cinnamon, baked sweet potatoes and fresh apple pie. My mouth involuntarily started watering. I smiled to myself, thinking of my brother. No wonder he was starving.

Zak interrupted my thoughts. "Hey, Grandpa, how about after we eat, you and I go outside and go for a walk? It's been a while."

I was shocked almost to the point of speechlessness. It was the last thing I expected to hear from my busy grandson. I almost put on my jacket right then and there, grabbed him by the arm and went back outside. Instead, I reached for him and enveloped him in a big bear hug as he good-naturedly squirmed to get away. "That'd be wonderful, Zak, just perfect." Our meal couldn't be over soon enough, as far as I was concerned.

Afterward, as Zak and I got ready to go outside, snow flurries started falling ever so lightly. The sun was setting, painting the western horizon dusty mauve, and the soft glow of street lamps was illuminating the drifting snowflakes like floating specs of glitter. It was so pretty that we were spontaneously joined by my daughter Janet (Zak's mom) along with Kath. Even my brother Tim dragged himself out of his easy chair and made it outside. I couldn't recall the last time all of us had gone for a nice family stroll together along a snow-covered street. It was way better than being at the mall. In fact, I wouldn't mind if we made a habit of it, all of us making time to get together and go walking. Winter, summer, spring, or fall, it wouldn't matter. I'd like that a lot.

But today was special, having us all together. And you know what? The whole time we were walking, I remembered where we were from beginning to end. In fact, I still do. It was unforgettable.

Pictures in the Sky

My earliest memory is of a sunny summer day with Mom and me sitting in our shady backyard. I was four years old, and she was holding me in her lap. Casually, she pointed and said, "Jerry, look up in the sky. What do you see?"

I looked and said, "Umm, clouds."

"Right, honey," Mom said. "Now look very closely. Do any of them remind you of anything?"

I looked again, starting to get the feeling I was missing something and maybe letting her down a little. "Maybe, pillows?" I ventured.

Mom grinned and hugged me tightly. "Oh, honey, I love you so much." I remember that distinctly. She always had a way of making me feel good about myself, which was nice, because, believe me, I was never the sharpest pencil in the box.

She pointed in a different direction. "Look over there. I see something that looks like a horse. Do you see it?"

I looked. All I saw were cotton-looking clouds. "I see cotton balls," I said.

Mom smiled, having fun I could tell, playing the art teacher that she was at the local high school. "Let's look again." She directed my gaze and with her graceful finger outlined the horse she saw. "There's the head, there's the body, there are the legs and there's the tail."

"I think I kind of see it," I said, hesitantly, even though I really couldn't.

"That's okay if you don't," she smiled and hugged me again. Then she stood up. "Just a second, I'll be right back." She hurried into the house and returned with a sketch pad and a pencil. "Here's what I see." And she sketched out a simple drawing of a horse, showing me each part as she drew: head, body, legs, and tail. When she was finished she said, "Now look in the sky again and this time use your imagination."

Oh, my imagination, so that's what it took. And that's what I did. I let my mind go free and when I did I was able to see the horse. Finally. I nodded happily. "Yes, Mom, now I can see it," I told her, getting enthusiastic. "Can I try and make my own drawing?"

"Absolutely." She gave me a pencil and paper. "Let's look at more clouds and find something special for you. What do you see?"

Now that I knew how to look, I let my imagination take over. I looked for a few moments and then pointed. "There. I see a doggy," I said, confidently.

"Can you draw it?"

"I'll try." And I did. I drew a doggy and that's how it all started, Mom and me drawing pictures of clouds together.

We passed that summer and subsequent summers thereafter, as often as we could, sitting outdoors looking at the sky and drawing pictures of what we saw. I'm glad we did because over time her vision began to fail little by little until, when I was in my early twenties, blindness from macular degeneration robbed her completely of her eyesight. After that, we'd sit together in the sunshine and she'd ask if there were any pictures in the sky, and I'd tell her what I saw and then I'd sketch them. I think she enjoyed imagining them as much as I did drawing them.

But it was more than the drawing for us, much more. It was us being together. We'd talk, I'd tell her about my day, and she'd tell me about hers. We shared our lives. She was able to instill in me a love of nature, the sky and the sun, and the passing of the seasons. And a love of clouds, of course. Always the clouds.

She was seventy-nine the last time we were together.

We were sitting outside of her senior living complex on a warm summer afternoon. The sun was shining and the sky was clear and bright and blue. "Jerry," she said, "how's the sky looking today? Any good pictures up there?"

I took her hand, thinking back over all those years of us together drawing pictures of what we saw in the sky." Yes, Mom, there are."

"Can you draw me one?" she asked, just like when I was young.

Today's sky was cloudless, but it didn't matter. "Sure, Mom. I can do that."

I used my imagination and drew a picture of a son and his mother, sitting outside on the patio on a warm sunny day. They were happy and smiling as if life would go on forever, or at least their memories would, of soft summer days when the two of them spent time together, enjoying each other's company and looking at the sky, imagining what pictures they saw there.

When I was finished I showed her what I'd drawn. She told me that she loved it.

Mr. Macaroon

"Sorry to have to tell you this," Doctor Jensen said, not looking all that sorry, "but you've got celiac sprue."

Celiac what? It sounded serious. "Am I going to die?" I asked, cutting to the chase along with starting to perspire. Heavily. Man, I was only forty-four years old. Way too young.

"No, you're not going to die, Frank, and before you let your imagination run away with you, let me explain: You've got an intolerance to gluten."

Never heard of it. "What's that?" I asked wiping away the sweat that was now running into my eyes.

"What it means is you can't eat anything made out of wheat. You've got to stop right now. If you don't, yes, you could die. It could kill you." He looked at me hard. "Am I making myself clear? No bread, no pasta or Doritos or cookies, none of that stuff. Only non-gluten foods like carrots, lettuce and raisins or things made with gluten-free flour." He peered at me above his wire-rimmed glasses. "Understand?"

I was picturing myself snacking on carrots and raisins instead of a bag of chips while watching Monday night football. For the rest of my life. The prospect was not pleasant. "Not even occasionally?"

"What about 'It could kill you' didn't you understand?" he stared at me.

Oh, yeah. Right. "Got it," I said, not really getting it at all. Nor happy about it, either, for that matter.

When I told my wife, Jenny, she looked me up and down and said, "Snacking on carrots and raisins? It might do you good, you know, Frank. You could stand to lose of few pounds."

So much for a sympathetic ear.

But she was right, I had kind of let myself go over the last few years, well five or six to be exact, ever since the twins were born. But I'm not going to use Carrie and Kylie as an excuse. They were the light of my life. This was all on me.

Dr. Jensen told me that I could investigate gluten-free alternatives to wheat and I did. To say the results were mixed was putting it mildly. Jenny and I shared the cooking duties so I was comfortable in the kitchen. I began to make cookies and bread and pasta with gluten-free flour, all to limited success: the bread was dry, the cookies tasteless and the pasta was so sticky, it was impossible to chew.

I admit that things looked bleak until the last day in May came around. It was a bright and sunny Saturday, we'd just planted some pots of geraniums, and Jenny and the twins suggested we go to lunch at a favorite restaurant. We made ourselves comfortable and I had my (now) usual salad with a side of rice crackers and hummus. Sound bland? Well, yeah, but by then a few months had passed since my visit to Doctor Jensen and I was getting used to it. The girls wanted ice cream for dessert (which I can eat, by the way,) so were ordered.

While we were waiting my daughters handed me a small box. They giggled with excitement.

"It's for you, Daddy," Carrie said.

"Yes, Daddy, for doing so well on your new diet," Kylie added.

I looked at Jenny. She just grinned and nodded toward the girls. It was their idea, she mouthed. I have to say, my kids are pretty sweet. "Why, thank you, girls," I said, smiling at them, intrigued. What was going on? I opened the box. Inside there were four round objects, flattened on one side. They were white with toasted edges and shaped like large golf balls. I looked at Carrie and Kylie and then at Jenny, the question on my face obvious. What was I looking at?

"They're macaroons," Jenny said, smiling. "Made from coconut. They're gluten-free, if you must know. The girls found them at a bakery and thought you'd like them."

I had no idea. Coconut cookies? I'd been a chocolate chip man all my life, but the girls were looking at me with heightened expectations. I took one out and held it up for all to see.

"Looks good," I said. The girls watched expectantly. "I think I'll have a bite."

Carrie and Kylie giggled excitedly. "Yea, Daddy!"

I bit in and the flavor exploded in my mouth. A sweet vanilla mixed with soft, chewy coconut, it tasted fantastic, maybe even more so since my girls gave them to me. I took another bite and then reached over to hug Carrie and Kylie. "Thank you, kids. This is the best gift ever."

I shared the rest of the macaroons with my family along with the ice cream. Everyone loved them. They were gone in about a minute.

That was years ago. I'm still gluten-free and have learned to make great meals using gluten-free flour and recipes. I even make macaroons. But you know what? Those macaroons the girls gave me? They're still the best I've ever tasted, and not necessarily just because they were gluten-free, but because they were a gift from my girls. We stop at that bakery on a pretty regular basis to stock up. My whole family loves them. In fact, my kids have a nickname for me now. The call me Mr. Macaroon. I love it.

Limerick Day

Growing up it never failed, and this year was no exception, the first day of school was always embarrassing. By that, I'm referring to class introductions, where the teacher went around and had us introduce ourselves and tell something interesting about said self. Being painfully shy, it was not my finest moment.

"And so now we have this young man," Mr. Strout said, smiling at me and rubbing his hands together in anticipation of I'm not sure what. Well, actually, I was. "Tell us your name."

Titters wove through the classroom like snakes through wet grass. God, I hated this, but Dad was kind of famous and I'd been taught to be polite.

"Edward Langston," I stated, trying to speak up and not mumble like I normally did. "Ed," I added, hoping this year in sixth grade I'd make the much-anticipated move up from Eddie.

"Ed Langston," the teacher said. (Thank you, Mr. Strout!) Then he turned to the rest of the class. "Do any of you know who Ed's father is?" My ears turned red, my face felt like it was on fire.

Of course, my best friend Mickey, class clown and goof-ball extraordinaire, had to raise his hand. "His dad is Arthur Devon Langston, the famous poet."

Mr. Strout smiled broadly. "That's right Mitchell." (Mickey was the nickname he'd chosen for obvious reasons.) "Arthur Devon Langston, the famous poet and lyricist. He's also well-known for his limericks if I'm not mistaken, isn't that right?" Now he turned toward me. "Isn't that right, Ed?"

I sighed inwardly. I wanted to crawl into my shirt and die. But, of course, I couldn't. Plus, Dad always told me to, as he put it, "Do our name proud."

"That's right, Mr. Strout."

Mickey chimed in. "He's really famous. He wrote that one about the guy's feet." Then he stood up next to his desk and recited dramatically, "There once was an old man from St. Pete. Who walked on his hands not his feet. He lasted one day. And then had to say. 'It's not a feat that I'd like to repeat.' "

And the class erupted in laughter. Just shoot me, I thought to myself. Please, someone, just kill me.

Despite that rather inauspicious beginning, sixth grade turned out to be a good year for me. I met Angie. Mick and I became even better best friends. I was able to keep a low profile and not have too much attention drawn to myself, which was always a good thing in my book. So all in all the year went well.

But then in May, Mr. Strout sprung the final assignment of the year on us.

"Class," he intoned, standing tall and proud in front of us squirrelly and anxious to be done with school for eleven and twelve-year-olds. "Class, your last assignment for the year is a writing exercise. I want you to write a limerick."

Groans from everyone. "Now, now, let's calm down." Mr. Strout held up his hands and waited for silence. He was muscular and bald, nearly six and a half feet tall with a full beard. Rumor had it he once played linebacker for Purdue or something. He really did command a presence. "And the best news is this," he added. We all waited in anticipation, thinking that the best news was that he was just joking and we wouldn't have to do the assignment. Of course, we were wrong. "Ed's father, Arthur Devon Langston, has agreed to judge them and read some of his favorites for us. Won't that be nice?"

Right then and there what had been a rather perfunctory year in sixth grade exploded into one I'd never forget. Dad was going to come to school and read our limericks? News to me. He taught English at the University so he was good in front of a class. Great, actually. He was an amateur thespian and enjoyed acting in local plays. He'd be in his element in our classroom. But my father coming to school to be an ad-hoc teacher? It couldn't get much worse. Adults like to say that it's all about character-building. "It'll be a good learning experience," they'll tell you. Maybe, but when you're eleven years old, it's just plain embarrassing.

In the end, though, it wasn't so bad. Dad was good with the class. Friendly. My classmates liked him. He told us that the name limerick most likely referred to the city or county by the same name in Ireland. He told us that the form first appeared in England in the early years of the eighteenth century and was popularized by Edward Lear in the nineteenth century. He understood that our attention span, not the best on a good day, was even shorter with the end of school drawing near. In short, he kept it short.

Then he went ahead and read a few of our limericks. He had a booming voice, and, like I said, he was good in front of people. The class loved him.

"This first limerick is by Angie Smith," he said. I glanced over at Angie and she shyly smiled at me. My heart went racing.

Dad recited:

> *She was a dancer at club Bet Your Bippy.*
> *She was talented, hardworking and thrifty.*
> *Men hooted and hollered.*
> *She saved all their dollars.*
> *Now she lives in a big house in the country.*

He smiled at Angie. "Well done, young lady." Angie's ears turned red. Mine, too.

Dad continued, "Next is a charming one about a kitten. It's by Kathy Anderson."

He cleared his throat, then read:

Jane loved her new little kitten.
Its fur was as soft as a mitten.
But when kitty peed on the floor
Jane ran for the door
With her kitten. Then Jane wasn't so smitten.

The class laughed a little. Dad smiled and said, "Very good rhyming, Kathy." She beamed.

"Next is by Susan Warner," he said. "I liked the imagery in this one."

He recited, dramatically:

A fierce storm blew in late at night.
The lightning made everything bright.
Thunder rumbled like a train
And the sound of the rain
Gave everyone who awoke such a fright.

He smiled at her. "Good job, Susan." She giggled.

Dad glanced at me before saying, "This next one is by Ed Langston."

Oh, man… I thought to myself, this can't be good. But it turned out okay.

Dad recited:

The daredevil was named Flying Red.
He walked a tightrope that others would dread.
When he performed the crowds cheered.
They never knew that he feared
Falling and waking up in a hospital bed.

Dad gave me a quick smile and a nod of his head. Whew, it was over. I appreciated he didn't say anything.

"And now I'm going to read the last limerick," he said. "I saved it for last because, as much as I enjoyed them all, this one I really liked. It's by Mitchell, excuse me, Mickey Johnson."

I looked at my friend. He was grinning from ear to ear. He'd told me earlier that he'd worked, as he put it, "Really, ready hard," on it. I hoped for the best for him.

Dad composed himself for a moment before lifting his voice dramatically, really getting into it, reciting:

My grandfather liked to drink beer.
Grandma said we had nothing to fear
'Cause after he was drunk
He smelled like a skunk
And the bad guys would never come near.

The class erupted with laughter. Dad smiled at Mr. Stout who grinned back and there was no doubt about it, the limerick writing assignment had been a hit. I'll never forget that day. All in all, it wasn't a bad way to end sixth grade.

After his success with the class, for several years Dad came back to school for, as he and Mr. Strout called it, Limerick Day. He helped out with the assignment and read limericks the students wrote. Everyone loved having him there. I went on to a career in computer science and never wrote another limerick in my life. Mickey ended up teaching middle school English. He's even had some of his poetry published.

Angie? Well, Angie and I married. She became a high school guidance counselor and together we are raising two daughters and one son. We leave it to their grandfather to teach them about limericks, something he loves to do and something my kids love to write and perform.

Here's one my ten-year-old daughter recently recited:

My best friend Sue has a yellow canary.
She's a pretty bird whose name is Sherry.
When she sings songs so sweet
Sue gives her a nice treat.
Then Sherry's songs become even more merry.

You know what, after all these years, they're fun to hear.

83

Neon in Our Veins

Dad stopped working on the combine, took off his cap, wiped his forehead and looked to the north. Grandpa and I stopped working, too, sweat dripping into our eyes, thankful for a break. It was blistering hot for early September, over ninety degrees, and out in the middle of our soybean field there wasn't a bit of shade. We all watched the old pickup spewing a plume of dust as it raced down the county road.

Dad put his cap back on and turned to Grandpa and me with a perplexed look. "That's Lilly. What can possibly be so all fired up important?"

Grandpa and I looked at each other and shrugged our shoulders, neither of us having a clue, but, we did know one thing, if my mom was in a hurry, there must be a good reason.

She turned off the road and raced across the edge of the field, the truck going air borne over deep ruts made by farm equipment, then pulled up to us fast, slamming on the brakes and sliding to a stop, dust billowing all around. Mom didn't even bother to get out, just yelled through the open window, "Dad, you've got to get to town quick. Jerry Jorgensen called. They've got an emergency with that big hotel sign of his."

My humble but talented grandfather was the most sought-after neon sign repairman in Redwood County. "What's the matter?"

"He didn't say, but there's some fancy pants guy, the governor, I think, and a bunch of his cronies coming to stay. He needs you right now."

Back in the fifties, the Prairie City Hotel, nestled on a picturesque bend of the Little Sioux River, was the premier place to stay in southwestern Minnesota. It was about twenty miles from our farm.

Grandpa looked at my father who shook his head and said, "I can't go with you. Take Jack Junior, instead. I need to get this combine un-jammed."

Grandpa scratched at the prominent blue vein on his neck, a move that caused me to subconsciously reach for the small vein just forming on my own neck. He nodded toward me and looked at mom. "What do you think, Lillian?"

My heart leaped to my throat. Grandpa had lived with us for several years and had his workshop in an outbuilding back behind the barn. From an early age, I had tagged along after him, showing an interest in the work he did with neon signs. He liked my company, I guess, and had already taught me about electricity and shown me how to bend glass to make tubes and how to add neon and lots of other cool stuff that you needed to know for neon sign repair. But I was only eight years old. Usually, Dad helped if Grandpa need it, but not today. We were in the middle of the soybean harvest and he was too busy getting that troublesome combine up and running.

I watched Mom. It was up to her to make the final decision. She and Grandpa held each other's gaze for a moment while I held my breath. I'd give anything to go along. Finally, she gave him a quick smile and then looked at me. I could see something in her eyes. I was pretty young and the real question was, was I ready? Mom hesitated only a moment before silently nodding, as if to herself, and then said, "Yes, J.J., you can go with Grandpa, but for Pete's sake, be careful." Inside I silently cheered.

It took us thirty minutes to get to the hotel located on the corner of Main Street and Riverview Avenue. It was an imposing three-story red brick structure with gleaming white trim that had a wide, twenty-step entryway adorned with a beautiful black wrought iron railing. A small crowd had gathered. When we arrived Jerry was waiting for us on the steps, literally wringing his hands. He ran up while the truck was still rolling and said, "Thank god you're here, Bill. The governor is coming soon. The sign's out. Oh, man, this isn't good."

Grandpa got out of the old pickup, put his hand on the distraught man's shoulder and calmly said, "Don't worry, Jerry, my grandson and I'll take care of it." He turned to me. "J.J., let's get going."

We dragged our ladders out of the back of the truck, set them against the side of the building and climbed up. Grandpa quickly deduced the problem; a transformer had blown, and he proceeded to fix it while I handed him the tools. We had the repair completed and the sign back in excellent working order in about half an hour; plenty of time before the governor and his entourage showed up.

Later, after the sun had set, Grandpa loaded me in the pickup and we drove back to town. When we got to Main Street, he parked a little way down from the hotel and we watched the hectic scene on the street. Nearly a hundred townsfolk had gathered and three or four different news crews were milling around, everyone eager to get a glimpse of the governor. I don't think Grandpa saw any of it. He only had eyes for the hotel's neon sign, *Prairie City Motel*, illuminated with glowing colors of red and green, and blue.

After staring in reverent silence for a moment, he pulled me close and pointed past the front windshield. "See, J.J., look at how pretty the sign looks. The reds and greens are so vibrant, and that blue is my favorite color."

"It reminds me of a castle in Wonderland," I said, thinking about my favorite television show.

"I couldn't agree more," Grandpa grinned. "It's magical." He paused touching the blue vein in his neck and then added, "I'll let you in a little secret. Neon makes me feel alive inside."

Grandpa was as much a poet as he was a skilled craftsman.

I'll never forget that day. For the next twenty-five years, I helped grandpa, traveling to the rural towns of southwest Minnesota, and repairing neon signs. I loved the work. After he passed away, I stayed with it. This year, I've started bringing my nine-year-old grandson Johnny along and he loves it as much as I do. There's lots of work for us. They don't make neon signs anymore, everything is LED. That's okay. Nostalgia for the old days is in fashion right now, and there are a lot of old signs out there. We're busy all the time.

We were driving home from a job the other day when Johnny turned to me and asked, "Granddad, do you think we have neon in our veins? You know, like blood?"

I laughed, thinking he was joking, but one look told me he wasn't. He was deadly serious.

I thought for a moment, thinking back over the years to all the signs my grandpa and I, and now, Johnny and I, had repaired. I took my time before finally answering, "You know what? Honestly? You might have a point. I think maybe we do."

He sat back in the seat of my old pickup and looked out the window. It was a warm, sunny afternoon in late fall and fields of golden corn were waiting to be harvested. For the first time, I saw a blue vein pulsing in my grandson's neck just like the one in mine. Like my grandpa's.

He smiled and nodded his head, as if to himself, and said, "Yeah, I thought so."

Music on the Wind

George and Ida Ferguson, my great-grandparents, were second-generation cattle ranchers in eastern Montana. Mom kept a framed picture of them on the fireplace mantel when I was a kid. It was taken in their parlor and you can just make out a piano behind Ida with a vase of cut wild flowers on it. They were dressed for the occasion, she in a calico dress, her long auburn hair wrapped around her head in a twirled braid, he in a white, snap button shirt, vest, and gray Stetson hat. The flat prairie land of the Yellowstone River valley can just barely be glimpsed through the billowing curtains of a window in the background.

I spent countless hours as a kid imagining what their life in nineteenth-century cattle country would have been like: herding longhorns, busting broncos, and mending fences. My tastes back then ran toward cowboys and Indians, so their romantic love was certainly not on my radar, but the true fact of the matter was that their love for each other was known far and wide.

"That's right, Stevie," Mom used to tell me. "They were hard workers and humble, salt of the earth people, busy with chores from dawn to dusk. But in the evenings they made time for making music. Ida played piano and sang while George accompanied her on the fiddle. I'm told that their songs brought joy to even the crustiest cowhand's heart."

As a kid, that kind of talk was embarrassing to hear and often turned my ears red. But as I grew older, I started to imagine a different scenario, one in which they not only lived the hard life of cattle ranchers on the western frontier but also found it within themselves to love deeply while creating beauty and harmony through their music in juxtaposition to that rugged land.

Years later I met Janie and we fell in love. While we were dating, I talked often about George and Ida. Did I idealize them? Maybe. But Janie told me she thought it was sweet they loved each other the way they did and that was good enough for me. It got me thinking that maybe she and I were kindred spirits like my great-grandparents were.

The summer after we married, Janie and I took a driving trip west to the great plains to see first-hand the land of my great-grandparents. We ended up parking our car outside the small town of Willow Creek, Montana, and spent the day hiking rolling pastureland amid pungent sage, prickly cactus, and golden fields of wildflowers, kept company by prairie dogs, meadowlarks, and a small herd of pronghorn antelope.

By sundown, we had made our way to the top of Buffalo Butte, the highest point of land in Stillwater County, and the overlook where George and Ida's ashes had been scattered. The sun was low in the west, the sky exploding in a fiery orange from the last light of day, the land stretching out to the horizon where we could just barely make out the shadowy peaks of the Rocky Mountains.

The peace and quiet was immense, so quiet I swear I could hear both of our hearts beating. I said to Janie, my voice a whisper, "Legend has it that you can still hear my great grandparent's music if the wind is right."

Janie turned from viewing the scene spread out before us and took in a deep breath of fragrant prairie air. Then she took my hand, her smile as wide as the big sky above us, and said, "I'm so happy you brought me, Steve. I love you. I love being here with you." Then she leaned in and kissed me.

"I love you, too, Janie," I told her. "Forever and all time." And we embraced, holding each other tight, our bodies molding into one.

Then, out of nowhere, we heard it. Faint strains from a piano, a fiddle, and then a soft voice singing. We stood together, our love growing stronger with every note we heard, listening to the heartfelt music played by my great grandparents, songs of love I somehow knew Janie and I would carry with us for the rest of our lives. Songs from my great grandparents brought to us from them on that gentle prairie wind.

Kite Flying

The flat, treeless, chunk of land on the cliff outside the town of Granite, Minnesota was the best place around to fly kites. It was the size of a football field and me and Joey were flying ours that summer when we noticed a new kite soaring on the wind. A pink one that made us laugh.

"Ha. Man, look at the thing," Joey guffawed. "What a sissy piece of crap."

"No kidding," I said, just to go along with him. We were eleven years old between sixth and seventh grade and peer pressure was alive and well in our little town.

My kite was a black winged batman and his was a red and blue Spiderman, both simple kites we picked up at the drug store in town. There were nearly twenty kites in the air that day, a lot of them fancy ones flown by the summer kids. Joey and I were townies. Our fathers worked in the Steel River iron ore mine fifteen miles inland. Cheap kites were the way to go for us. They worked just fine.

Later in the afternoon, everyone else had left and we were by ourselves. We had lost interest in the pink kite and were talking about baseball when we heard a scream. It came from the far side of a rise near the edge of the cliff. We quickly pulled in our kites and ran to see what was going on.

What I saw made my blood boil. About five or six older kids had surrounded a young girl and had her pined up against the side of a huge boulder. They were taunting her, pulling at her clothes and making rude gestures by grabbing their crotches. Their laughter reminded me of hyenas I'd seen on some nature program. I looked at Joey. He was frightened. We were both small for our ages, no match for a group of big guys that looked to be in their early teens at least.

"Let's get out of here," he whispered.

We'd stopped about fifty feet behind them. They had their backs to us, but the young girl could see us plain as day. I could see in an instant that even though she had to be scared, she was defiant, trying to hold her own. She even had a stick in her hand that she jabbed out whenever someone tried to attack her. It was only a matter of time before they descended on her like a pack of those hyenas I'd seen on the television.

I looked around for a weapon. The ground was bare, just smooth granite and lichen, but I did find a fist-sized rock. It'd have to do.

"Come on," I said to Joey, "let's help her."

Joey... Man, to this day I still think of that moment. He could have run and saved himself, but he didn't. He picked up a rock even smaller than mine and said, "Okay. Let's do it."

Screaming at the top of our lungs, we ran at them. I'm not sure what we were yelling but we startled the hell out of them. I remember them turning toward us, looking perplexed. Then they looked bemused. Then they looked angry.

But by then it was too late. The girl had taken their distraction as her chance and she bolted toward us. We turned and ran with her and didn't stop until we got to the safety of the wide-open space on the top of the cliff.

We stood panting, nervously looking over our shoulders to see if we were being followed. We weren't. They must have decided we weren't worth the effort. We were safe.

She was the first one to speak. "Boy, you guys were amazing," she said. She was maybe a year older than us, and taller by a head. She had short-cropped dark hair and green eyes and skin so smooth I had to stop myself from reaching out and touching her to see if it was real. In that instant I felt myself tumbling down a slippery slope I'd only heard about.

She hugged us both. "I owe you guys my life." Her smile was so sweet I thought I'd die. Instead, I swooned. She smelled like vanilla.

She looked at each of us for a moment and I felt like she was looking into my soul, a soul I never knew I had until that very instant. Then she grinned, turned, waved her fingers, and said, "Well, thanks. See you around."

I watched as she sauntered away toward the road. I could see her bicycle parked there and I panicked, not wanting her to leave. I yelled, "Say, was that you flying that pink kite?"

She stopped and turned. "Yeah, that was mine." She pointed. "Those bastards wrecked it. I'm going to have to get a new one."

Joey and I looked at each other. He mumbled, "Go ahead, ask her."

"Do you want us to go with you?"

She took a stick of gum out of her pocket, slowly pealed the wrapper off, and started chewing. My heart rate went through the roof. All I could think of was being close to her.

"Sure," she shrugged her shoulders. "Why not?"

That was good enough for me.

We joined her and went to the drug store in town and helped her pick out her kite. Superwoman. By then it was dinnertime and Joey had to go home but I just couldn't bear the thought of leaving her. She told me her name was Angie. We went back and flew kites until sundown.

And we flew them every day afterward for the rest of the summer, some days joined by Joey. Those were great times. Just before Labor Day her parents put her on their sailing yacht and left for their home somewhere on the Saint Lawrence River. We never saw her again.

Joey and I stayed in Granite where we eventually finished high school and went to work in the mines like our fathers. We still live there, raising our families and making lives for ourselves. This summer we've been teaching our kids to fly kites outside of town on that same spot we met Angie.

We were there a few days ago when Joey turned to me and asked, "I wonder whatever happened to her, you know, Angie." He was helping his four-year-old son launch his blue and red Superman kite.

"I have no idea," I told him, tugging at the string, helping my five-year daughter save her Wonder Woman from crashing to the ground. "I liked her a lot. I just hope she's happy."

"Me, too," Joey said, thoughtfully, before adding. "That was a great summer, though, wasn't it?"

"It really was," I told him smiling. "One of the best."

And we were quiet then, lost in our own thoughts, standing in the sun, the wind blowing clean off of Lake Superior, enjoying the day and having fun with our kids, our minds drifting back to that long ago summer, a time that with every passing year faded a little more from our memories.

Just then the wind died and the kites started to fall. We hurried to help the kids, each of us grabbing a string and running backward, the kids racing alongside laughing at our antics, us laughing with them. Finally, the breeze returned and the kites lifted into the air. We handed the strings back to our kids and grinned at each other, completely in the moment, this summer rapidly becoming more and more memorable.

Joey gave me a high five. "Nothing better than flying kites."

"No kidding," I said, watching Superman and Wonder Woman dip and dance on the wind, feeling like this was one of the best days I'd had with my young daughter in a long time. I knew Joey felt the same way about his son. I turned to him. "Say, I've got an idea. How about if the wind is right, let's grab the kids and come back here tomorrow?"

Joey smiled and nodded. "Absolutely. I was just about to suggest the same thing."

I laughed. "Great minds…"

He laughed, too.

And the next day, we did.

Big Air

My nephew and I had always been close, but when he called instead of texting and asked me to meet him at his home, I knew something was up.

I drove to where Josh and his partner lived, high in the foothills, a few miles from me. He answered the door with a smile and a "How you doing, Kenny?"

I told him I was fine, but quickly cut to the chase. "What's going on? You doing okay?"

For the last six months, he'd been undergoing treatment for prostate cancer. It was in remission, but still, you never knew.

"I'm good, I just want to talk to you about something." He motioned me inside. "And no," he added with a grin, "it's not cancer-related. The treatments are working just fine." We walked through the welcome coolness of his stucco home to his shaded back patio. "Have a seat."

I was getting antsy but did as I was told.

He looked past me down the long sloping hill toward Lake Havasu, five miles away. The fresh, clean desert air seemed to invigorate him. "I've got a big favor."

"What's up?"

"Funny you should put it that way," he laughed. "I want to go on a hot air balloon ride for my fortieth birthday. I want you to come with me."

I gulped. Jesus, that wasn't fair. I loved Josh with all my heart, but I have to be clear: I was deathly afraid of heights. I paid a guy to climb a ladder to clean debris off my one-story roof, for Pete's sake. Elevators at the mall made me queasy. Ride in a car in the mountains? No way. But this was my nephew asking, a man I'd helped my sister raise ever since his father died when Josh was five. My wife and I never had any kids, and I looked at him as my own son. Fear of heights or not, it didn't take but a blink of an eye to decide to go. Besides, it's not every day you get to face your biggest fear, especially, with someone who's dying. The way I looked at it, it'd be a once-in-a-lifetime experience. Turns out I was almost right.

"I'd love to go," I told him. "I only have one question."

"What's that?"

"Do they provide air sickness bags?"

"Funny."

It was good to hear my nephew laugh. Six months ago the doctors had told him he had between six months and six years to live. Josh was a fighter and definitely had his sights set on the six-year option, if not longer.

Three weeks later, at dawn on Josh's fortieth birthday, I pulled my jeep into the tiny parking lot for Big Air Balloon Rides, located at an abandoned airfield on a spit of land that jutted out into Lake Havasu, a half-mile wide stretch of the Colorado River on the border between Arizona and California.

We got out and headed for the rainbow-colored balloon tethered a hundred feet away near a dented Winnebago that I assumed was the office, if not also the home, of Galen Pickle, the owner of the company.

Galen was checking out the basket but stopped and walked over extending a callused hand. "Hi, Josh. This must be Kenny. Welcome," he said, shaking our hands. Then he spent more than a few moments looking me over. Josh was tall and lean and, in spite of his cancer, still remarkably fit. He worked for Desert Adventures, a company that led outdoor excursions around the Lake Havasu area, primarily hiking, camping, and kayaking. Me? Well, think the opposite of my nephew and you'd get a pretty good picture. I was short and stocky, a little doughy to be honest, and retired after teaching geography at Lake

Havasu High School. I thought Galen was being kind when he said to me, "You look like you'll be able to handle this just fine."

Josh grinned and gave me a high five. "See, Uncle. This'll be great."

Thirty minutes later we lifted off and were soon soaring high above the southwest desert. Did I mention I was afraid of heights? Well, for some reason that morning the fear disappeared. I was having the time of my life watching the desert landscape unfold beneath me with ragged hills stretching to the horizon set against a fiery orange sunrise. It was a thrill I'd never anticipated. I'm sure having Josh with me helped. But then…

Josh said, "Here, Kenny, help me put this on." I looked. He was holding a parachute and a harness. He grinned. "We're jumping together."

That's right, jumping. Together. Seems Josh had a little joke up his sleeve to play on his old uncle. He'd been taking skydiving lessons for a year. Who knew? One minute I was enjoying a mellow morning sunrise, silently congratulating myself on conquering my fear of heights, the next minute I was air born, strapped to my nephew's chest, silently screaming.

Just kidding. Once I got past the fear of losing my stomach, I have to say, jumping out of that hot air balloon was the most exhilarating adventure of my life. We went out at six thousand feet and opened at four thousand. It was a fifteen second drop of unrelenting terror followed by three minutes of magical floating that I never wanted to end. The whole experience was fantastic beyond words.

We landed a mile from where we'd lifted off.

"What do you think?" Josh grinned at me after he'd wrapped the chute up.

It took a minute to get my thoughts in order, not to

mention my equilibrium. Finally, I grabbed him in a tight bear hug. "I loved it."

"Want to go again?"

"Anytime."

That was ten years ago. Since then, we've jumped every year on Josh's birthday. A once-in-a-lifetime experience every year for the last ten years. In spite of his cancer.

First Step

A black hole, that's what it felt like. Depression sucking the life right out of him. He hated it, tried to fight it, but lost the battle that morning and ended up lying in bed unable to move, feeling sorry for himself and missing them both.

An hour or so later the phone rang and he forced himself to pick up. It was his son.

"Dad, it's been a while. I miss talking to you. Can I take you for coffee?"

Yes or no? Decision time. Leave the comfort of his bed, or be a father to his boy? Drown in his own sorrow, or set a good example for his son. In the end, it was Jake's voice that did it, just the jolt he needed. "Please?"

"Yes, I'd like that," he said, clearing his throat and forcing himself to sit up. "I'll see you… when?"

"I'll pick you up in an hour. I'll drive."

"That'll be good, Jake. See you then."

He hung up and took a long moment to collect himself before thinking, I've got to get dressed. He looked at the door leading from his bedroom. It seemed like a long way, a long dark tunnel.

He swung his feet from the bed to the floor and got ready to stand. One step at a time, he told himself, one step at a time to climb out of the depression he'd been mired in for the last six weeks, ever since his wife and daughter had been killed in that car accident.

He struggled to his feet, stood shakily, and steadied himself. He might be depressed, but at least he could walk. He lifted his foot, put it down, and stepped tentatively forward. Then he did it again. He wanted to take a shower and get into some clean clothes and be ready for when his son arrived. It felt good to have something to look forward to. He took another step. He had a long way to go, but at least it was a start.

The Drive around Phantom Lake

"Nicki, look." Frank pointed. Dust billowed as he slowed the car to a stop. Out on Phantom Lake, about one hundred yards from shore were a pair of trumpeter swans and their four young. "See how white they are. Big, too. Aren't they beautiful?"

Frank was taking his time driving up the west side of Crex Meadows, a thirty-thousand-acre wildlife refuge in northwestern Wisconsin. He had driven to the area that morning from their home in Orchard Lake, Minnesota, a three-hour journey, just to see birds in their fall migration. It was mid-September and already the oaks and maples were turning rusty red and orange.

Frank pointed again, becoming excited. "Look at all the ducks. I can see blue-wing teal, redheads, and shovelers." He peered through his binoculars and added, "There's also some common mergansers farther out and a few golden eye. Bufflehead, too." He smiled. "That's very cool." He silently gazed over the big lake, a half mile across and a mile long, a well-known stopover for hundreds of thousands of waterfowl feeding and resting on their long flight south for the winter. He was enthralled.

After a while he put the car and gear and continued at a slow pace, stopping frequently to watch the ducks, dipping and dabbling in the calm water. Overhead bald eagles and red-tail hawks soared in a robin's egg-blue sky.

A movement to the left caught his eye. "Look, Nicki, there's a marsh hawk," he pointed, "and a sharp-shined, too." Both raptors were gliding over the marsh grasses the area was named for, Crex being short for carex, the grasses common in the huge wetland and at one time used to make rugs.

He drove on. "You having a good time?" he asked. The

loop around the refuge was seventeen miles of gravel road and he was enjoying puttering along, moving slowly, pointing out clusters of sandhill cranes feeding in nearby corn fields, various songbirds, more eagles and hawks, and even some osprey. It took two hours to make the circuit and he loved every minute of it. He was sure Nicki did, too.

The end of the drive took him past a modern-looking visitor center remodeled ten years earlier with donations from the one hundred thousand visitors to the refuge each year. He and Nicki had generously contributed and had become friends with many of the staff.

Frank parked and walked through the front door, glancing to the right into a small office. His friend Bob Jensen was at his desk working on a computer. He was the game warden for the area including the refuge. "Hi, Bob," he called, waving.

Bob grinned and walked out to greet him. The two men shook hands. "Good to see you, Frank. Beautiful day, isn't it?"

"Can't beat it. But give me a minute, will you?" Frank held up one finger and shuffled his feet. "I need to use the little boy's room."

"Go for it," Bob smiled.

On his way back, Frank joined Bob who was talking to a high school girl running the cash register in the gift shop. The three of them chatted for a few minutes about the waterfowl migration before Frank said, "Well, I'd love to talk some more but I've got to hit the road. Long drive ahead."

"I'll walk you out," Bob said.

Outside, the scent of pine was pungently pleasing in the warm, late afternoon sun. They walked quietly until Bob touched Frank's shoulder and said, "Say, before you leave, I just wanted to say how sorry I was to hear about Nicole. I couldn't make it to the funeral last spring, but I was thinking of you both. That congestive heart failure is a bitch. I guess her old heart finally just up and gave out. That's too bad. She was a great person; a fine lady."

Frank laughed. "What'd you mean, Bob? She's doing just fine. She's great."

Bob just stared at the old man, bent with age, withered with not only arthritis but also the years. He decided not to push it. "Okay, whatever you say, my friend. See you next year?"

"You bet. We'll be up for spring migration. Maybe even participate in the April sandhill crane count."

"Sounds good. See you then."

Both men shook hands once more. Bob watched Frank get into his car and pull away, wondering if the old guy would even be alive next spring. He'd aged considerably since his last visit. Oh, well… Bob headed inside to the sound of geese flying overhead and crossed his fingers, saying a silent prayer. *We can but hope.*

It was dark by the time Frank got home. He fixed a grilled cheese sandwich for dinner and fed Hootie his seven-year-old tabby cat. The two kept each other company for the rest of the evening.

He began nodding off while watching the ten o'clock news so he got ready for bed. Breathing a heavy sigh, he slid under the covers, lay on his back, and stared into the darkness. It'd been a long day and he was exhausted. He felt the kitty cat jump onto the bed and make herself comfortable down by his feet. In a moment he heard her purring. He smiled. She was a good companion. Then he turned to his side, put his hand on the empty spot next to him, and said, "Good night, Nicki. What a great day we had, didn't we?" The only reply was the soft purring of the cat.

He pulled the covers tightly around him, happy he'd made it through another day without succumbing to the crushing loneliness he'd felt ever since his wife's death. Each day was a challenge. Each day he did the best he could.

He closed his eyes and drifted off to sleep. Tomorrow he'd get up and face the day. With Nicki's help, of course. With her forever and always by his side, he'd find a way. He was sure of it.

The Greeter

Jerry and his wife Jane have been next-door neighbors of Lauren and me for many years. He and I talk regularly, usually while one or the other of us is working in the yard or doing something else outside. He's a nice guy, maybe a little conservative for my tastes, but he's kind and decent and a good neighbor. Over the years I've heard many stories about his strong-willed mother. So when he told me about Helen and how she first got her job at Macy's, and then how she'd been injured and unexpectedly laid off before finally becoming a volunteer Greeter at Macy's, it prompted Lauren and me to do something we hadn't done in a few years – we decided to take a drive into downtown Minneapolis to see the holiday lights and displays. Maybe we'd even run into Jerry's interesting-sounding mother.

We went on a Thursday afternoon, the second week of December, driving on I-394 for half an hour into downtown and then parking our car in the lot A ramp. We walked five blocks across the city with the expressed purpose of going to Macy's to view the recently opened "Old Thyme" Christmas exhibit on the eighth floor, but as we came through the Seventh Street revolving doors we were lucky enough to see Helen. We'd never met her before but Jerry had described her well; there was no doubt the friendly, white-haired lady who welcomed us with a "Merry Christmas! Thank you for visiting our store" like we were long lost friends, was her. We introduced ourselves as friends of Jerry and she was charming and gracious and couldn't have been nicer.

We only chatted for a moment or two before more people crowded in so we left and made our way through the crowded aisles to the escalator and then up to the Christmas exhibit on the 8th floor. That's' where the Old Thyme

Christmas theme was really put on display for all to see. A bustling, cobbled stone street scene had been created, and we walked along wide-eyed, admiring the quaint shops on both sides with workers inside illuminated by the glow of warm yellow lights. There were mounds of cotton snow all around, and the scene was populated with men and women out and about, carrying packages, dressed for winter in old-time woolen jackets and coats with colorful scarves and hats. There were children playing – ice skating and pulling sleds, and dogs running and cats hiding behind corners, and trees everywhere decorated with pretty ribbons and bows and ornaments and lights that twinkled. And, of course, softly playing in the background were the melodic strains of traditional Christmas music.

After Lauren and I viewed the exhibit we wandered around on various floors, window shopping and looking at other festive displays. We even saw a jewelry counter decked out with sprigs of evergreens adorned with tiny silver and golden ornaments and red bows. In a word, the effect of the entire store was enchanting.

When we were finished with our browsing we made it a point of making our way through the crowds back to where we'd entered, just to say good-bye to Helen, but we didn't get the chance. She was talking to a young Somali man with "Asid" on his name tag. They were carrying on an animated conversation and seemed to be enjoying themselves immensely, and we didn't want to interrupt them. I noted she was wearing a red carnation on the lapel of her jacket, a gift, no doubt, from one of the many friends of his mother Jerry had told me about.

Lauren and I left then, feeling good and infused with a little more Christmas spirit than we'd had before we entered the store. It was nice to see the older lady and the young black man together. With all the crap on the news lately about people not getting along, and everyone freaking out over the color of someone's skin or their choice of religion, it was good to see those two together and how comfortable they were with each other. It was really good.

We walked through the crowded downtown sidewalks toward our car. The sun had set and every building had displays of Christmas lights on, filling the night with a festive glow. If it were to start snowing, it would have made the scene perfect. And then it did. We smiled at each other and Lauren took hold of my arm. Was it the time of the year? The seasonal festivities? Or could it happen anytime or anyplace? We didn't know, but for one brief moment the world felt right and in sync with itself, and we walked along smiling and nodding greetings to complete strangers. Sound weird? Maybe, but it felt like it was the right thing to do and that was good enough for us.

We took our time walking to our car, talking about what we'd seen at Macy's and about Jerry's mom, enjoying each other's company and the fresh snow drifting down and the pretty, colorful lights of the city – even the cold bite of winter in the air. And, most especially, the growing feeling that maybe Helen was on to something. Maybe it really was all about opening your heart to others and putting differences aside. Maybe it was about seeing those who were not the same as we were as people first and foremost, and not getting hung up on the color of their skin or where they worshiped. Maybe it was all about being humane and treating people with decency and respect like Helen was doing; and like her friends were doing. And if that was the case, we were more than happy to join her. Which gave me the inkling of an idea.

Make no mistake, the city was loud. There were buses blasting by and cars speeding, kicking up slushy snow, and horns honking almost non-stop. In a way, it was kind of a madhouse. But, balancing the mayhem, there were also carolers on the street corners and bell ringers for the Salvation Army, and people like us, out having a good time, enjoying the soul of the city, and finding joy in the season.

Foremost in my thoughts was Helen. In my mind, I saw her back at Macy's talking to Asid and how comfortable they were with each other, and how happy they seemed. It was little things like what she was doing that was making the world a better place, and she was doing it for no other reason than it was the type of person she was. And so was Asid, as well as all of the other friends Jerry had told us about: Clare, Simon, Leon, and Rico. They were open and generous with each other. Skin color and religion didn't matter. The type of person you were was what counted the most. I wanted to be part of that world.

My idea suddenly crystallized. I stopped dead on the sidewalk and told Lauren about it and she agreed. We turned around and headed with a quick step back to Macy's. Thankfully, Helen, thankfully, was still there in high spirits and just as cheerful as before.

I walked up to her when there was a break in the crowd and re-introduced myself and Lauren as friends of her son. She immediately remembered who we were. We chatted for just a minute before I asked her the question we'd come back to ask.

"Lauren and I were wondering if we could take you to dinner this evening when you're done working," I said to her. She didn't bat an eyelid and nodded enthusiastically as I was talking, but before she could agree out loud, I added, "And maybe bring some of your friends from work along, too."

And she did. And that's how we got to meet Asid, Simon, and Rico (Clare and Leon couldn't get away). We had a nice meal together, good conversation, and, before we parted, made plans to get together for the following Thursday. Hopefully, it was the beginning of something permanent for all of us.

And that may have been the end of the story except for one final thing. The next day I was out shoveling the five inches of snow that had accumulated since it had begun falling while Lauren and I were downtown. It had continued during our dinner with Helen and her friends as well as during our slow drive home and then long into the night.

I had worked my way out to where the driveway met the street, and was clearing what seemed like ten tons of the stuff left behind after the city plow had gone past, when Jerry drove up, slid to a stop, and beeped. He rolled down his window and greeted me with, "So when are you going to break down and join the twenty-first century?" I was nearly too tired to laugh, but I did anyway. This was our long-running joke about my insistence on shoveling my driveway and sidewalk by hand. Jerry, on the other hand, had used his powerful snow blower earlier, finished quickly, and then had run out to open his hardware store before stopping home to drop off a gallon of milk he'd bought on the way for Jane. I was happy for the break since I'd been out for almost an hour and a half. The snow had been wet and heavy, our driveway was long, my arms were sore, and I was beat.

I laughingly told him, "Never!" Even though I'd been silently wishing for one for the last half hour, picturing myself jauntily prancing up and down my driveway gripping a big, red snow-blowing machine with both hands, merrily flinging snow fifty feet into the air.

We chatted a while, being neighborly, before he turned serious.

"So how'd your evening downtown go?" he asked.

"Good," I told him. "Really good." I took my hat off and wiped the sweat from my forehead. "The holiday displays were great. Really pretty." But I knew that's not what he was really asking about. "The best part, though, was that we saw your mom and even met some of her friends."

"Really? How'd that go?" He had a look between wanting to know and driving straight home without hearing my answer.

Well, don't ask if you don't want to know and he asked, so I went ahead and told him about our evening, specifically about how happy his mother seemed and how nice her new friends were. "There's a guy from Somali named Asid and he and Lauren talked about cooking. We came away with the recipe for a dish called Qado that sounded delicious. We talked with Simon about the conflict in the Middle East. He used to live in Lebanon but he's been in the States for fifteen years. He's a Christian and had a pretty unique perspective about the different factions of Muslims and all the fighting going on between them. And her friend, Rico, gave me a hint on how to get rid of those Japanese Beetles that were feasting on my Morning Glories last summer. He said all I needed to do was brush them off the flowers into a bucket of a little dishwater soap and water."

When I was finished with my re-cap of our dinner, Jerry was silent for a minute, looking straight ahead through the windshield, doing some heavy-duty thinking, I figured. I told him, "Your mom said she wished you'd come down there. She'd like you to see where she works and meet some of the people she works with." I paused. He was quiet, thinking hard, I'm sure weighing the pros and cons, so I added, "They're good folks, Jer. You'd like them."

Finally, he turned to me. I always felt Jerry had a kind nature and I knew he cared a lot about his mother. "I'm glad you saw her down there. I've been thinking about maybe going down there for a while now. My mom can be a force of nature, that's for sure."

"I don't think you have anything to lose. When was the last time you and Jane were downtown, anyway?"

"A long time ago. Thirty years at least."

I didn't want to make a big deal out of it, but I felt a little nudge wouldn't hurt. "The eighth floor Christmas show is done up old fashioned and is kind of fun. Jane would like it," I said, just to push him a bit more.

He looked past me to his home, thinking some more. Then he said, simply, "Well, what the hell. Why not?" I realized, then, he must have been ready, all he needed was a reason to convince himself. It was really that simple.

We chatted a bit more, and I told him about parking in Lot A. Then I waved good-bye as he drove down the street to his driveway and turned in. I may have been mistaken, but I could have sworn there was a look of relief on his face. Like he'd told me many times before, he and his mother had always gotten along well. He must have come to the conclusion that it was time to move on and accept this new phase of her life. Besides, like I'd told him, her friends really were good folks. It wasn't going to hurt at all to get to know them.

I finished my shoveling and walked up my driveway to the back door. I was thinking about Jerry and Helen. It was good he was going to make an effort to accept what his mother was doing and the new friends she was making. I know it sounds like a little thing and it may have been a long time coming and, yeah, I know change is hard, but you had to start somewhere. And that's what he was going to do. You couldn't ask for anything more than that. And, who knows, when all is said and done and for everyone concerned, next year might turn out to be a pretty good year.

Ice Skating on Christmas Eve

On Christmas Eve the two brothers got together to go ice skating. Once young and full of pep, they were now old and just this side of decrepit, not to mention both widowers and grey-bearded for longer than they cared to remember. That was okay. Skating was something they'd enjoyed all their lives though this was the first Christmas Eve they'd thought to do it together. It was soon apparent it had been a good idea, for they reveled in the moment, enjoying the crisp winter air and the late afternoon sun casting long shadows on the frozen pond as they glided over its smooth surface.

After a while, Tim took a break and bent down close to the surface. "Hey, these bubbles in the ice are kind of cool. I'm going to take some pictures."

"All right," Joe called to him. "Go for it. I'll just skate."

"Don't fall," Tim cautioned.

Joe laughed as he started skating backward, showing off. "Don't worry." He turned and took about six glides before he stumbled and fell and landed hard on his butt. "Damn!"

Tim looked up, concerned. "You okay?"

Joe lay on his back looking into the clear blue sky. It felt good to be outdoors. It felt good to be skating with his younger brother, too, though he'd probably be stiff in the morning – the fall certainly wouldn't help. "Yeah, I'm fine," he said, struggling to his feet and brushing some snow off as he skated over to see what Tim was doing.

His brother was on his knees, his camera inches away from a bubble in the ice shaped like a heart and framed by the blade marks of ice skates that had cut through a thin dusting of snow. "What do you think? Think this'll make a nice picture?"

Joe had long ago given up trying to offer suggestions to

his artistic brother. Tim had a unique gift, especially when it came to seeing the beauty found in nature. He used to be an accomplished landscape artist. Used to be, that was until his eyesight began to fail him. Now he could barely see to drive, let alone paint. But he could see well enough to take pictures like he was doing now.

"Looks good," Joe said, meaning it. "It's kind of surreal."

"Yeah. I like it. I'm going to take some more."

And he did, all the while Joe skated around the small pond located in a wooded park a hundred yards behind Tim's small home. They were out on the ice for nearly an hour, until the sun dropped low behind the trees. Even though he fell a couple more times, Joe couldn't remember when he'd had a better time skating.

Finally, Tim said, "We should probably get back home." He struggled to stand. He'd taken at least a hundred pictures. "It's getting cold. Maybe I could make us some hot cocoa when we get back. Do you have time for that?"

Joe lived in an efficiency apartment in a small town twenty miles to the west. He had nowhere he had to be. "Sounds good," he said, skating over and plopping down on the shore in the snow next to Tim to take off his skates.

Then they walked through the cold winter afternoon to Tim's home. Later they'd have their cocoa, maybe build a fire, listen to Christmas music, and enjoy the evening together. They might even reminisce, remembering Christmases long ago when they were young boys, and their family and grandparents and aunts and uncles had all gathered together around a festive tree decorated with colorful lights and handmade ornaments, sharing laughter and the goodwill that comes from being together this time of year.

Times long ago, but not like now. Joe and Tim's children and grandchildren were scattered across the country and preferred to stay put, while their young brother Will happily did the same in the warm sunshine of his home in Arizona. Now it was just the two of them, these two brothers, older, quieter, but not any less appreciative of the season and the chance to be together on this Christmas Eve.

As they walked the path leading to Tim's home, Joe suddenly had an idea. "Hey, how about if we do this again next year? You know, go skating on Christmas Eve. It's been fun."

Tim smiled, patted his brother on the shoulder, and said, "I was just thinking the same thing, and you know what? I'd love to."

Joe thought for a moment. "You know, maybe we could invite Will next year. We could call him up and talk him into leaving warm and sunny Arizona for a couple of days. If he could stand the Minnesota cold, that is."

"We could buy him some long underwear to entice him," Tim added.

Both brothers laughed good-naturedly. Will had a thing about cold weather, and it wasn't a good thing, either.

"All we can do is ask," Tim said. "Let's do it."

"I'm all for it," Joe said.

So, they called Will that night and he immediately said yes, he'd be happy to join them. And he'd be happily accepted their offer of long underwear, too.

Just like that, a new tradition was born, and in a season of traditions, a new one for these two old brothers was the best thing that could have happened. It gave them something to look forward to, something to count on, something hopeful to live another year for. Next year it'd be the three brothers together. For the first time in who knew how long. It was all they could ever have hoped for.

"We'll have to get him some skates," Tim said after they'd hung up. He was enjoying his hot cocoa, savoring every sip.

"Not a problem," Joe said, moving closer to the fire crackling in the fireplace. He thought for a minute. "How about the day after tomorrow? After Christmas? We could buy them then."

"That'd be perfect, Tim said, rubbing his eyes. "Okay if you drive? You know these old eyes of mine aren't getting any better."

"Not a problem. Be happy to."

They sat back, sipped their cocoa, listened to quiet Christmas music, and watched the fireplace fire crackling merrily away. It had been a pretty good Christmas Eve as far as the brothers were concerned. In fact, it was the best one each of them had had in a long, long time.

The next one just might be even better.

The Park Bench

The October wind suddenly gusted and blew leaves swirling along the pathway causing the old man to pull his worn fedora more tightly on his head. His battered cane kept him company as he shuffled along, feeling the sun's rays on his face, the fleeting warmth of the last days of fall. He hadn't been out of his tiny apartment in days and it felt good to breathe the fresh air.

Up ahead an elderly lady sat in her wheelchair, dozing near a park bench in the sun, her head wrapped in a colorful scarf of bright green and scarlet red. He marveled at her peacefulness, then wondered for a nervous moment if she was dead. But no, as he shuffled closer, he could see the rise and fall of her shoulders, the slight twitch of her knurled fingers. *Just resting.*

She awoke as he passed and smiled a greeting. "Hello," she said in a foreign accent.

He nodded in return, his perpetual frown unbroken, and continued on walking, realizing as he did so that it was the first time in days he'd interacted with another human being. He didn't have many friends or acquaintances anymore. Nobody, really, ever since his dear Emma had passed away nearly three years ago.

Emma. Like a tidal wave crashing, the memories came flooding back: his darling wife, their marriage for fifty-seven years, the pure joy of their long, fulfilling life together. A sharp, crushing pain suddenly pierced his heart. He stumbled. Fortunately, his cane propped him up, maintaining his balance. He put his hand to his chest ignoring the plaintive voice behind him calling, "Sir?"

After a few moments, his heart rate slowed and his breathing returned to normal. It wasn't a heart attack he was having, it was much worse; a heart broken by loss and still struggling to bear the weight of his ongoing sorrow. Still healing.

He steadied himself and gripped his cane, equilibrium restored. It was then he heard the voice drifting into his consciousness. The lady in the wheelchair.

"Sir? Can I help?"

He turned and saw her look of concern vanish as she realized he was all right. She smiled and gave him a little wave, fingers fluttering like butterfly wings.

He took a deep breath and let it out. She seemed nice. It might be good to talk to someone. Emma wouldn't mind, would she? Just to talk?

He took a tentative step forward. Then another as he slowly made his way toward the old lady, his cane tap-tapping through the leaves.

When he was next to her, he tipped his hat and introduced himself. "Hi. My name's Earl," he said.

"I'm Sophie," she answered, smiling. Then she motioned to the bench. "Why don't you sit?"

Something about her caused his frozen facial muscles to thaw and relax. He returned her smile, obliterating his perpetual frown. It felt good.

After only a moment's hesitation, he said, "Thank you."

Then he sat down and joined her.

Surface Tension

He remembered it from biology class. Surface tension. It meant *the tendency of water molecules to shrink into the smallest area possible.* He remembered something else, too, about a water bug being able to walk across the surface, which at the time he thought was pretty amazing.

He'd never been the best student and probably failed the science test back then, just like he'd done years later when their marriage failed. He'd shrunk, become smaller as a human being, while she'd grown and blossomed like the flowers he grew in his carefully tended garden. He'd stayed safe and secure in his IT job. She'd grown like the bright blooming lilies in that same garden, excelling as a fast-tracked manager in a prestigious marketing firm, making new friends, traveling both home and abroad and even joining a running club and completing a triathlon. She'd grown and he hadn't. Pure and simple. He'd taken the safe way, kept his head down, and played it safe. She'd moved on like that water bug, moving ever forward, fearlessly into the unknown.

Sure, they'd tried, especially during those early years. They'd made time for date night once a week and together planned three getaway vacations each year. But now, nine years in, their interests had changed, and they'd drifted apart. Their marriage had died. He hadn't been enough for her. She'd given up and now was leaving; moving on.

He watched as she came down the stairs.

"Already, Bill," she said, shifting her suitcase from one hand to the other. It didn't appear to be all that heavy. "I'm done packing. I guess this is goodbye."

He had nothing to say; knew her leaving was inevitable, yet he was now emotionally unprepared and stunned speechless by the finality of it all.

"But… But…" he finally mustered.

"No buts, Bill. It's over."

He watched her eyes slip off his to some unknown, but for her, eagerly anticipated future. A future that didn't include him. There was a twinkle there. And something else he hadn't seen for years. A spark. She was on fire with her passionate desire to leave him.

She picked up her laptop satchel from the table by the door and slung it over her shoulder. Then he kissed him on the forehead, turned, and walked out.

He watched as the door closed, leaving him alone. She was gone, gone for good. The reality finally setting in, a heavy weight in his chest. Man, how he still loved her. Man, how he wished he could change. Man, how he knew that he couldn't.

He went into the kitchen, filled the teapot with water, and set it on the stove. Some tea would be nice, some nice soothing chamomile perhaps. Relaxing. Maybe. He sat down, looking out the window toward his garden but not seeing it. Time slowing to a crawl.

A little while later, the water began boiling, the teapot whistling, but he didn't hear a thing. He stared into space, remembering the rest of the definition for surface tension. How it allowed for objects to float on the water's surface. Suspended and driftless.

Just how he felt now.

Migration

When Phil arrived at the viewing platform there were maybe twenty people. Half an hour later, as the sun was sinking low in the western sky, there were over a hundred with more arriving by the minute, all excited to see one of the greatest spectacles of the bird world: the nightly flight of sandhill cranes to their roosting spots along the Platte River in central Nebraska.

Phil watched in awe as huge flocks of cranes boiled out of the stubble corn fields north and south of the Platte where they'd been feeding all day and made their way to the river. They were big yet graceful birds with six-foot wing spans, the tips of which barely moved as they skimmed the tops of riverside cottonwood trees before dropping low and coasting to a landing on one of the many sand bars scattered up and down the river. There they would spend the night, safe from roving coyotes and the occasional bobcat. In the morning they would rise in unison and head back to the fields to feed. At any one time between mid-February and the end of March, there were as many as three-hundred thousand sandhill cranes in the area, half a million all total during migration. People came from near and far to view them.

Count Phil among those coming from afar. He'd spent the day making the nine-hour drive from his hometown in Long Lake, Minnesota, and he was happy he had, but there was more to it than seeing the cranes. He'd also made the drive to help alleviate some of the loneliness he'd been feeling. Divorced now for just over a year, his ex had taken their two kids (along with her boyfriend) to Cancun for spring break. They shared custody but this was the longest he'd ever been separated from ten-year-old Jason and six-year-old Sara, and he'd been unprepared for how lonely he felt. He'd come to Nebraska to see the crane migration, sure, something he'd always wanted to do, but as stunning as it was he still missed his kids. A lot.

Toward sunset, the crowd of crane watchers in the viewing area swelled to over five hundred, and for Phil, it got to be a little too much. He shouldered his backpack and walked along the riverbank to nearby Alda Bridge where there were fewer people. The river was a quarter of a mile wide at this point and he savored the relative calm before stepping onto the bridge. The sun hung poised on the horizon and the sky was on fire in blazing orange. The rattling, prehistoric voices of the cranes drifted through the ever-deepening twilight. The air was clear and clean and the river murmured in poetic harmony with nighttime falling over the land. It was like being in another world and Phil loved it.

Groups of three to twenty cranes coasted over his head as he walked along the wide concrete bridge. Some were so close he could hear their wing beats and see the amber irises of their eyes. The only people around were couples wanting to be alone and families with young children and babies. He was walking by just such a couple when he couldn't help but overhear the frazzled voice of the mother.

"Frank, could you do something with your son? Frank Junior is driving me nuts."

"He's just excited to see the birds. I'll take him for a walk, maybe that will help."

"Well, do something. Emily's getting fussy," the mother said, bouncing a small bundle wrapped in a blanket. "We might have to leave soon."

"Okay. I won't be gone long," Frank said. "Come along Frankie." He took his son, an eight-year-old boy it looked like, by the hand. "Let's go check out the other side of the bridge."

They fell in a few steps behind Phil.

"Dad, where do all these birds come from?" Phil heard the young boy ask.

"I think they come from South America," the father said. "I'm not sure."

"I like them," Frankie said. "They're cool."

Phil smiled. He liked hearing the exchange between the father and son. For eighteen years he'd taught tenth-grade biology at Long Lake High School. He liked kids and liked being around them. He was also a dad who missed his own children and felt drawn to this young father and his boy.

He turned and smiled by way of greeting. "Nice night," he said to the father.

"It sure is," he smiled back. "Great night to be out."

"It is," Phil responded, slowing down so he was walking next to them. "Do you guys live around here?"

"We do." He pointed behind them. "Five miles that way. Over across the highway in Wood River."

Locals, then. "Cool," Phil said.

They started talking, talking and walking all the way to the end of the bridge where they turned around and came back. Phil told them about the cranes, how they migrated to the Platte River from Mexico and Texas, and that they were stopping over in the area to feed and rest before continuing their journey to their nesting territory in northern Canada and Alaska. He talked about his job teaching tenth-grade biology. The dad talked about working for the highway department and his wife working at the local grocery store. They'd lived in the area their entire lives but this was the first time they'd taken their young family to see the cranes.

"By the way, I'm Frank. That's my wife Kathy and daughter Emily," he pointed up ahead. "And this here is Frank Junior. He likes to be called Frankie."

"Nice to meet you, Frank. Frankie," Phil said. He

introduced himself and he and Frank shook hands. When he extended his hand to the young boy Frankie chose not to shake. That was all right with Phil and he put his hand down.

"Frankie, come on," his dad encouraged. "Be polite."

Reluctantly, Frankie put out his hand and they shook. When he let go his eyes brightened. He looked at his dad and then at Phil, a wide smile forming. In his palm was a bright and shining quarter. "Wow! How'd you do that, mister? he asked.

"Magic," Phil said, laughing.

"Can you show me, mister? How to do it, I mean?"

Phil made eye contact with Frank to see if it was okay. He didn't want the father to think he was a weirdo pervert or anything. Frank nodded, yes, and Phil showed Frankie how the trick was done.

By the time they got back to Kathy, the twilight had deepened and there was just enough light to see.

Frank introduced Phil. "He's from Minnesota and he's a teacher. He taught Frankie a magic trick."

Phil chuckled. "Hi. I teach biology. Magic is just a hobby."

Even though she was distracted with her daughter, Kathy was gracious. "Nice to meet you, Phil," she said, bouncing her little girl.

With the last light fading and night settling in, Phil took a flashlight from his backpack and used it to light the way back to where Frank and Kathy's car was parked. They chatted for a few minutes and then said their goodbyes. When Phil shook little Frankie's hand he came away with a tiny matchbox car. He was impressed. "Looks like you've got the makings of a real magician here," he told Frank. Then he smiled at Frankie. "Good job." Frankie beamed.

Phil stood in the dark watching the young family drive

away and then used his flashlight to walk to his car. All the other crane watchers had left and the peace and quiet was breathtaking. There was a light breeze from the south, bringing with it the pungent aroma of moist, fertile farmland. It smelled heavenly. Nearby, he could hear the nighttime sounds of the cranes on the river, quietly talking back and forth, their voices sometimes rising in volume calling out and alerting others to possible danger, a coyote perhaps.

The proximity of the cranes had a calming effect on him. He thought about the family he'd met, Frank and Kathy and Frankie Junior. Even baby Emily. Nice people. Salt of the earth. He was glad he'd spent time with them. He thought about the cranes resting nearby preparing in a few days to fly nearly two thousand miles north to their nesting territories, a feat in and of itself. As he gazed into the darkness, he could feel the immensity of the big land around him stretching horizon to horizon with stars filling the sky to overflowing, unlike anything he'd ever seen; constellations spinning in a never-ending cosmic dance; verdant fields waiting to be tilled and planted with this year's crop. Let his ex have Cancun, he'd take Nebraska in the spring anytime.

He got into the backseat and wrapped up in his sleeping bag. He'd sleep here tonight so he could watch the cranes rise from their roosts at dawn. Then he'd head home. As he closed his eyes he knew for sure he'd be back next year. He'd be back but he wouldn't be alone. He had a sudden, passionate desire to share the experience of seeing the cranes and this country with his children, a father's innate feeling it was the right thing to do. Maybe they'd even make it a yearly event and come down together every spring. Just like the cranes, he and his kids could make their own migration to the Platte River. He had a feeling Jason and Sara would love it. He knew he would, being here with his kids, the three of them together like they were supposed to be. Having the cranes around would just make it that much better. In fact, then it'd be perfect.

Is There Such a Thing as True Love?

Dave Callahan's browser was set to scroll through various news stories of the day. He was idly looking at them when one caught his eye: *Is There Such A Thing As True Love?* The story was based on an article a psychologist had written looking into the nature of true love. Dave was intrigued so he read it, but it turned out there wasn't anything astounding there. The psychologist had done a twenty-year study and written an article detailing his findings. It all came down to what, in Dave's mind, was your basic psycho-babble about the nature of love and how everyone was different so every relationship was different and some relationships had stronger feelings of love than others, and blah, blah, blah, on and on, until Dave had just had enough. The author never even answered the question about whether or not there was such a thing as true love.

But what Dave found to be interesting was the "Comments" section at the end. There were over a thousand of them. A nerve had definitely been touched and reading some of them was quite interesting. The gist of it was that the vast majority of the people writing in were of the opinion that yes, in fact, they did believe in true love. By a margin of at least twenty to one. Easily.

Crazy, Dave thought to himself. *Lots of romantic people out there.*

Many of the comments were from women but there were a surprising number from men, and he found he couldn't stop reading them.

"I found my true love after divorcing my husband of fifteen years after years of neglect," one woman wrote.

A guy said, "I married my high school sweetheart but it didn't work out. We just drifted apart. After we divorced, I met my true love."

Another female wrote, "We met in college and hit it off right away. We've been together ever since. It really is true love."

There were positive comments by straight couples and gay and lesbian couples and transgender couples. All types. In a way, it was kind of cool, Dave thought, that there were so many happy couples out there.

As the days went by, Dave found he really couldn't stop thinking about the article and the concept of having one true love. He knew a lot of happy couples, and, if he had to guess, all of them would subscribe to the belief that their relationship was one based on true love. They *did* seem happy together, and Dave had no reason to doubt them. But there were also many people he knew who had been divorced or had been in bad relationships. How did the idea of true love fit into their view of things?

He remembered a conversation he'd had with his mother shortly before she passed away. His parents divorced when he was ten. His father had left his mother for another woman, whom he subsequently married. They were together for five years before his father died. Some years after his death, Dave's mother remarried and she spent the rest of her life in a happy relationship with her new husband. But when Dave asked his mother if she ever had experienced true love she answered without hesitating, "Why, yes, your father."

"How could that be?" Dave asked. "He left you for someone else."

"He was the first man I truly loved. Even after he left, I thought he might come back."

Dave was shocked. "Would you have taken him back, after all he put you through? Put us through?"

"Yes," she replied. "In a heartbeat."

She was adamant in her belief and would not budge. In

the end, Dave wasn't sure if he was happy for her or sad for her: happy that she had experienced true love, or sad because her true love had left her for someone else.

The article also caused Dave to look more deeply into his own past relationships. From an early age, he had always wanted to marry and have a family. He had been married twice. Once when he was in his early twenties to a woman with whom he'd had two children. They had grown apart and divorced. A few years later he married a woman whom he'd been together with for over twenty years, before they, too, had grown apart and divorced.

He was a good father, but the marriage hadn't worked for him. Had true love been a factor in each of his marriages? Not really, if he was honest with himself. He'd felt a great deal of affection toward each of his wives in the beginning, but that changed over time as other insurmountable life factors got in the way. Some of his conversations with friends over his lifetime had hinted that maybe he'd married and had a family to prove to himself that he could do better than his father had done with his mother. There was probably some truth to that, except that deep down he really did want to be a father and husband. The father part had been wonderful. The husband part, not so much.

A couple that he knew were both on their second marriage. They'd been together for over twenty years. He was convinced that they would say that their marriage was based on true love. Why was that? Because they both were devoted to each other, supported each other, and enjoyed each other's company, as well as giving each other space and time to grow.

Maybe that's what it came down to when it came to true love. More than the depth of feeling one had for the other person, it was also the ability to accept that person for who they were and to be a positive part of the growth in that person's life.

A friend of Dave's often talked about her idea that relationships weren't designed to last longer than twenty years. People maybe had three good relationships in them in their lifetimes. One, early on in a person's twenties before kids were born. Then, a second, middle period, where two people had children and raised a family together. And, finally, a third relationship toward the end of one's life when the child-rearing and intense job years were over.

"Successful marriages, maybe combine all three relationship elements," she said.

"What about true love?" he asked her.

"What about it?"

"How does that fit in?"

She was divorced after nearly thirty years of a less-than-fulfilling marriage. She laughed. "I don't believe in true love. I'll leave that to you romantics."

Is true love, then, only for romantics?

Dave asked some of his male friends and most of them were very uncomfortable with the question, looking at him in a weird way with a kind of "What's wrong with you?" look on their faces. Only one said that he believed in true love. Others had never really thought about it, and, when pushed, didn't really have an answer. But some of the comments on the article from guys said that they believed in true love, so that said something.

Dave wasn't sure why he was obsessing over the question. It all came down to the fact that even though he hadn't experienced true love, he still felt that maybe it was out there. That maybe it did exist. It did for others. Why not for him?

He was in a long-term relationship that had been going on for over ten years. It was the kind of relationship where the two of them had met and been friends before falling in love and committing to each other. Friends told him that she was the kind of person he should have been with all along. He didn't disagree. He felt a depth of love and affection for her that he never had felt before, and he was one hundred percent committed to the relationship. They were mature adults and each had their own interests, but they loved sharing their life with each other. It was the happiest he'd ever been and she told him that being with him made her happier than she'd ever been. He could easily see them being together for the rest of their lives. She wanted it too. Neither of them had a desire or need to be married.

When Dave asked her whether or not she believed true love, she told him that she didn't. "Look, I'm just happy we're together," she said. "What more do you want?"

"As long as you're happy, I'm happy. I guess I'll just have to be the romantic one in the relationship," he laughed.

She smiled, getting what he was saying. "So it sounds like you believe in true love."

"You know, I believe I do, the more I think about it." He was trying to be honest. He told her about the article and the impact it had on him. Maybe true love really was different for everyone. Maybe the point wasn't about true love forever and ever, but, instead, was the idea of committing to the relationship through the good times and bad; to be with the person no matter what just for the simple joy of being together and having the fulfillment of a loving and caring relationship. Which was how he felt about her.

"Does it bother you that I don't?" She asked, "Believe in true love?"

"No." He liked that they were talking about it. "Just don't hold it against me that I do," he added and grinned.

She laughed. "Don't worry. It doesn't matter to me that we see things differently. How about you?"

"No. I appreciate that we are different and have our own points of view. I'm just happy being with you. I like our life together." He paused and then added, "I'm just glad we found each other."

She looked at him for a few moments and then reached over and squeezed his hand. "Me too," she said, her voice honest and true.

At that moment Dave realized that whether what they had was true love or not, he didn't really care. The important thing was that they were together and committed to each other and that was good enough for him. As to the question about whether or not true love really existed, well, he'd leave that for the psychologists to figure out. He had all he needed to know right there beside him with her.

At the Platte River Motel

"Matt, could you please get me a can of pop? I'm kind of thirsty." Janie was sitting in the one chair in their tiny motel room.

"Sure. Let me just check outside." He pulled the curtain back and quickly shut it. "Shit. I think the owner saw me."

Frightened, Janie cradled their newborn daughter to her chest. "Matt, don't let anyone take Naomi away from me. I couldn't stand to lose her."

Matt looked at his backpack in the corner of the tiny room. His gun was in it. "Don't worry," he said, making up his mind right then and there to use the weapon if he had to. "I won't."

Across the parking lot from room number seven, and outside the manager's office, Linda Creeklow held her two-year-old son Ronny. She'd seen the curtain move and now she was starting to get mad. "God damn it. What's going on in there?" she muttered to Ronny, who, by way of response, stuck a finger in his mouth and sucked on it.

Earlier that morning, Clara, the housekeeping lady, told Linda that for the last two days, the young couple staying in room number seven wouldn't let her in to clean.

"I don't know what's going on," she said when Linda asked her about it. "I knock but they just say for me to go away, so I do."

"That's okay, Clara. You did the right thing."

Linda checked her watch before setting Ronny down in the sandbox. Her husband Jack was due home any minute. She'd put him on to it.

A little while later, Jack's ten-year-old white Dodge Ram pickup sped into the parking lot kicking up a cloud of dust. He pulled to a stop in front of the office and got out, looking forward to a cold beer and a chance to play with

Ronny a bit before looking into the leaky faucet in room number fourteen. His wife and son were playing in the sandbox with a Tonka-toy dump truck.

"Hi, sweetheart," he said, reaching into the open window of the truck and grabbing his lunch bucket. He worked the middle shift at Nebraska Cattle, a meat processing plant north of Grand Island. It was hard work, but that was okay, it paid good money. "How's it going?" The look on his wife's face told him he'd better forget about playing with Ronny. And having that cold beer, too.

Linda left Ronny and came up to him. "We've got an issue with number seven."

He turned and looked across the parking lot to the string of seven units. Number seven was at the far end. "That young couple that checked in the day before yesterday? What's up?"

"Clara said they won't let her in to clean. I'm worried something weird is going on in there."

Jack grinned. "Like what? Maybe they want to be left alone and have a little private time." He tried to hug her. "Like we hardly get anymore." He glanced at Ronny, who was oblivious to his parents and completely occupied with his dump truck.

Linda squirmed away. "Not funny. They could be doing drugs in there. Or making drugs, like speed. Hell, someone might be dead in there for all we know."

"We'd smell the speed, honey," Jack said, joking a little and trying to placate her.

Linda was having none of it. "Jack, I'm serious. I want you to go check them out."

"Check them out? What do you mean?"

"Go knock on their door and find out what's going on."

He shuffled his boot in the dust, not enthused. "I'm not sure that's a good idea. They deserve a little privacy, don't they?"

"Not on my watch they don't. I want to know that everyone is safe in there." She pointed a threatening finger at him. "Go. Now!"

Jack knew from experience when Linda had her mind made up there was no stopping her. Or arguing with her. He went.

As he walked across the dusty parking lot, Jack started thinking about how good things were for him and Linda. They were in their early thirties and had a long life ahead of them. They had Ronny. They'd been together since high school and married soon after graduation. In those early years, they both had jobs, were frugal with their spending, and worked hard at saving their money. When the motel had gone up for sale five years ago, they'd been able to secure a loan, purchase it, and get on with their dream of becoming independent business owners.

The motel was situated near the Platte River just off Interstate 80 in the rolling farmland of central Nebraska. There were fourteen units in two buildings that faced each other across the big, unpaved, parking lot. They catered mostly to cross-country travelers. It was out in the wide-open spaces, which they both loved, and they could occasionally take little Ronnie down to the river for a picnic. Jack's job at Nebraska Cattle paid enough to cover expenses, while Linda ran the motel and kept the books. One day the loan would be paid off and he could quit his job and they could both work the motel. Business was good and they'd never had much of a problem with any of the customers. Not until this.

Jack, hummed a little tune to try and settle himself down and fought a desire to light a cigarette. He slowed his gait as he approached number seven. Inside he could hear two people talking. He took a deep breath, let it out, and knocked on the door. In less than a minute it opened.

Across the way, Linda watched as Jack stood in the doorway and talked to the young man. She remembered the couple when they'd checked in. The guy was tall and skinny with long greasy hair and a wisp of a goatee. Not much to write home about, as far as she was concerned. The girl stayed in the car, but Linda could see her through the office window. She was a waif of a thing and looked about fifteen but was probably older. The guy seemed fine, though. Polite. Paid with cash through tomorrow. She'd taken his money, given him a receipt and the key, and hadn't thought anything more of it. Not until today when Clara voiced her concern.

As Linda watched her husband and the guy, it appeared everything was going smoothly: no problems or hassles. Hopefully, Jack would find out what was going on.

After talking for a few minutes, Jack shook the guy's hand and started back across the parking lot. He took out a cigarette from the pack in his back pocket and was lighting it as he came up to Linda.

He'd just taken his first drag and was grinning when she grabbed it and threw it away. "What'd I tell you about smoking around Ronny?"

"Oh, yeah, sorry." He looked chagrined.

"Now, what happened over there?" She pointed across the way.

Jack turned and looked at number seven and turned back to her. "You'll never believe it," he said, grinning.

"What? Are they doing drugs? I knew it. Should we call the police? The highway patrol? What's going on?" She slugged Matt in the muscle on his arm. "Tell me!"

"First off, ouch!" Then he smiled. "And, secondly, everything is fine. You don't have to worry. All is well."

By now, Linda was angry. "What do you mean all is well? What kind of a statement is that to make?"

"Well, remember what we went through to get this little guy?" he said pointing to Ronny, still playing in the sandbox.

"Yeah. So what?"

"Well, that's what they're doing in there."

"You mean they're screwing?"

"I think they prefer to think of it as making love."

Karen was silent for a moment, thinking. Then she said. "I don't believe it. Something doesn't sound right." She thought for a moment. "Did you see her? The wife or girlfriend or whatever?"

"No. She was in the bathroom, but the guy, whose name is Matt by the way, had her call out to me and I heard her voice. She sounded fine."

"Hmm." Linda was unconvinced.

"Oh, sweetie, they're just young and in love. Like we were. Are." He smiled and grabbed for her, but she dodged away.

"I don't know…"

He reached into his pocket and pulled out a wad of bills. "Look, they paid for another week. They're harmless. Let's just leave them alone."

Linda took the money and counted it.

From the sandbox Ronny said, "Mommy. I'm hungry."

"Okay, honey," Linda said to her son. "Jack, you get Ronny and let's go in. I've got a hamburger casserole for dinner."

"Great. I'm starving."

Linda was just turning to go into their living quarters when she happened to glance over her shoulder. She saw the curtain on number seven quickly being pulled shut.

"Damn. I've had it." She stuffed the cash in her pocket and said to Jack. "You watch Ronny. I'm going to find out what's really going on."

"Oh, honey…"

"Don't 'oh, honey' me," she said, looking him in the eye. "Something's not right over there, and I'm going to find out what it is."

She turned and began marching across the parking lot. Jack watched her. There was going to be hell to pay, and it occurred to him she might need help. Then again, knowing Linda, probably not. He picked up Ronny and followed close behind anyway, just to be on the safe side.

Matt had been watching the events unfolding over by the office. When he saw Linda come storming across the parking lot, he knew he had to do something fast, so he reached for his backpack and took out his gun. Janie looked at him, horrified.

"Jesus, Matt! What are you going to do?"

"I'm going to protect you and our little girl."

Janie stood up and cradled Naomi to her chest. The little baby was only five days old. She'd been born in Omaha and both Janie's parents and Matt's parents had wanted them to give her up for adoption. That wasn't going to happen. The young couple loved the little girl too much to let her go. Plus, they wanted to build a life for themselves: Janie away from her drug-using mother and stepfather, and Matt because he loved Janie so much. And now Naomi.

Matt checked the cylinder of the twenty-two pistol. Six bullets. His grandfather had given it to him on his tenth birthday, nine years ago. He hadn't shot it much, but he was ready to use it.

He said to Janie, "What if they call the cops? Or your parents? What then? They'll take Naomi."

"No, they won't, Matt. We won't let them."

"That's what this is for." He waved the gun in the air.

Janie ducked, shielding her daughter, and whispered loudly through clenched teeth, "Geez, Matt, what is it with you and that thing?" Still holding Naomi tightly, tears started running down her cheeks. "Don't, Matt. Please don't do anything stupid," she begged him. "We'll figure something out. Maybe the owners will just let us stay here. We aren't doing anything wrong." She wiped her eyes. "Put the gun away. Please, Matt. Please. For me." And she held out their daughter to him. "And for your little girl."

Matt lowered the gun. He looked at Janie and Naomi and his heart went out to them. They were his little family and he needed to take care of them. Using a gun wasn't going to help. It could only come to a bad end. He should have known that.

He put the gun into the backpack and buckled the flap tight. Then he took Naomi from Janie and held her in his arms and kissed the little baby's bald head. Then he kissed Janie. "I love you," he said.

"I love you, too," she said, holding him tight.

Pounding began at the door. "Open up. It's the manager. We've got to talk."

Matt handed Naomi to Janie and gave her a quick squeeze before letting her go. Then he turned to the door.

And opened it.

Covid-19 Lunch

Larry looked up. "Okay, I'm pretty psyched. I'm going to try something different.

His wife of fifty years looked at him across the small table and smiled. "What, not beans and rice, like usual?"

They were having their first lunch, their first real outing, since the pandemic started six months earlier and they were both a little giddy.

"Nope. I'm having the salmon with roasted spinach and fried yucca."

"That's very adventurous for an old fart." Shelia grinned.

He laughed. It was Saturday and the middle of August with a bright sun, a light breeze, and the temperature in the high seventies. It felt good to be at their favorite restaurant, Café Enya, a quaint little place in south Minneapolis. Larry had made reservations three days earlier, just to be on the safe side. He needn't have bothered. They were seated outside, all by themselves.

He'd also printed out the menus they were both perusing.

"What are going to have, my dear," he smiled, feeling suddenly very romantic. The sidewalk seating on a quiet street made him imagine they were in Paris or somewhere exotic; someplace they'd probably never ever get to, not at this stage of the game, especially with the pandemic and travel restrictions in place for who knew how long. Minneapolis would have to do and that was fine with him. At least they were together. That counted for a lot, especially after the scare they'd had last year with Shelia's breast cancer and her courageously winning the battle with it just before the pandemic hit. Right now they were happy to be alive, relatively healthy, and, more importantly, able to share a nice meal together.

"I'll have the curried chicken," Shelia said in answer to his question.

"Like always," he laughed. "Look who's in a rut."

Shelia smacked him on the arm and then pointed. "Better put your mask on."

Larry looked up and saw their waitperson coming toward them. "Okay, got it." He slipped his black face covering on as Shelia put on her floral one, the one she had made for herself when the pandemic had started last March.

A young black man came up adjusting his red face mask and said, "Hi. My name's Roland." He handed them each a menu. "We've cleaned the menus so they are ready to go for you." In spite of the mask, the old couple could see his eyes crinkled up in a smile.

"Thank you very, much," Shelia said and then held up the print-outs. "My husband was a jump ahead of you."

Roland looked at Larry and gave him the "thumbs up" sign. "Well, good for you! In that case, would you like something to drink?" He tucked the menus under his arm.

"Water would be fine," Larry said.

Shelia could see her husband grinning. He was having a good time being out. It was nice to see.

"And we're ready to order," she said.

"Awesome. Let me know what you want, and then I'll bring your water. How's that sound?"

"Great," Shelia said.

After they'd given him their orders, Roland was about to step away when Larry offered, "This is our first outing since the pandemic began. We're pretty excited."

Roland paused and turned to them. "I'm glad you see you here," he said, the sincerity evident in his voice. "Business is still pretty slow." He looked around at the empty tables. Then he waved his hand to nothing in particular and said, "At least it's a nice day out. That counts for something."

Shelia nodded and agreed, "It certainly does."

"You got that right," Larry added.

"Okay, let me go get that order in and bring your water. I'll be right back."

Larry and Shelia had a lovely lunch. They chatted with Roland and learned that he had a girlfriend and they had a baby and the three of them lived only a few blocks away. "Within walking distance," he told them.

After their meal was over Roland brought the bill and Larry used his credit card to settle up. As they were getting ready to leave, Shelia said, "What a nice young man."

"No kidding," Larry said, then paused, thinking, then said, "Say, I was wondering. Since this is our first time out in six months, how about if we do something nice for him?"

"Like what? Leave him a big tip?"

"Yeah, that's what I was thinking."

Shelia smiled, stood up and leaned over the table, and hugged him. "Perfect. Go for it."

Larry took out his wallet, thumbed through the bills, and said to Shelia, "You want to contribute?"

"Absolutely."

He and Shelia stood up, put on their masks, and got ready to leave. By now a few other diners had shown up and Roland was getting busy. Larry waved at him. "I left the bill right here." He pointed at the table.

Roland waved. "Thanks so much. Come again." Then he went back to taking an order.

Shelia looked at Roland. "Just put his tip under the plate." And he did.

A few minutes later when Roland was clearing their table, he noticed the bills. Curious, he picked them up with a trembling hand and counted them. Then he counted them again. "Oh. My. God," he said out loud. Embarrassed, he looked at the nearby customers and smiled. "Sorry about that. I'll be right back."

He ran around the corner looking for Larry and Shelia but didn't see them. On his way back to the restaurant he took out his phone and made a quick phone call. "Katrina? Hi. It's me. No, everything is alright. In fact, it's fantastic. Guess what happened? No, I've still got my job. Get this. A customer just gave me a super tip. Two hundred and twenty dollars! Can you believe it? Yeah, it'll help out a lot. Just thought you'd like to know. Yeah, love you, too. Give little Naomi a hug from her daddy. See you in four hours."

Roland hung up and took a moment. He hadn't felt this good since the pandemic began. He and Katrina and their little girl just might make it through the Covid -19 crisis after all. Thanks to people like that old couple. He went back to work, the smile behind his mask never leaving his face. Life had suddenly gotten lots better.

Christmas Magic

I hurry to the back door, put on my gloves, boots, and jacket, and rush outside, just as the Prius is sliding to a complete stop three feet in front of the garage door. I see Lea in the back seat and she smiles and waves a greeting. She's looking a little haggard, which I attribute to the journey from Minneapolis. (It's a known fact that she doesn't like driving in inclement weather.) Other than that, though, she looks happy. She must have had a wonderful time at Nate's, just like I knew she would.

I help her out of the car and give her a hug. "Have fun?" I ask, even though I know what her answer will be.

"I did. It was the best," she says, hugging me back. "Let's help Mom and Dad out and get them inside by the fire." She looks at me with a sly smile. "You do have one going, right?"

"Of course," I say magnanimously, spreading my arms wide and joking with her. "It wouldn't be Christmas Eve without one."

"That's for sure. Mom and Dad will love it." She squeezes my arm, an intimate gesture that feels really nice.

I'm stepping over to help Ed get out of the passenger seat when Lea stops me. "Wait a minute. How about you? Are you doing okay?"

I know what she's getting at, especially with me mooning over those albums of mine like I've been doing lately, reminiscing and, frankly, feeling more than a little sorry for myself. Well, after tonight, all of that is past. My talk with Dad (whether I imagined it or not) showed me that I've got a lot to live for. It's up to me to put the past aside and make the most of what I have right here and now. I hug Lea again. "I'm doing great," I say, squeezing her tight, thanking my lucky stars that we'd found each other fifteen years ago. "I've never been happier."

We get Ed and Barb inside and situated on the couch in the living room. Lea makes tea for everyone and I stoke up the fire. We stay up for a while, talking, relaxing, and enjoying each other's company. Lea and her parents all have fun looking through the photo albums I'd left on the coffee table. Both Ed and Barb comment on how much they enjoy catching a glimpse into my past, saying the photos bring them closer to me. Lea, god love her, only jokes about all the cookies that had been consumed while she was gone. Me? I tell her that they were so good, I just couldn't stop eating them.

At one point, Lea goes to the freezer and takes out four more cookie containers to thaw. I followed her into the kitchen. "Good thing I planned ahead," she laughs. Then she turns to me and adds, "You know everyone's coming over tomorrow, right?"

I nod my head as I munch on one of her sugar cutouts. "Yeah, I do remember." Then I mention what I've been thinking about off and on throughout the evening. "Say, about everyone coming tomorrow… I wanted to talk to you about that." I point back toward the living room. "Maybe later after your folks go to bed. Is that Ok?"

"Absolutely," she says, giving me a quizzical look.

I wave off any concern she might have, saying, "It's no big deal, just something I've been thinking about tonight."

"Ok," she says. "Sounds good."

She takes a list off the refrigerator and starts to review what she's going to be working on in the kitchen tomorrow morning, getting ready for when Nate and Emily, and their families come over. One thing I appreciate is that she doesn't say anything about the two empty tea mugs, even though she does give them a funny look as I take them to the sink and quickly wash them out. Then we both go back to the living room and join Barb and Ed.

Upstairs there are three small bedrooms and a bathroom. Whenever Ed and Barb stay with us, they prefer the one on the north side of the house. It's a cozy little space that once was Lea's brother's bedroom and they don't seem to mind sharing the small, full-sized bed. Around eleven or so Ed starts yawning. Then Barb.

"Well, time to hit the hay," Barb says. "Tomorrow's a big day."

Lea and I help her folks upstairs and get them settled. Then we go back downstairs. I go into the kitchen to make us some chamomile tea while Lea makes herself comfortable in her chair. I bring the tea out and for a while we sip it companionably while we watch the final coals of the fire, now glowing red hot and throwing off tons of heat. Then I look at Lea and she looks at me. We both smile, happy to be together.

I'm wondering if now is a good time to tell her about how I spent my evening and the things I thought about and the conclusions I came to concerning my father when Lea says, "What was it you wanted to talk to me about?"

Oh, yeah, there's that. I shift mental gears and say, "You know, you've got your family coming over tomorrow."

Lea has turned toward the fireplace, watching the coals and enjoying the warmth they are giving off. I can see her visibly relaxing as she sips her tea, but she's still a little revved up from the evening spent seeing her kids and grandchildren and her mom and dad. In other words, she's in a super good mood. "Yeah, I'm going to be busy in the kitchen in the morning. Moms' going to help. Why?"

"Well, I was wondering if that offer still stands. About me joining you all. You know, me being a part of it." I pause and then add, "With your family, I mean," emphasizing the obvious.

"Why, of course," Lea says, suddenly perking up. I can

tell she's happy I've decided to be part of her family's get-together. Then she thoughtfully takes a step back and looks at me, curiously. "What's brought this on all of a sudden? Usually, you just go to a movie."

"Oh, I don't know," I say, knowing I'm sounding vague. Now is the perfect time to tell her about talking to my father, whether I imagined it or not. I think about it for a split second and then decide to let it go. Maybe some other time. For now, it's best to just focus on tonight with Lea and tomorrow and getting ready for Christmas Day with her family. So, I say, "I just think that maybe it's about time."

However, Lea is more than a little perceptive and wise to me to boot. She's not ready to let me off the hook. She points to the dining room table where the stack of the three albums has ended up. "Does it have something to do with those photo albums of yours?"

I stand up and go to her and kneel down and hug her tight. "Yea, sweetheart, it kind of does."

Lea hugs me back. I'm sure she's wondering what is going on with the man she has chosen to live with for the rest of her life. She seems to be enjoying the moment, though, and the closeness. She does have one final question, however, and I'm not surprised when she asks, "I know I sound like a broken record, but please, tell me one more time. Are you sure you're doing all right?"

I don't have to even think about it when I tell her, "Yeah, I am, Lea. I really am."

A fleeting image of my father passes before my eyes. It's not the image of him from when I was just a kid, only nine years old, and didn't know any better. Instead, it's an image of Dad as an old man. The image of the man who was here with me tonight. When he and I sat by the fire, had some tea and cookies, and looked through the past, reliving both of our lives.

Right now, my evening has jelled into a sort of pact with myself. My talk with Dad has revealed that, like him, I'd made some mistakes in my life. No one is perfect, that's for sure. But, in the end, my life has been a good one. A great life really. I just need to stay vigilant and not get lazy; not forget to pay attention to the things that matter most. To that end, I'll call each of my kids tomorrow and wish them a happy holiday. I'll encourage them to make time to see me next year because I'm planning to come out and visit each of them. I'll tell them that I miss not seeing them and want to establish physical contact. Soon. I'm pretty sure they will agree. I hope so, anyway. I'm going to do all I can to stay in close touch with each of them: Ethan, Sara, and Lucy. After all, they are from my blood. They are my children.

Just as importantly, there is Lea and how much she means to me. Our life together is more special than I could ever have imagined. By the end of his life, my father had failed to find someone to love and commit to. I hadn't. Call it luck or fate or what have you, but I've found Lea. We have each other and for that, I will be forever grateful. I'm going to do all I can to make her happy and prove to her that she made the right choice when she decided to let me into her life.

After a minute or so, we release from our embrace. I return to the couch and Lea goes into the kitchen. As she passes through the dining room she glances at the cupboard. The door is ajar. She goes to it and before closing it looks in. "Hey, Jack, what's with the backgammon game? It's been moved. Did you have it out?" She gives me a funny look which after a few moments turns a little wistful. "Remember, we used to play, didn't we? We haven't played in years."

"Yeah, I know," I tell her. "I was just looking at it

earlier." I look into the fireplace, contemplating the red-orange coals, and then back to Lea as I have a sudden thought. "Say, maybe we can start playing again. At least for old-time's sake. You know, we used to play a lot."

Lea laughs. "As I recall, I beat you quite often. You sure you're up for it?"

Another fleeting glimpse of my dad passes before my eyes. "Sure thing," I say. "Absolutely. Anytime."

"You're on. It'll be fun. But after the holidays are over, okay? I've got things to do tomorrow." She pauses, thinking, and then adds, "Maybe while Mom and I are busy in the kitchen, you can build a fire and you and Dad can play. He used to be pretty good. He's the one who taught the game to me. I think he'd like it."

If Ed and I played, it would be the first time I would have ever done anything with Lea's father. Just the two of us. Ever. Amazing as it may seem, we'd never even had a one-on-one conversation together in the over thirteen years we've known each other. *Well,* I thought, *no time like the present.*

"Sure," I tell her. "It'll be fun."

The next day we set up the game board and play. I sit on the couch where I sat last night, and Ed sits in the chair where my father sat. He beats me two games to one. I was right, it was fun. Really fun.

I'm already looking forward to next year.

The Covid Toad

It hadn't been the best year that was for sure. First, there was the Covid-19 pandemic followed by a nationwide lockdown.

Then my wife Amy got tired of being cooped up in the apartment with me, saying, "God, Jack, I can't tell you how sick I am of seeing your ugly face. I'm going to go insane if I have to spend another minute with you."

No beating around the bush with her. Okay, message received. We'd been in lockdown for about three days when she left. At least she lowered the boom when both the kids were asleep. No sense hurting their feelings along with mine.

My boss had furloughed me along with the rest of the sales staff at the car dealership so I was enjoying hanging out with Willie and April, having the freedom to be with them more than I'd ever had in the past. Being with Amy more? For sure I'd have enjoyed that but, obviously, the feeling hadn't been mutual.

Anyway, a week went by which turned into a month until I finally came to the realization that my wife of fifteen years was gone for good. I got a few texts from her indicating she was living in a different state and, as she put it, "Enjoying my freedom," so what could you do? I decided to move on and focus on the kids.

Twelve-year-old Willie occupied his free-time playing video games. He was a bright kid and would finish up his distance learning assignments quickly. Then he'd curl up on his bed, fire up *Fortnite* with his buddies online, and happily game to his heart's content.

But my ten-year-old daughter, April, was a different story. "When's Mom coming back?" she asked at least ten times a day that first month.

"I don't know, honey. I really don't." It broke my heart to see her so sad.

"Dad, was it your fault, do you think?" she asked, once, looking so forlorn I had to fight back my own tears. I mean, geez, she was ten. "Your fault that Mom's gone," she added as if I needed it put any more clearly.

"I don't know, sweetheart. We probably both had something to do with it."

She gave me a look only a ten-year-old girl could give her father and said, "Yeah, right, Dad."

So, things weren't the best between us, but they weren't the worst either. We did her distance learning together sitting side by side at the kitchen table and started preparing meals together, and after that first month, we started to get a little closer, especially as the pain of Amy's leaving receded somewhat into the background.

After school let out, we had more time on our hands so we started going outside for walks. The weather in Minneapolis in June could be nice and this year was no exception. Which was good. Our neighborhood was near a large park that featured a good-sized pond rimmed with cattails and just about every day we'd leave Willie with his video games and April and I would mask up and walk a couple of blocks to it.

One day we were sitting on a bench overlooking the pond watching some ducks swimming around, dipping, and diving for food. A walking path was nearby and most everyone was being pretty good about social distancing and wearing face masks. For us, it was nice to get out of the apartment and get some fresh air.

After a while, April got up and walked down to the shore, idly poking around in the weeds.

Suddenly she turned to me and pointed. "Dad, look a toad."

I hurried to join her. Sure enough, it was a toad. A nice big one with bumpy, olive green skin and liquid, languid eyes. April studied it and ask, "Do you think we could take it home?"

Ordinarily I'd have said, "No, Sweetheart, we should leave the toad in its own environment, in its own home, and let it live like it's supposed to live." Or something like that. But these were extraordinary times what with April's mother having left and all. Not to mention the pandemic. I gave in.

"Sure," I said. And just like that, the toad joined our little family.

Willie didn't care one way or the other. "Do I have to do anything with it?" he asked that first day, poking at it with his finger.

April pushed him away. "No! And quit bothering her," she stated emphatically. "She's all mine."

"Fine with me." He shrugged his shoulders and went back to *Fortnite*.

"She?" I asked.

"Oh, yeah. She's a she, Dad. Duh. Anyone knows that." Well, alright then.

April took to calling the toad Terri right from the get go, and I honestly thought she'd tire of it after a day or two but she didn't. At first, we kept her in an old shoe box I scrounged up from my nearly empty closet. (Amy had taken all of her clothes.)

"She doesn't seem happy, Dad," April said after a couple of days of close observation. "I'm going to see if I can find out why." After sending most of the day on the internet April came to me and said, "She needs more space, Dad. And she likes to be able to look around." She did some more research and then told me as we were preparing dinner, "I think we should buy her an aquarium."

Thanks to online shopping it wasn't long before Terri had a nice new glass home set up on a table by the front window so, as April put it, "Terri can look outside if she wants to."

It wasn't long before Willie started getting into the act by helping to collect food like bugs and flies. Of course, he had to go outside to do his gathering, which he started to enjoy, and I was happy to see him start to play his video games less.

In fact, in a day and age of video games and other electronic distractions, it was nice seeing the kids occupied with something natural. The toad, sorry, Terri, took their minds off the pandemic as well as Amy being gone, and they were happier for it. April used my phone to take photos of Terri and kept a journal about what she did during the day, which to my way of thinking wasn't much, but April seemed to find a lot to write about, even the kind of food Terri preferred; dead flies were her favorite.

Then she started making up stories and writing them down in which she and Terri were the main characters. She'd read me one most nights before going to sleep. My favorite was when the two of them went exploring in the African jungle. Terry rode in a little fanny pack kind of thing that April made for her and they fought off pythons and wild boars and other creatures, eventually finding a magical waterfall made of lemonade they were looking for. Where she came up with that stuff, I have no idea but it was fun to see her use her imagination and be so happily occupied.

Toward the end of the summer, April asked, "Dad, do you miss Mom?"

"I do," I told her. "But I'm adjusting." I hugged her. "Having you and Willie around really helps."

"What about Terri?"

I smiled. "Yeah, Terri, too."

April grinned and went back to watching her in the aquarium and writing in her journal.

Since she had brought it up, I ventured, "How about you? Do you miss your mom?"

She was silent for a few moments, and then said, "Yeah. Yeah, I do, but having you around is good." Then she smiled. "And having Terri with me helps a lot."

I gave her another hug. "You want to help me with dinner?"

"Sure. What are you planning?"

"Spaghetti."

"Great."

With Fall on the way, I wasn't sure what we were going to do about Terri, but April came up with a solution. She learned that toads needed to hibernate or else they would die.

"I think we should take her back to the pond and let her go."

"That's a really good idea," I said, "but won't you miss her?"

She got a faraway look in her eye before saying, "Yeah, but no. It's okay, Dad."

"You sure?"

"Yeah, I'm sure. I'll let her go and she can go to sleep for the winter and then next spring we'll come back and find her again and bring her home."

I smiled and said, "And save her a big bug to eat to celebrate her homecoming. How about that?"

She smiled. "Yeah, a big old fly!"

As soon as the weather gets colder, we'll take a walk down to the pond, me and April and Willie, and we'll set Terri free. We'll say our goodbyes and I, for one, will give her a silent salute and thank her for how she helped April and Willie get through those first hard months after Amy left. She was a good toad, and she was good for my family, and you know what? There's no doubt in my mind that next year we'll go down to the pond and find Terri and bring her home. She'll be there for sure. She's become a part of our family. Some things are just meant to be.

Boron

I don't remember much about being a kid and even less about my dad. But my earliest memory is when he and my mom and my two younger sisters and I went to a 4th of July fireworks display down by the Minnesota River.

"Come on, kids," he said, helping Mom load us into the backseat of the beat-up, grey and white, 1951 Oldsmobile sedan.

"Frank, make sure Marty and Sherry and Jenny are secure," she said.

Dad lit a cigarette, a sign he was peeved. "Don't sweat it, Bev. I've got it covered."

I'm making up part of the conversation, but not the bad feeling between Mom and Dad. It was there, that's for sure. Sometimes their jabbering at each other was just a prelude to a knock-down argument. And yes, sometimes punches were thrown.

I remember holding my breath because I really wanted to see the fireworks that night, and a fight between them would ruin it for sure. I watched Mom. She had her shoulder-length, dark brown hair pulled back with a white headband. She was wearing a yellow, sleeveless dress and a string of pearls. She'd dabbed some perfume on for the occasion and the car smelled like heaven. Or at least something special.

She lit her own cigarette but didn't respond to him other than to say, "Let's just go see the fireworks, okay, Frank? The kids are looking forward to it."

Whew! I didn't know about Sherry or Jenny, they were pretty young and as I recall didn't care one way or the other, but I had been looking forward to these fireworks ever since Dad brought it up at the dinner table a month earlier.

"Yeah, they shoot 'em off down by the river and it's supposed to be a big deal," he'd said at the time. He ignored

Mom and looked at me. "What do you think, Marty? Want to go?"

Did he even have to ask? What nine-year-old boy would say "no" to fireworks? None that I knew of. "Sure," I said. "You bet."

I tried to catch Mom's eye but she was staring at Dad with what could only be described as daggers. Or lightning bolts. I guess she wasn't looking forward to going. I realized much later it wasn't the fireworks she didn't want to be around, but Dad. But that was much later. For now, we were going, and I for one was ecstatic.

Dad drove us out of town from our home in Minneapolis on a two-lane blacktop highway. After nearly an hour, we parked on a bluff overlooking the Minnesota River Valley. We were the only car there. Way down below on the other side of the river was the small town of Jordan where Dad had grown up.

"They'll shoot them off right there," Dad told me, pointing. "It's where the ballpark is.

He and I were sitting on the hood of the car, and he was drinking a beer. Mom was in the backseat with the girls staying away from the bugs. They didn't bother me at all. I was enjoying being with Dad. He was gone a lot, driving around the upper Midwest selling lawnmowers to hardware stores, so I didn't see him much. He was in a good mood and told me stories of life on the road. He even gave me a sip of his beer. I didn't like it.

But most of all I was excited for the fireworks. By the time the sun had set, I was getting antsy. Finally, I asked, "When are they going to start?"

"Pretty soon," said, opening up another beer. He looked at his watch just as one shot up into the sky. "See," he grinned at me and mussed up my hair. "What'd I tell you?"

I watched, my jaw hanging open. The rocket seemed to

sail out over the river for a mile, trailing green and golden sparkling colors before exploding and raining down all over the valley. Then four more were shot off, five all total.

I was enthralled. "Yea," I yelled and clapped my hands.

I remember Dad lighting another cigarette and drinking more beer and smiling. "Pretty cool, huh?"

"Yeah," I exclaimed. "Really cool."

My sisters were asleep in the backseat so Mom decided to stay in the car with them. The night was completely dark and every now and then I could see a firefly flickering in the weeds. One after another of the fireworks rose in the air, exploded, and echoed throughout the valley, raining down rivers of color and firing my imagination of pirate ships and space travel. Dad and I sat on the hood watching the display and for those few minutes it was just the fireworks and him and me, like we were the only people in the world. It was wonderful.

At one point he turned to me. "What color is your favorite?" he asked.

I didn't have to think twice. "Green."

He grinned. "There's a chemical found in the earth called boron that they add that makes it that color."

"Really?"

"Yeah."

"Wow." I had no idea.

Years later I still wonder what else I might have learned from Dad, but I never got the chance. Later that night after we got home Mom and Dad started drinking and then started fighting and throwing things. My sisters were frightened and came into my room and we made a tent under the covers and I told them made-up stories about fireworks and dragons and rocket ships and anything else I could think of to take their minds off all the yelling. Finally, they fell asleep. So did I.

He was gone the next morning and I never saw him again. I missed him for a while, but then his memory faded. But I'll always remember that night and sitting on the hood of the car with him. Always. And the fireworks, too. For sure. Especially the green ones.

Model Airplanes

Was he high on glue? No, not at all. The young boy scooted the chair over to be closer. It wasn't glue he was high on but being together, he and his dad, and that model airplane they were building.

"Here, son. Let me help." His father guided the boy's hand. "There you go." A slight adjustment of two fingers, a turn of the wrist, and the wing fit tight, just like it should. "That's great," he said. "You did it perfectly."

The boy can't get over how good it is to be close like this. His dad's knowing hand, the firm but gentle touch. The aroma of his aftershave, something subtle and spicy. A lingering scent. Secure and gentle.

Later that fall his dad made a shelf for the planes they'd built, three in all: A Texan, a B-17, and a Spitfire. All lovingly made by the two of them.

With his son's help, he put up the shelf. It was right before Christmas just before he left his boy and his wife for good. He left an unfinished Flying Tiger behind as well. The boy completed it by himself that January. It wasn't the same as with his dad, not even close.

He was an airline pilot. One of the best, it was said.

The boy cleaned that shelf for the next couple of years, those planes. His mother never had to ask. He was drawn to the task by an emotion he didn't understand deep within his breaking heart. He thought about building those models as he dusted each plane one after another, gently caressing the lonely plastic. *Those were such good times. Why'd they have to end?*

One day he packed up the airplanes and took them out to the trash can. It was a painful experience but had to be done. He felt like he was throwing away not just those models he and his dad had built, but something of his father as well. But what could he do? He'd begun thinking about how one day things would be different. Especially when he got older, and he and the son he planned to have would build their own model airplanes.

Yeah, that'll be good, he thought to himself, as he dumped the models in the bin. *Really good.*

A roar in the sky caught his attention. He looked up. A 747 just like his father flew had taken off from the nearby airport and was flying overhead. He watched for a moment and then turned away. He secured the lid on the can and started walking back to the house thinking of the future; of himself and his son. One day they'd build their own model airplanes. He was sure of it. And, when they did, they'd be the best planes ever. He was positive.

The Lens

His boss was a crotchety old guy who ran the Texaco gas station with an iron fist and a greasy hand. The boy liked him even though he never once saw the old man smile. It was a good part-time job and he learned how to change oil and grease cars, two skills he never used much as he got older but were good to know nevertheless.

For high school graduation that year, his boss gave him a telephoto lens for his camera.

"Thought you could use this," he said, handing him an unadorned cardboard box while they were taking a break from working in the garage. Then he went back to changing a head gasket.

The boy was stunned. "Thank you!"

The old man just grunted and said, "Hand me that ¾ inch socket wrench, will you?"

"Sure!"

The next day the boy went into the woods with his camera and new lens. He climbed a tree and waited. And waited. And waited some more. He was looking for the perfect shot, but it never came.

Back at work the following day, he told his boss he'd used the new lens, and that even though he hadn't seen anything worth photographing he'd had fun anyway. The old man wiped his hands and nodded. "Good," he said. "I thought you'd like it." He was quiet for a moment, then said, "Come here. I want to show you something."

They went back into his cluttered office. His boss opened a file cabinet and took out a folder. He handed it to the boy. "Here. You might enjoy looking at these." The boy opened it up. It was full of outdoor color photos. To the boy's untrained eye, they were beautifully composed. There were photos of lakes, landscapes, and mountain ranges. There were sunsets and moonrises. Storm clouds and flowering meadows. The boy was speechless. The old man smiled. "If you stick with it, you'll take better pictures than these."

When the boy finally found his voice, he said, "I'll never be this good."

The old man grinned and clasped him on the shoulder. "Sure you can. You just need to practice."

And back to work they both went.

Words could not express the boy's gratitude for the lens, nor the hidden friendship shown by the old man; the kind and caring concern hidden beneath his greasy demeanor.

That perfect shot? It never came, although the boy always kept his camera handy just in case. And that was fine with him. He learned over the years to enjoy being outside and looking at birds and animals and trees and the seeing world in a different way. Kind of like an artist might.

He took a lot of photos too. Some of them weren't too bad. They captured the feeling of the scene and the beauty of nature. Like the old man had done in the photos he showed him on that long ago day. Deep down in his heart, he has the feeling his old boss would like the ones he's taken throughout his life. Especially the ones with the lens the old man had given him. All those outdoor landscapes. Yeah, especially those.

Goal Post

It's a late fall afternoon with the scent of burning leaves hanging in the crisp, cool air. There's a ten-year-old boy in the backyard practicing kicking a football. Twenty yards away is the goalpost made from one-by-fours he and his father built together in the garage.

The boy sets the brown leather football on the orange rubber tee and concentrates, picturing the ball spinning through the middle of the uprights just like his dad had taught him. It takes a moment, but soon the visualization is complete, and he is ready.

He steps back, takes a breath, and lets it out, centering himself. Then he steps forward counting *one, two, three.*

Suddenly he stops and skids on the grass. In his mind's eye, he sees his father's smiling face. He remembers when the two of them built the goalposts. They'd spent a weekend in August a few months ago on the project. He smiles at the memory of them working together: measuring and sawing the wood; screwing the pieces together; laughing at the occasional joke his dad told. What good times those were.

Why did you have to leave?

Rattled now, concentration broken, the boy bends to his task. More than ever he wants to become the place kicker on the team. With little fanfare, he steps forward and kicks the football. It sails straight on through the goalposts. Just like it was supposed to do. Success!

Excited he turns to tell his father, but, of course, the man is not there. It's then that the painful reality strikes the boy, sinking deep. His dad is gone. Still. After these past few weeks, he still has not returned. More to the point, the boy knows deep down in his heart his father is never coming back. No matter how much he wishes he would. He can't explain how he knows that for a fact, he just does.

The boy retrieves the football and holds it in his hand. The leather is warmed by the sun and feels good to the touch The day is calm. Overhead a flock of geese is winging its way south for the winter. The boy tosses the football up once and catches it. He looks at the goalpost and thinks of his father and building it together. He misses him so much. He smiles momentarily at the wistful memory of him and his dad completing the project, taking the goalposts out to the backyard, and setting them in the ground. His dad had turned to him and said, "You do good work, son."

His eyes well up with tears at the memory. He wipes them away, promising himself not to cry.

He walks back and carefully sets the football on the tee and prepares to kick again. Practice makes perfect. That's what his dad always told him. Who knows, maybe his father is out there somewhere watching.

He steadies himself and concentrates. Then he takes a step forward and kicks the ball and watches as it sails through the uprights again. It's a perfect kick. He smiles and looks around.

Dad?

Home to Evergreen

"Glenn." My wife Sue handed me her phone. "It's your mom. She wants to talk to you."

I leaned back in my chair, slightly peeved. "What about?"

It was Saturday and I was grading my class of tenth graders' life science tests. It was the test I'd given them before the Christmas holiday, and I just wanted to get it done with so I could enjoy the next week with my family. First on the agenda was to try and talk my son Will into going ice skating together. Once close, over the past few months, I'd felt him drifting away from me; much like I did when I was thirteen and his age. I didn't want to lose him. Like my dad had lost me.

Dad.

Sue gave me a look, one that I was quick to figure out after nearly twenty years of marriage.

"You should talk to her," she said, handing me her phone.

Yes, I should. "Hi, Mom. What's up?"

To make a long story short, my dad was dying. Okay, that happens. But the kicker was that he wanted to see me.

Here's the deal. In the late 1880s, my great-grandfather was in the logging business in northern Minnesota. He was very successful. So successful he founded the town of Evergreen. You may have heard of it. It's the *Christmas Tree Capital of the World*, or so my great-grandfather liked to say. "Best Christmas trees you'll ever see," he'd tell anyone who'd listen. Lots of people did, and to this day it's still the town's motto.

He bought land and planted more pine trees and business thrived. So did the town. He passed the business on to his son, Quimby, my grandfather, who passed it to my father who wanted to pass it along to me.

I wasn't having any of it.

"No way," I told him over thirty years ago. "Not on your life."

I fancied myself a free spirit back in those days. Not wanting to be tied down, I left home and never looked back. In essence, my dad disowned me, not wanting anything to do with my "devil may care" attitude. Which was fine with me. I moved to Minneapolis, smoked a lot of weed, hung out, and played guitar in coffee shops. In short, I was going nowhere fast.

Then met Sue. It was love at first sight. At least for me. We were definitely not on the same wavelength romance-wise, and she made it clear she didn't want anything to do with me.

"Clean up your act," she told me. "Then we'll talk."

So, I did. I quit the weed, trimmed my hair, and looked to the future. I started taking classes and eventually graduated with a bachelor of science degree majoring in biology. I also obtained a Minnesota teaching certificate which allowed me to get a job in the Minneapolis school system. I'm happy to say I've been teaching Life Science at Metro High School for over twenty years, and I love it.

Anyway, although Dad and I never reconnected, Mom and I stayed close. She kept me apprised of the family business, and business was good. Great, even. Dad was a firm believer in sustainability, long before it became a media buzzword. He had about five thousand acres and rotated his pine trees through them on an ongoing basis. He recognized that good forest stewardship was the best way to conduct business. That's where we differed.

Dad saw his forest of evergreen trees as a commodity. I didn't. I saw them as a place to go for a walk, observe nature and maybe write about the experience. He was a capitalist. I was a poet. We had vastly different philosophies and neither of us figured out how to connect with each other. So, we did the guy thing. We avoided talking.

For thirty years.

Thank goodness for Mom. We stayed in touch and talked often on the phone. When she came to the city, she stayed with us. She and Sue were very close, and Will adored her. She was a kind and generous person, and I loved her. So much, in fact, that I didn't mind her being married to my dad.

But I'll tell you this, when she talked, I listened. So, that day on the phone, I listened for a long time.

Afterward, I went into the kitchen where Sue was busy dicing tomatoes, getting dinner started. I hugged her from behind. "Smells great. Spaghetti?"

"Correct." She smiled. "Here." She gave me the knife. "You take over."

"Aye, aye, captain." I grinned and started chopping.

She leaned against the counter. "What'd your mom want?"

"It's Dad," I told her, trying for some reason to sound blasé. "He's dying."

"I'm sorry to hear that." I could tell she was. In fact, I got the feeling she already knew. Like I said, she and my mom were close.

"She wants me to come up there. He wants to see me. Will, too, since they've never met."

Sue poured a glass of wine and sipped. "Makes sense. What are you going to do?"

"I don't want to go all the way up there, but I think I should."

Just then Will came in. "I think I should what?" he asked, grabbing a handful of cookies. Sue slapped his hand good-naturedly. "Only one, buster. It's almost dinner time."

I turned to Will. He was thirteen years old and had short red hair. Tall and thin, it seemed he grew taller every day. "Go visit my dad," I told him. "Your grandma called. He's dying."

"He's dying?" Unexpectedly, tears formed in his eyes.

"What's wrong," I asked, confused. "You don't even know him." I know it sounded cold, but, honestly, I didn't know what else to say.

Will wiped his eyes. "I know. But I always thought one day I'd meet him." He set his cookie down. "After all, I never knew Mom's mom and dad." Which was true. They had died before he was born. Car accident.

"So, what are you saying? You want to go met him?"

His eyes brightened. "Yeah, I would. I'd love that."

Wow. I looked at Sue. She met my gaze and raised her eyebrows. I could tell she was thinking, *you'd better do this, pal. You may not get another chance like this to not only be with your son but to mend fences with your dad.*

She was right.

"Okay," I said to Will. "Let's do it."

"Yeah!" he jumped up and, surprisingly, hugged me. "Thanks, Dad."

I hugged him back. I guess I'd made the right decision. I hoped when we got back home, I'd still feel the same way.

Christmas was five days away. I did a quick calculation, thinking out loud. "Okay. I'll call Mom and tell her we're coming. We'll go tomorrow. Stay maybe a night or two. See how it goes." I looked at Sue and she gave me the thumbs-up sign. I looked at Will. "Okay with you?"

He smiled at me. A smile I hadn't seen for quite a while. "It's great, Dad. I'll go pack."

Now, I was excited. Evergreen, here we come.

The drive took about four hours, and we arrived around noon. Before we went to Mom's, I took Will on a quick tour. Evergreen is in the middle of Moraine County. It's a quaint town of four thousand hardworking souls who love the out-of-doors. They also love to decorate the town for the yearly pageant which runs the week before Christmas. We'd hit it just right. Main Street was lined with beautifully lit Christmas trees and decorated with hanging evergreen garlands interwoven with shiny red ribbons. All of the storefronts were decked out in twinkling Christmas lights and some of the windows had colorful displays of Santa and his elves. Everywhere we looked there was a feeling of festive joy in the air.

Will was enthralled. "Wow!" he said, pointing to a horse-drawn sleigh with four people in it being pulled along the snowy street. "I've never seen anything like this."

I had to admit it was very cool. The town was done up even more than I remembered. Back then, I thought it was an ostentatious display of extravagant commercial Christmas hogwash. Now, though, seeing Will's face light up, I realized that there was a feeling of magic in the air. Maybe it's because I was older and less jaded, but I really felt like I'd entered a different time and place; a Christmas wonderland full of the spirit of the holiday. It felt good.

"Shall we go to Grandma's?" I asked.

"Sure," Will said, looking out the window, his eyes wide with wonder. He turned to me. "Dad, I'm glad we came. This is way cool."

The fact that we were even talking after not communicating much over the past year was, to use his term, "way cool" to me. I grinned. "It sure is." I reached over to muss his air in a show of affection like I used to do.

He let me.

"Okay," I said. "Let's take this sleigh to Grandma's."

"That's pretty bad, Dad," Will said. But he grinned anyway.

"Giddy-up," I said. And off we went.

Mom and Dad lived near the town square in the house my grandfather Quimby built. It's a beautiful, two-and-a-half-story wood-frame farmhouse-style home with a wraparound front porch.

We pulled up front and parked. It was wonderfully decorated, of course. But beyond all of that, beyond the memories and emotions having to do with the house I grew up in, and the father I hadn't seen for thirty years, was the memory of what Sue had said to me the night before.

We were lying in bed. I was restless, unable to sleep. She'd put her hand on my shoulder and said, "Glenn. I know you've got a lot on your mind."

"That's putting it mildly."

"Well, here's something else to think about when you see your dad tomorrow."

I turned the bedside light on and sat up. "What?"

"Think of it as if the situation was flip-flopped."
"What do you mean?"

"Like if the roles were reversed. Instead of you and your dad, think of it as if it were you and Will."

"Me and Will?"

"Yes. Think what you'd feel like if for some reason you and Will had a falling out and he left and you hadn't seen him for thirty years. Think what it'd be like if I contacted him for you because, heaven forbid, you were dying. What would you want to have happen?"

Well, when she put it that way, the answer was easy. "I'd want him to come home and makeup."

"Exactly."

That conversation was in the front of my mind as Will and I walked up the steps and across the porch and I knocked on the front door. It was early afternoon. The sun was shining and the temperature was around twenty degrees. From a few blocks away on Main Street carolers were singing. But I was aware of none of that.

Mom opened the door and smiled. "Glenn." She hugged me tight. "You came."

"I did, Mom." I hugged her back. "It's great to see you. Merry Christmas."

"Merry Christmas to you, too." Then she stepped aside. "Here's your dad."

Standing just behind her, teeter-tottering on unsteady legs was my father. Once a robust man who could lift fifty pounds in each hand, he had shrunk at least six inches. He was bald, his full head of hair gone. His cheeks were sunken, and I had the fleeting thought that he'd lost all his teeth. Next to him was a wheelchair. He'd obviously stood up to greet me and was using a cane to keep his balance. He was not the same man I'd left thirty years ago.

But he was my dad. And always would be.

"Hi, Dad," I said. "It's great to see you."

He took a tentative step but suddenly lost his balance and fell forward. I caught him in my arms and held him. He was emaciated, just skin and bones. He buried his head into my neck. He smelled like an old man with a hint of aqua vela shaving lotion. He smelled wonderful.

His first words to me were, "Thank you for coming, son. It's great to see you, too."

Then we both broke down in tears.

We spent the afternoon talking. Dad was in his wheelchair and often nodded off, napping, but that was okay. It was like nothing had happened between us. The expression "let bygones be bygones" kept coming to mind. Whatever had caused our estrangement (which was basically our different ways of looking at life) meant nothing. The important thing was that we were together.

After we reminisced about when he coached my

peewee hockey team and I told him about coaching Will's, he looked at me and said, "Okay. Getting back to one of the reasons I wanted to see you…"

"I'm glad I came, Dad."

He grinned. "Me, too." Then he cleared his throat and said, "I really have only one request, son. I'd like you to consider the business. It pretty much runs itself these days. I've got two good operations managers, a young couple named Gabe and Kris Jenkins, and a good accountant doing the books. I'd like you to take over my role and oversee the operation." I looked at him, touched, frankly, that he'd made the offer. In that speechless moment, he added, "You could even keep teaching. Just think about it, okay?"

I told him I would.

The next day we visited the tree farm. I helped Mom load Dad into their handicap-accessible van and off we went. It was mid-morning and two days before Christmas Eve. It was a beautiful winter day, clear and cold, probably fifteen degrees. We'd had a fresh inch of snow overnight and crystals sparkled in the sunlight, turning the world into an enchanted fairyland.

Evergreen Tree Farm was bustling with business. There were sleigh rides, and a seasonally decorated kiosk giving away (giving away!) hot apple cider and Christmas cookies. The parking lot was sectioned off for those who wanted to buy trees already cut, or those who wanted to cut their own. It was a place full of joy and good cheer. Bursts of laughter filled the air and mingled with piped-in Christmas music. Seeing all the smiling faces made me feel incredibly happy. I couldn't believe I had turned my back on all of this so many years ago.

I said to Will. "What do you think?"

He grinned. "I love it." Then he said, "Dad?" He pointed to the horse-drawn sleigh. "Can we go for a ride?"

"Absolutely," I said.

Before we did, though, I met Gabe and Kris and a number of the other workers. It was an experience I'd never had before, being around happy employees. Most of the people I knew were disgruntled in one way or the other with their job, so it was amazing having all those people compliment my dad and mom, many of them pulling me aside and telling me how wonderful it was to work for them. Even though the circumstances were extraordinary with everyone knowing Dad was dying, it was easy to see the honesty in their heartfelt sentiment.

While Dad sat in the van with Mom talking to their employees as well as customers who were stopping by to pay their respects, Will and I slipped away and went for our sleigh ride.

Our horse's name was Lightning Bolt, a misnomer if there ever was one. But what the big gelding lacked in speed, he made up for in durability and endurance.

We got an up-close tour of the tree farm.

"It's got nearly two million trees," our driver, Becky told us. "They add not only half a million tons of oxygen into the air every year but also provide homes for birds like the endangered Kirkland Warbler." She turned to me. "Your dad is doing a good thing here."

I smiled. "I know. I can tell."

As we made our way back to the parking lot, Will turned to me. "Dad, I've got a question." He'd overheard all of the discussions between my dad and mom and me. He was also sharp as a tack.

"What is it?"

"Are you going to take over for your dad? Like he asked?"

"No beating around the bush with you, is there?" I grinned at him.

"I just want to know."

"What do you think I should do?"

He didn't have to think. "You should do it." He waved his arm. "Look at all the trees. This is a great place and if you don't help keep it, who knows what might happen? It might get sold to some developer and then a bunch of houses will go in and all of the trees will be gone and all of the birds and animals too." He paused and looked at me closely. "I'm serious, Dad. You should do it."

I'd called Sue the night before and we had talked. She'd agreed with my thinking, but knowing Will's feelings helped.

"You know what? I'm going to do it."

"Yeah!"

I was told later by Mom that you could hear him a quarter of a mile away in the parking lot.

Evergreen Tree Farm was always about two things. One, it was about protecting the forest through sustainable planting and providing a home to birds and animals. Years ago, I was too self-centered to see that, but I saw it now. Very clearly.

It was also about building a family business. One I almost turned my back on. Almost.

That Christmas I can home. Mom and Dad and Sue and Will were glad I did. Me, too.

Real glad.

The Pandemic Year – A Novella

January

From under the covers, I checked my phone for the outdoor temperature. The reading came up and I blinked twice to convince my disbelieving eyes. Oh, wow. I honestly didn't expect it to be so cold out there, but, minus twenty-eight degrees? Man, that's brutal.

The curtain on the window at the head of our bed had frozen onto the pane of glass. My wife Meg yanked it free and used her fingernail to scrape ice off the window to try and look outside.

I watched the ice shavings fall to the sill.

"Cold out, I guess," I said, trying to strike a congenial tone.

It fell flat. "Geez," Meg said. "You think? The ice is so thick I can't see a thing."

From the next room three-year-old Allie heard us talking and cried out. "Daddy, I'm freezing."

"Yeah, Dad. It's like the north pole in here." Five-year-old Andy was not known to mince words.

From their muffled voices, I could tell they were both huddled under their covers for warmth.

"Coming!" I yelled.

Meg gave me a shove to get me going. "You see to the kids. I'll get breakfast started."

"I'm on it." I swung my feet out of the warm covers (flannel sheets, cotton blanket, wool blanket, thick quilt) and onto the floor. "God. It's freezing in here." I could see my breath. "Damn. The stove must have gone out."

"Welcome to the Northwoods," Meg said, standing up and pulling her thick robe tight. Then she grinned. "Are we having fun yet?"

I raised my eyebrows and shook my head. "No comment."

"Good," she said. To make her point, she blew out a cloud of vapor. "None needed."

She went off to the kitchen while I hurried into the kid's room. We were living in a tiny, four hundred square foot cabin, on the edge of the small town of Esker, located on the shore of Lake Moraine in northcentral Minnesota. We were on the main highway between Bemidji thirty miles to the north and Park Rapids thirty miles to the south. Our plot of land was one-hundred feet by one-hundred and fifty feet and in a grove of about one-thousand dead or dying jack pine trees, average diameter of four inches, an average height of eighty feet. At one time it might have been dense and lovely, but now it was, frankly, mildly depressing, if you thought about it, which I tried not to. You could see right past the bare trunks of the trees to the boarded-up building across the highway and the empty homes on either side of us. In other words, it was kind of a forest, kind of not.

It was January 2021, and we'd moved up here to get away from the pandemic. So far so good. None of us had been infected, but that was beside the point. We hardly saw anyone, let alone interacted with them, so getting Covid wasn't a huge concern. The pressing issue was that it was so cold the very real possibility of us freezing to death kept rearing its ugly, frozen head.

We'd been here a week, and it seemed like a year.

I helped the kids get dressed and got the fire going in the wood stove that provided our only source of heat. I'd done a crummy job banking it with logs when we'd gone to bed the night before and the fire has burned out. Lesson learned, hopefully. The kids helped with the re-starting process for about a minute, handing me a stick or two, before beginning a rambunctious sword fight.

By the time the fire was roaring and the little cabin was starting to heat up, Meg had put together a warm and filling breakfast of oatmeal and pancakes.

The kitchen was small, but we were all four able to squeeze around a table shoved against the wall across from the sink.

"What's on the agenda today, Lee?" Meg asked.

"Firewood. I'm going to cut some more," I told her, dumping maple syrup all over my pancakes before adding a dollop to my oatmeal. "We're going through it pretty fast."

The woman we'd rented the cabin from, Gladys Hawkinson, initially wanted to sell the one-hundred-year-old structure. She'd had no takers, but when we contacted her about renting, she'd agreed.

"You'll have to cut your own wood, though," she told Meg on the phone. "I'm done with that BS."

Meg and I agreed to her terms. I mean, seriously, I was twenty-nine and in shape from working out at the health club and running. How hard could cutting wood be?

Well, I'll tell you, if it were sixty degrees in the middle of October, it'd be fine. But way below zero in the first week of January, chainsawing firewood was another story.

"Okay," Meg said, leaning over to Allie and wiping syrup from her chin. "Sounds like a good idea. Make sure you dress for it."

No argument there.

Our landlady had had ten chords of fifteen-foot logs delivered as part of the rental agreement. It was a mix of poplar, birch, oak, and pine. "Here's a chainsaw," Gladys told us when we'd met in Park Rapids where she lived to finalize the agreement.

"Thanks," I told her. I'd never run one before, so she gave me a quick lesson. *Piece of cake*, I thought to myself.

"Still want to rent?" she asked.

The pandemic was getting worse. Vaccines were on the way, but because of our age, we'd have to wait a while. I looked at Meg and she nodded. We were all in. "Yep," I said. "Bring it on."

She shook hands with us. "It's a deal." And we signed the lease.

Later, I will swear on a bible with my frozen fingers that under her Covid mask, she was smirking. *Suckers*, I'm sure she was thinking. *You're signing a year's lease to live in that dump. It's your funeral. Just make sure you pay me on time and we'll be fine.*

We waved goodbye and drove our Honda Fit north thirty miles to Esker. It was twenty-nine below. We had no idea what we were getting into.

That had been a week ago. The temperature had stayed way below zero and our days were spent with me cutting firewood and Meg running an at-home preschool for the two kids. When she needed a break, she came out and cut wood, and I took over with the kids.

We shared cooking and cleaning and kept reminding ourselves we doing this for the safety of our family from Covid. Especially for Andy and Allie. We hadn't had our shots because the vaccines hadn't been released yet. My parents had gotten Covid early on in 2020 and Mom and Dad had both died. All over the world, people were dying every day and it was scary, so not many begrudged us moving north, and the ones that did, too bad for them. For us, it was the right thing to do for our children.

That morning, I used the chain saw to cut a good supply of sixteen-inch-long logs. Then, after lunch, the next step was to use my axe and split them. Once that job was completed, I'd load up the wheel barrel and haul split wood to the back porch where I'd unload it and stack it inside, ready to be used in our stove. All of this while navigating through two feet of snow on the ground.

The one good thing? Cutting firewood was hard work but warm work. I actually worked up a sweat even though the day had warmed to no more than ten below. I'd even taken my insulated jacket off.

The bad thing? It was exhausting work and by late afternoon my arms were like two lead weights hanging from my stiff and sore shoulders. I'm sure that had something with what happened. I was coming down the home stretch on splitting the logs and not paying attention. (Another lesson learned, hopefully.) I took a mighty swing and managed to NOT hit the log exactly dead center like I should have. The axe deflected and hit me square in the shin bone. Oh. My. God. The pain was unimaginable. Not to mention the blood.

Later that night after we'd gotten the kids to bed, Meg and I sat on the couch in the living room which was the main room in the cabin. It was also where the woodstove was located and the warmest room we had.

"How are you feeling?" Meg asked, sipping from her nightly glass of red wine.

I set my book aside, and, grimacing, tried to sit up straight. I had my leg stretched out, resting my foot on a stool. "Not too bad." I'd opened a three-inch gash in my right leg. The doctor at the clinic in Park Rapids had stitched me up and said, "You've got a nasty bruise, but at least you didn't break any bones. Go home, rest, and let it heal."

I got the feeling he'd seen this kind of thing before.

Meg looked at me. "This is going to make cutting firewood difficult."

"I know."

She was quiet, thinking, then asked, "What do you think? Should we break the lease and go home?"

I didn't have to think. "No. We made a commitment, remember?"

Meg smiled. "We did."

"We'll stay for the kids, even though," I pointed to my bandaged leg, "it'll be even harder."

"I don't care," she said.

"Me neither."

"I still think it's the right thing to do."

"Me, too."

She stood up and kissed me and helped me stand. I put my arm around her and we headed to the bedroom. "Hold it," I said.

"What?"

"Let's not forget the fire."

"Right."

We added more logs and went to bed.

Tomorrow was another day. There was wood to cut and bring in. We didn't have any choice. Somehow, we'd figure out a way to make what we were doing work. We really didn't have any other choice. We had a pandemic to try and beat. I just had to be more careful outside. Especially with that damn ax.

February

Five-year-old Andy ran out the back door of the cabin and dove headfirst into the big pile I'd shoveled after yesterday's snowfall. Three-year-old Allie was right behind him.

Giggling, she climbed out and brushed snow off her pink snowsuit. Andy lay on his back laughing.

"That was fun!" He got up with a big grin on his snowy face. "Let's do it again!"

I watched from my woodpile and smiled. It seemed like it snowed every day up here in the Northwoods, so keeping paths clean was another chore I was adding to my ever-growing list of work that needed to be done to deal with the elements. But that was okay. We'd been at the cabin for six weeks now and were adjusting to life pretty well. My leg was healing from being wounded in an accident with my axe, and Meg had picked up some editing work from Charlotte's Press, the publishing house she worked for, so we had some money coming in. Which was always a help.

With my leg feeling better, I was back into the rhythm of cutting firewood and helping out with the kids. Plus, a vaccine was being made available soon to fight the pandemic and that was welcome news. So, life was good. Was it challenging to live in our little cabin on the outskirts of tiny little Esker? You bet. But we wouldn't change a thing. We'd closed up our house in Minneapolis and had my brother stopping by every week to check on it. My research job at Zylon Labs had shut its door in April last year after the pandemic hit, but I still got a partial paycheck with the idea that they would eventually reopen. (No word on that happening anytime soon, though.) We had savings we could tap into if we needed, but now with Meg picking up some extra work, money wasn't as much of an issue as it had been. We didn't spend a lot. The rent was cheap. For entertainment we had Wi-Fi. We were adjusting and enjoying the challenge of it.

We'd moved up here to limit the kids' exposure to the coronavirus and so far, we'd been doing a good job. The only time we were around people was when we did our grocery shopping. We went to the nearest big town, Park Rapids, located thirty miles south of us. I'll never forget the first time we went there. Let me tell you, that was an experience.

The county we lived in was not completely sold on the idea of masking up and social distancing, so when all four of us walked into the Northwoods Grocery in downtown Park Rapids with our masks on, people stopped and stared. Other than the two clerks running the cash registers and a couple of employees stocking the shelves there wasn't a mask to be seen.

We grabbed a cart, loaded three-year-old Allie in the child seat, cleaned out hands with Clorox wipes (provided by the store), and began making our way up and down the aisles. We made as much of our food from scratch as we could. In fact, we both liked to cook, which in the city was sort of a hobby, but up here it was a necessity. The food we cooked was healthy and fulfilling, pasta and beans and soups and stews, just the thing on these cold winter days. It was also a pastime. I'll tell you, and I'm dead serious, working together and preparing a thick lentils stew chock full of root vegetables was entertaining in its own way. The kids were even learning how to help in food preparation, although baking cookies was a task much more preferred by them than stir-frying snap peas – you get my drift. It was a fun family experience.

That day at the grocery store, we were able to stock up on the essentials, beans, rice, and potatoes. We also added an array of canned goods. We even scored some decent-looking broccoli, cauliflower, and Brussels sprouts. So, in addition to apples, oranges, bananas, raisins, and dates, our shopping experience was a success, and we were pretty happy.

The entire time we were shopping, though, I have to say it was hard to ignore the looks we were getting. Looks of disdain, to be frank, and not friendly at all. It made me mad, and not for the first time, to think how sad it was that this pandemic had been turned into such a hotly debated political issue. I'll always remember my dad telling me how happy he was as a kid to be able to get a vaccine for polio.

His best friend at been stricken with it and walked with a limp, so Dad was scared to death he'd get it. He told me he lined up outside the school with his parents and gladly took the vaccine. "It was great, Lee," he told me. "Oral. Orange flavored." He grinned. "I actually would have had more. Orange was my favorite drink back then." He smiled. "We also got a shot for smallpox and the DPT. Diphtheria, tetanus, and pertussis. Didn't like the shots, no kid did, but we didn't want to get sick, so, we took the jab. None of us got sick at all." He smiled. "Always give yourself and your loved ones a fighting chance, Lee. I'm all for getting a shot." He and Mom died last year before the vaccine became available. He'd have taken it for sure. God, did I ever miss that man.

Anyway, here we were in the store, just wanting to get our shopping done and get out of there and away from the maskless locals when I rounded the corner and accidentally bumped into another cart.

Speaking of locals… Meg had taken five-year-old Andy around the corner already so it was just me and a guy who looked like Paul Bunyan. He had a full beard (no mask) and wore a black stocking cap. He was dressed in a black snowmobile suit, zipped partially down to reveal an insulated long underwear top. On his feet were calf-high leather boots with felt liners sticking out of the top. He looked like he was born to be a lumberjack and definitely looked like he belonged here, in this store, and in this town.

He also had a little girl in his cart about the same age as Allie.

"Sorry," I said. "Tricky corner," I added, making a little joke, hoping to lighten the mood.

He looked at me with deep-set, unblinking eyes, sizing me up. His sizing didn't take very long. I could see him thinking: "Here's some liberal jerk up from the city taking up space in my store. Some guy who knows nothing about the Northwoods." He'd have been right (except for the jerk part. I hoped.) I wore a forest green insulated jacket, blue jeans, a burgundy stocking hat, and hunting boots I'd bought at a big box store. To be honest, I looked kind of like a tourist and I'm sure Mr. Beard felt the same way.

Who knows how long we'd have stood there, him glaring at me, me wondering what I should do next if Allie hadn't grinned at his daughter and said, "Hi."

Then she turned and glanced at me with my scraggly six-week beard poking out from under my Covid mask and then back at the little girl's father (I assumed) and asked the little button of a girl, "Is your daddy Santa Claus?"

I couldn't help it. In spite of a potentially tense situation, I laughed.

So did he.

He looked at me and grinned. "Kids," he said. "They say the damnedest things." He smiled, then, showing me his white teeth. He seemed like a nice guy.

I held up my hand in sort of a half-wave of resignation. "Yeah, no kidding." It actually felt good to chat a little. Other than the doctor at the clinic last month who stitched my leg, I hadn't talked to anyone local.

The bearded man turned to Allie and said in all seriousness, "No, sweetheart. But sometimes I fill in as one of his elves."

Allie's eye went wide. "Really?"

"Sometimes," he said, grinning. He looked at me, winked, and then said to Allie. "But I know what Santa would say if he was here."

"What?" Allie asked, her voice almost a whisper.

"He'd say, 'Remember to always mind your parents.' "

Allie glanced quickly at me over her shoulder, then back at him. "Oh, I will," she said. "I really will."

That'll be the day, I thought to myself, but appreciated the sentiment.

"That's good," he said. "Santa will be happy." We were probably a safe six feet apart, me in my mask, he with none. He turned his attention to me. "Jack Camden," he said. "That's my daughter, Samantha." He smiled and roughed up the little girl's hair. "We call her Sam."

"Lee Acton," I said. "This is Allie."

Allie waved. "Hi."

So did Samantha. I mean, Sam.

Jack grinned. "Nice to meet you both." Then he did something I didn't expect. He leaned over and put out his elbow and we elbow-bumped. Like you're supposed to do. And, just like that, I'd met someone.

Meg and Andy came up just then with a couple of gallons of milk and put them in the cart. Meg glanced at Jack. "Hi."

I introduced Jack and Sam to them and we talked a bit. He was a little older than Meg and Me. We were both twenty-eight and Jack looked to be in his early thirties. (We found out later he and Linn were both thirty-five.) Jack told us that he lived with Sam and his wife Linnea on Turtle Lake about fifteen miles north of town, not too far from us.

"Linn takes care of Sam and does bookwork for me and my partner and for some of the businesses in the area," Jack told us. We had walked through the store and were in the check-out line next to each other. "How about you guys?"

He was so friendly! Way more than me. By nature, I'm very quiet and withdrawn, but Jack was friendly and easy to talk to. I told him that I did research for the Zylon Labs, a company looking at ways to improve the biological degradation of plastic. "I've been laid off for nearly a year with the pandemic."

"Yeah, I hear you," Jack said. "It's a bitch."

"Meg is an editor," I said.

"Yeah, I just picked up some more work," she said. Then glanced at me. "Every little bit helps, right, Lee?

"Exactly." I didn't want to get too deep into our finances with a guy we just met no matter how nice he seemed.

He surprised me when he turned to Meg. "An editor, huh? Really?"

"Why?" Meg asked.

"Well, my partner and I work cutting pulp wood for Blanding's. You know, that big paper mill up north by Bemidji."

"That's cool," I said. Mainly for something to say. I have to admit, occasionally it bothered me I wasn't working, even though technically I was. I did still get a paycheck.

"Yeah, it is," Jack said. Then he looked at both of us as if sizing us up. Finally, he made his decision. "I also write books."

"Really?" Meg said, interested.

I was interested as well. I loved to read, but write books? No way. I tried once. Didn't work out too well.

"What kind of books," I asked.

He looked at us. Then he looked at Allie and Sam. "Kids books," he said.

"Really," I said, and just barely stopped myself in time from adding, "That's cool". I went with "That's great" instead.

He looked at us and smiled. "Thanks. I do the illustrations, too."

Wow.

And in the middle of a pandemic, with lockdowns and social distancing the order of the day, that's how our friendship with Jack and Linn and Sam began.

And it was a good thing, too, because when we went outside there was a group of three maskless guys in their mid-thirties waiting by our car. I won't go into everything they said to us but the gist of it was that me and Meg were a couple of freaks and didn't belong in "their town".

The thought raced through my mind, *What? Is this the wild west?*

"Look, guys," I said, pushing my cart up to them. "If you'll just excuse us, we'll be on our way."

I was just trying to avoid the whole thing and get the groceries in the back of the Honda and Allie and Andy settled in their car seats. Meg was standing her ground nearby. I knew she was getting angry. So was I. But, frankly, I'm not much for confrontation. I really just wanted the whole thing over.

Then Frank walked up to us, his cart loaded with Sam and his groceries. He stopped between us and the three guys and stared at them. There were all dressed pretty much like Frank. "Problem, boys?" he asked.

It was like a motion picture in my mind. A standoff. A confrontation that could have gone two ways, one of them not so good. Fortunately, the three guys backed down. They took one look at big Jack looming over them and hurried away, one of them mumbling, "No" under his breath. Thank God.

Frank looked at us and shook his head. "Sorry about that. They're a bunch of idiots."

Later that night, Meg and I were relaxing in the living room of our cabin. The kids were asleep and the fire in the wood stove was warm and burning brightly. Meg took a sip of her nightly glass of red wine and said, "That was pretty cool about Jack and those jerks back in Park Rapids."

"No kidding. Who knows what would have happened?"

"I know. It could have been ugly." She was quiet for a minute, then she said, "You know, I was thinking."

"About what?"

"You know, Jack gave us their number. I was thinking about maybe calling their place and talking to Linn and seeing if I could set up a play-date with Sam and Allie." She turned to me. "What do you think?"

I didn't have to think long. I liked Jack, probably because he was so different from me. The fact that he didn't wear a mask, I guess I'd have to learn to deal with that. I kissed the top of Meg's head. "I think it's a great idea."

"Great." She smiled at me. "I'll call them in the morning."

The next day Meg called and Linn said, "Yes."

Just like that, we'd made some friends and our Northwoods world had gotten a little bit bigger.

March

To be honest, I've never been much of an outdoorsman. Oh, I liked to take the kids for walks in the park near our home in Minneapolis, and we had a little garden in the backyard where we grew some petunias and marigolds. That was all well and good, but I'll tell you, moving up north to our little cabin in the small town of Esker has changed me big time. I'm outdoors for hours every day, cutting firewood, shoveling snow, and playing with Andy and Allie. I've even started ice fishing. Yeah. But no matter what activities we're engaged in, it's challenging to be outdoors, especially when the temperature rarely gets above zero for months at a time (like for the last two months.) To make it all bearable, you have to dress for it.

When I'm outside, I wear a pair of sweat socks and a pair of wool socks under my felt-lined leather boots (suggested by my new friend Jack.) Waist down, I wear thermal long underwear over my regular underwear and a pair of thick wool pants held up by wide red suspenders. Waist up, I wear a tee-shirt, long sleeve tee-shirt, a flannel shirt, and a thick wool sweater. Then my insulated jacket. If it's really cold out, instead of the insulated jacket, I wear a snowmobile suit that Jack gave me. "It's a good one," he told me the day he handed it over. "I just sort of outgrew it." He laughed. Jack was taller than my six feet by three inches and outweighed my hundred and seventy pounds by at least sixty pounds. As Meg and I liked to say, he was "A big boy!"

But his brother-in-law, Arnie Blackhawk was even bigger. Arnie was Jack's wife's older brother. Linnea and Arnie were members of the Turtle Lake tribe of Ojibway. She and Jack met while attending college at Bemidji State University and had been married for ten years. Jack and Arnie had a pulp-wood cutting business. They were big, strong, hard-working men.

Arnie and his wife Amber lived with their daughter Willow on ten acres of land five miles from Esker. Like Jack and Linn, Arnie and Amber were independent-minded people who grew as much of their own food as they could and kept a variety of animals to supplement their diet. For them, the pandemic was a minor inconvenience. They didn't spend much time around people anyway.

All four of our new friends kind of chuckled at me and Meg and our Covid masks. "You guys do what you want, Lee," Jack told me when we were talking shortly after we'd first met. "It doesn't bother me at all."

When Meg first met Linn, it was on the phone shortly after I'd literally bumped into Jack's shopping cart in the Northwoods Grocery store in Park Rapids. The next day Meg had called her to suggest organizing playdates with our two kids Andy and Allie and her daughter Sam. Linn had readily agreed, and the two women bonded right then and there talking about kids, raising them, and taking care of a family.

"How about if I include my brother Arnie's child Willow?" Linn asked. "She's four and I'm sure she'd love it. She's over here a lot anyway."

Meg readily agreed and, just like that, our lives expanded some more.

Which was great. It was nice to at least talk to other people and occasionally get together, and none of them minded at all that we masked up.

After I met Jack in the grocery store and he and I had become friends, he introduced me to Arnie. He was a few years older than Jack's thirty-five, and, like Jack, he was a likable guy. The two of them seemed to get a kick out of me, this greenhorn city dweller who had moved his family to the Northwoods.

"We'll make a woodsman out of you yet," they joked with me whenever we got together. I laughed along with them. Good clean fun is what I figured.

A few weeks later they took me ice fishing.

It turns out Lake Moraine, on the shore of which our little town is located, is a great place to catch panfish like sunfish and crappies. Who knew? So, on a Saturday in the middle of March Jack and Linn and Arnie and Amber showed up at our cabin with their daughters. Linn and Amber went inside to be with Meg while me and Allie and Andy and Sam and Willow squeezed into Jack's pickup along with Arnie and we all drove out onto the lake to go ice fishing.

Onto the lake!

Jack's truck is a super-sized Ford F-350 with a raised chassis. He drove onto the ice at the public access and then plowed across the lake through six inches of snow like driving down a freshly cleared highway. He pointed up ahead and off to the right. "See those guys? That little village over there?"

There were about a dozen ice-fishing houses set up in the middle of the lake. They would stay up until the season closed at the end of the month. "Yeah. I've seen them. They've been here since we moved in."

"I know those guys." Jack shook his head. "They think they know what they're doing."

Arnie grinned. "But they don't." He was one of the biggest men I'd ever seen, maybe six-feet-five inches, and weighed close to three hundred pounds. He was a friendly guy with a quick smile who wore his long black hair in a ponytail. He was also kind and thoughtful, and I enjoyed being with him.

"Let's head to our spot," Arnie said to Jack.

"I'm on it."

Jack shifted into four-wheel drive and yanked the steering wheel to the left. We were now off the beaten truck path and on our own. He plowed away from the ice-house village through two feet of snow, tires spinning, kicking up a ten-foot-high rooster tail plume of white behind us. After about five minutes he pulled into a secluded bay at the north end of the lake and shut off the engine.

"Okay," he said, opening the driver's door. "Let's get some fish."

Arnie grabbed an ice-auger from the truck bed and fired it up. It took him only a few minutes to drill 9" wide holes in the ice, one for each of us men and one for each of the kids, seven in all. I was impressed to see that the ice was nearly two feet thick.

Jack baited the hooks of our poles with a colorful little jig and a piece of mealworm. He set out buckets for us to sit on and in less than fifteen minutes we were doing something I'd never dreamed I'd be doing; we were ice-fishing.

You might think that sitting on a bucket in the snow in the middle of winter and looking at a hole in the ice would be the definition of boredom, and you might be right. But, in this case, you'd be wrong. We weren't just fishing, we were bonding. Yeah, it might sound strange, or new-age, or whatever, but we were. And, I must say, for someone like me, who didn't mind being by myself and who really didn't have any close male friends, it was kind of nice.

The sky was deep blue. There was no wind. The temperature was in the mid-twenties. Above zero, for a change, I might add. Crows kept us company calling back and forth, often landing nearby looking for handouts. Even a pair of bald eagles circled overhear in a mating flight (Jack told me.)

Arnie told stories about growing up on the reservation, or "The Res" as he called it. Jack talked about the business of cutting pulp wood and hauling it to the pulp mill in either Bemidji or further north to International Falls. They were both interested in my job at Zylon doing lab research on the degradation of plastic in the environment, both of them agreeing that it was a necessary endeavor to be involved in, but that it would drive them crazy.

"I couldn't stand being inside all the time," Jack said.

"Me neither," Arnie added, pulling up a small bluegill, carefully removing the hook, and releasing it back into the lake. "Or being around all those people."

"No kidding," Jack concurred. "Give me the great outdoors anytime."

With the nice weather and the setting and the comradery, it might have a perfect day. Except…

Our conversation was suddenly interrupted by the girls when Allie and Sam and Willow started screaming.

"Help! Help!"

We all three jumped to our feet.

The four kids had wandered off. I know, I know, we should have been paying better attention. And, in our defense, we were, but, obviously, not enough. The girls had stayed close but not Andy. A dog had come onto the lake and Andy had decided to follow him. The girls had stayed put. Andy had not.

Ironically, he had followed the dog to only a hundred feet or so from the shoreline where unbeknownst to him (and us) an underwater spring had softened the ice. It only took Andy's extra weight to cause it to give way and in he went.

He was about two-hundred feet away. I ran like I'd never run before, leaping through the deep snow and keeping my eyes glued to my son's red stocking hat. He was screaming at the top of his lungs, hanging on the edge of the ice, and doing all he could to stay afloat. It seemed to take forever to get to him but probably was only about a minute.

As I approached the hole, Andy saw me and yelled, "Dad! Dad, help me!"

"Hang on," I called out. "Don't move. I'll save you."

The more he struggled, the more the ice gave way. My biggest fear was that he'd sink in his water-logged clothes.

"Help! Dad. I'm freezing."

Oh, my god. Let me save my son. I said a silent prayer as I struggled through the deep snow toward the hole. What to do? I had no idea. Water was puddling around him and I could see his little hands slipping off the ice. He was starting to sink!

Then I did the only thing I could think to do. As I came close to him, I went into a full belly slide, stretched out over the snow, and right up to the hole. "Grab my hand, Andy! Grab on tight."

He was soaking wet. He'd lost his mittens, and his lips were turning blue. He was going numb. I grabbed his hand to keep him from sinking further into the water.

"Hold on, son," I said. "I've got you."

He looked at me. His eyes were rimmed with ice crystals. "Dad," he moaned.

He kicked his feet frantically to try to get out of the water. Reacting quickly, I pulled on him. Bad move. The ice underneath gave way. Oh, no! Still holding on to Andy's hand I started sinking into the water. In a matter of moments, the icy water soaked into all of my layers of clothing, instantly numbing my body and dragging me and Andy down, down, down. A terrifying vision of the two of us sinking into the black depths of the lake passed before my eyes. Instinctively, I held my breath. I thought it was all over.

Then I heard a voice behind me. Was I dreaming? Then, I heard it again. "Hang on there, partner. You aren't going anywhere. I've got you."

It was Jack. He had me by my feet. Together he and Arnie pulled Andy and me out of the water and onto solid ice. We were saved.

We were also freezing to death. The two men got us to our feet helped us to the pick-up and loaded us and turned the heat on full. Hypothermia was setting in and Andy and I were shaking so badly, I thought our teeth would rattle out of our heads. We held on to each tightly for warmth.

Then they loaded Allie and Sam and Willow in the back and we raced the truck across the lake to the public access and onto the main road and eventually to our cabin. It only took five minutes but by the time we got there Andy and I could barely move we were so cold. Jack and Arnie hurried us inside, me carrying Andy. Finally, out of the cold and into the warm cabin we started to start to thaw out.

Then the fireworks started.

Meg freaked out when she saw us, and I didn't blame her. Linn and Amber weighed in as well, all three women berating me and Jack and Arnie up and down and fifty ways to Sunday. Us men? What did we do? We kept our mouths shut. Which was a good move on our part. The women gave it to us with both barrels, the gist of which was that we should have been paying better attention.

They were right. Lesson learned.

And next time we did pay attention. Big time. In fact, we went ice fishing the following weekend and caught our limit. We fried up a batch of sunfish and crappies for Meg and Linn and Amber to make up for the week before. It helped.

A little.

April

On April 19, we got word that the Pfizer vaccine was available for our age group and we took advantage of it. Meg called down to the clinic in Park Rapids and made an appointment for us. We drove there on April 22nd and got our first shot. It was an interesting experience.

The clinic was on a side street, one block off Hwy 34, one of the two main roads through town. It was a low-slung, tan brick building built (the sign said on the side of the entrance) in 1934. It was one of the Works Progress Administration projects (WPA) provided by President Roosevelt's New Deal which brought jobs to the area. The building had obviously seen a lot of history and today was no exception.

We showed up at our appointed time, 10 am, and stood in line with Andy and Allie, both of them masked up and quietly standing with us. There weren't many people, which was too bad. We wore our Covid masks and nodded to those in line that made eye contact with us. Not many did, but that was okay. We weren't there to make friends. Or in the North country either for that matter (even though we had.) There was still a huge stigma in rural Minnesota about mask-wearing and people freaking out about what they felt was the government infringing on their right to do whatever they wanted to do. Like suggesting citizens wear a mask to stop the spread of the coronavirus. It was a heated discussion, let me tell you, with unwavering lines drawn on both sides of the argument. Meg and I had long ago given up trying to convince people of the right thing to do: follow the science, wear a mask, social distance, wash your hands – that kind of thing. And, now, finally, we could get vaccinated! For us, it all came down to doing what we could to keep our kids healthy and safe.

I should say that we hadn't entirely given up. Meg had been talking to Linn and Amber over the last month or so about not only the advantages of the science side of Covid but also the benefits of being safe and doing the right thing for the sake of the kids. The two women had finally seen the light of what Meg was talking about and had made a commitment to wearing Covid masks in public. Same with their kids. They also had agreed to get vaccinated. That was a big step for them. Even more so when they informed Meg that they'd talked their husbands into getting shots, too.

"For Linn and Amber, once we talked about the good science practices, it made perfect sense to them," Meg told me. "Plus, of course, it's good for the kids. And that's what got Jack and Arnie on board."

"That's great," I told her. "Linn and Amber get much of an argument?"

Meg smiled and shook her head good-naturedly. Like me, she liked her friend's husbands. "You know Linn and Amber. If the boys did put up an argument, it probably didn't last for long, if you know what I mean."

I kind of did. I was getting to know Meg's two new friends fairly well. All three of us couples were getting together pretty often and I could see how strong-willed the two women were. Even though Jack and Arnie were big, husky, powerful woodmen, petite Linn and tall and thin Amber were just as strong but in their own ways. It was obvious each woman ran their family with an assertive, "take no prisoner's" kind of love that bordered on the obsessive. But in a good way. It was great to see that aspect of their personalities because Meg was that way as well. With all those shared traits, it was easy to see why the three women were forming a strong bond.

At the clinic, the line was slowly moving forward. I unzipped my jacket and did the same for the kids. It was kind of hot in there. "When are they all coming in for their shots?" I asked Meg, referring to our Linn and Amber and their husbands.

"A couple of days from now. I guess the boys are trying to get some more trees cut before the snow gets too soft."

Over the last few months, I had been finding out a lot about pulp word cutting from my two new friends. Not only was it hard work, but it was work that could go on almost all year long. The "boys" as Meg referred to them, applied for permits with the Department of Natural Resources (DNR) and cut where they were told. They especially liked cutting in the winter because it was relatively easy to get into and out of the forest. Plus, there were no black flies and mosquitoes, the bane of the north woods, to contend with. Just the cold, the mind-numbing, fingers freezing off if you weren't careful, cold. But they were tough men and could easily handle the frigid conditions. They just dressed for it in wool long underwear, wool pants, and Carhartt Overalls. They told me that oftentimes they'd break out in a sweat even if the temperature was twenty degrees below zero.

When working in the woods in the winter, they'd ride snowmobiles over the snow to pack it down and then use them to drag the felled trees over it to their huge truck where they used a claw-like crane to load the wood. Then they'd haul it to either Bemidji or International Falls for processing. Once set up, they might be at a site for a day, sometimes a week. However, when the temperatures warmed and the snow started melting, moving heavy logs through the forest was hard work due to the soft conditions.

Or so I was told. It was the third week in April and the snow wasn't melting yet, but it was getting soft, with daytime temperatures sometimes getting into the thirties. Sometimes.

"We've still got a few weeks," Jack told me a few days ago when I last talked to him. "There's a good two or three feet in some places in the woods."

"Then what happens?" I asked.

"Then we wait for the land to dry out."

"How long's that take?"

He shrugged. "Who knows? Last year it was done by the middle of May."

"Really?'

"Yeah, but that's okay. It gives us time to work on the trucks."

Don't ask if they applied for unemployment. I did once and got a derisive look. Question asked and answered. They didn't.

I'll tell you one thing: Those guys were proud and independent men.

Anyway, back at the clinic we got our shots and went into town and did some grocery shopping. We'd had no run-ins with any of the locals since that one time in February. I attribute it all to Jack. Apparently, he was quite well known in the area as a tough, fair, but no-none sense person. It was nice to know he was friends with us.

With our errands run and feeling good about being vaccinated, we headed home to Esker. The temperature was in the high thirties, the sun was shining and the snow was melting. There was a definite feeling of spring in the air. We even stopped at the drive-up Dairy Queen on the way out of town and got the kids each an ice cream cone. Us, too. What the heck, why not? We'd gotten our first shot. Why not celebrate?

Heading north on the highway, Meg was driving and I was checking my messages. Nothing new or out of the ordinary. I set my phone aside and was chatting with the kids in their car seats in the back when I received a "ping". I picked up my phone and took a look.

"Oh, oh," I said.

"What?" Meg looked over, concerned.

"It's from work." I was a research scientist with the Zylon Group, a company that was dedicated to searching for ways to help make plastic degrade faster in the environment. I'd been there for nearly six years, ever since I'd graduated from college. The president of the company, Bob Jenkins, was in his mid-forties and a dedicated environmentalist. He'd built the company from scratch and employed about two dozen of us like-minded people. Since the pandemic had begun, he'd had to close the door to business but kept us all on the payroll. He also kept in touch with us all with a monthly newsletter.

I could see Meg's knuckles turn white on the wheel. "Better check it."

I did, reading it quickly. When I was done, I turned to her. "Shit."

She glanced at me. "What?"

"It's from Bob. He's got news for us. He's closing the lab. For good. I guess there are supply chain issues right now and we can't get what we need to do reliable work."

Meg kept her eyes on the road, but slowed down considerably. "Does he say if they might re-open?"

I read further, the sinking feeling in my stomach growing heavier with each line. "He's hanging it up, I guess."

"What's that mean?"

"He says, and I quote, 'I'm leaving to pursue other avenues of environmental work.' " I stared at the email. Not really seeing the screen. "Damn. This is not good."

"Don't you get some kind of severance or something?"

I read further. Whew. "Oh, good. Yeah, I do. Three-quarter salary for a week for each year I worked there."

"Six weeks."

"Yeah,"

Meg did a quick calculation. "So, until the end of May, early June."

"Yeah."

I looked out the window watching the forest go by. I was thinking about Jack and Arnie and the independent loggers that they were. The hard work that they did. At least they didn't have to worry about being laid off.

Meg interrupted my thoughts. "Hey, don't worry about it, okay, Lee? I've still got my job with the editing company. We got money in savings. We'll figure something out."

"Oh, I know," I said. Although I had no idea what form "figuring it out" would actually take.

I turned and used my thumb to wipe some ice cream off Allie's chin. She grinned at me. So did Andy.

"Can we go sledding when we get home?" he asked.

"Yeah. That'd be fun," Allie said, excitedly.

In spite of having just been let go from my job and having no prospects for another one, my kids' suggestion sounded awfully good.

"You know what? That'd be a great idea."

I looked at Meg and she gave me the thumbs-up sign.

So, when we got back, we went sledding on a little hill overlooking the lake. We all had a great time. Then we went back to our snug cabin, made some hot chocolate with tiny marshmallow's and played Candyland. Our little family.

We were healthy. Meg and I had had our first jab. We were together. So what if I didn't have a job anymore? Somehow, we'd figure out a way to make ends meet.

We really didn't have a choice.

May

This year Mother's Day fell on May 9th, the same date as Andy's birthday. When I left for work, I hugged Meg. "Happy Mother's Day, sweetheart."

She hugged me back. "Thanks." Then she held up Allie, who she'd been holding. "Kiss Daddy."

"Bye, Daddy," she said.

I gave her a slobbery raspberry smooch, which she loved. "Bye, bye, Goofy One," I told her.

She crossed her eyes and made a face. "Goofy, goofy," she said and scrambled out of her mother's arms. It took one second for her to gear up to top speed as she began running around the room yelling, "Goofy, goofy, goofy" at the top of her lungs.

"Thanks for that," Meg said. But she was laughing. She and Allie had a special bond.

Kind of like me and Andy.

Speaking of... I looked around. "Say, where's the Birthday Boy by the way?"

"In the back by the garage, building a fort or something."

"Okay, I'll touch base with him on my way out." I kissed Meg again. "The party still on for four this afternoon?" Our friends Jack and Linn and Arnie and Amber and their kids Samantha and Willow were all coming over for a dual Mother's Day/Andy's birthday celebration. The weather was pleasantly mild in the sixties, and we were going to fire up the grill and do venison steaks that Jack was bringing and filleted walleye from Arnie. I was going to do up a big salad, bake some potatoes and steam some pea-pods. For dessert, we'd have Andy's homemade birthday cake that Linn was bringing.

"Yep, we are," Meg said, chasing after Allie. "Watch out! Mommy's coming to get you!"

Allie screamed and ran laughing into the bedroom she shared with her brother. "Nooooooo!"

Meg and I both smiled at each other, silently sharing the same thought: It was nice to see our daughter so happy. We shared a quick hug.

"Okay," I said. "I'm off. See you a little after three."

"Have a good day."

"I'll try."

I'd been working at Esker Quik-Stop for a couple of weeks. It had taken about a month to find the job and get hired after I'd found out that Zylon Labs, the company where I'd been a research scientist for the last six years, had closed its doors for good. The conclusion I'd eventually come to after bemoaning my loss of employment for about a day? That's life. Get on with it. So, I did.

Of course, Meg was a little more direct. "It's no time to feel sorry for yourself, Lee." Looked me in the eye and spoke in the direct way she has when she wants me to be perfectly clear I understand the point she is making. "Time to move on."

Message received. I started looking the next day.

I usually worked two or three days a week at the station, most often from ten in the morning until three in the afternoon. I was paid ten dollars an hour. It wasn't much, but having a little extra cash never hurt.

Meg was making good money as an editor for *Charlotte's Press*, a small independent publishing company, but I wanted to contribute. With the onset of warmer weather, we didn't need as much firewood to heat the house, so with less wood to cut, I had some extra time.

The Quik-Stop station was two blocks west of us on the corner of our highway and country road 2. It'd had a sign in their window that we'd seen coming home from getting our second Pfizer shot a few weeks ago.

I'd pointed it out to Meg. "What do you think?"

She'd slowed and read it as we drove past. "You working at a gas station?"

"Yeah. We could use the money, right?"

"Right."

"You don't sound too enthusiastic." I thought for a moment or two. "Is it because of the extra kids?" In addition to Andy and Allie, Meg was now watching Linn and Amber's girls, Samantha and Willow.

"No, that's not it. I love those two little ragamuffins."

"So, what is it?"

"I don't mind you working at all." She turned and smiled as she pulled into the parking space behind our cabin and near the garage. "In fact, it'll be nice to have the place to just myself and the kids." She joked. I think. "I'm concerned about you being around so many other people." She waved her hand arbitrarily. People up here aren't the safest you know when it comes to Covid."

She was right. Mask-wearing and social distancing were still frowned upon by the vast majority of rural Minnesotans. But by being conscientious and masking up and social distancing and avoiding crowds we had managed to stay healthy and keep the kids from getting sick with Covid for the nearly five months we'd been up here.

"I see your point," I said, helping the kids get out of the car. I watched them run laughing to the cabin. I pointed and commented, "It's nice to see how well the kids have adjusted."

"It is."

Meg took my hand as we followed behind. The wind was warm blowing through the pine trees. The ever-present crows were around squawking up a store. The sun was shining and the sky was blue. It was a pretty day. "The kids are doing great." She hugged me. "We all are." She sighed. "I just want you to be careful. That's all."

"Don't worry. I will be. I'll wear my mask and use hand sanitizer. Plus, they've got a plexiglass barrier between me and the customers." I smiled and opened the door for her to go inside. "So, you're okay if I apply."

She shrugged. "I know you'll be safe. Sure, go ahead."

So, I did. The next day. Mr. Sven Jorgenson, the manager, hired me on the spot. So far it had worked out fine.

I checked my phone as I went out the back door. I still had some time before I had to leave. "Hey, Andy," I waved. "How are you doing?"

He waved back. "Fine, Dad. I'm building a fort. Come look."

"I will."

"I found something."

"Cool," I said, not really thinking about what he'd found, but more to the point, thinking about getting to work. It was only my second week and I wanted to make a good impression. Plus, I was one of those people who was obsessed with being on time. I checked my phone as I walked across the worn yard that at one time probably used to be grass but was now mostly dirt and low-growing weeds.

He was playing with some of the boards that were part of the collapsed garage next to the single-car one that we could have used if it were empty of junk. Which it wasn't, hence us parking the Honda Fit outside. The garages were about a hundred feet from the cabin.

On the way, I eyeballed the last of the wood Gladys our landlady had left for us in January. The pile was tiny compared to the ten cords that had originally been there. We'd used most of it up but still had enough to take the chill off any cold nights or days. I made a mental note to cut it all up, split it and store it on the porch in the next week or two to clear the yard. Maybe then we could plant a garden.

With those thoughts in mind, I walked up to Andy. He was squatting down with his back to me looking at something.

"Hi, buddy," I said. He was dressed in a dark blue sweater under worn bib overalls. He had on rubber boots because the ground was soft and muddy in a few places. And on his head, he wore a Minnesota Twins baseball hat. His hair was long and curly and spilled down to his shoulders.

He turned and grinned. "Hi, Dad." Then he pointed. "Look what I found."

I put my phone away. "What?"

He stood up and pointed. "There."

I bent close and looked. "Where?"

"Under that board."

I squatted down and looked underneath. "I don't see anything."

Andy got on his hands and knees next to me and lifted the board.

"Oh, my god!" I yelled, scrambling backward and falling over myself to get away. It was a twisting, writhing, mass of snakes.

Andy laughed. "What? You don't have to be afraid. They just gardener snakes."

Now let me tell you something about me and snakes. It won't take long, and it's not a pretty story. Nor one I'm proud of. My mom was terrified of them. So was my dad. Together they instilled a reptilian fear of them in me while I was growing up that not only filled my days with terror but my nights with nightmares. "They'll come in your sleep and eat you," Mom sometimes said.

"Or crush you to death by suffocation." Dad would add.

Thanks, Mom and Dad.

The idea was to fill me with a fear so great I would stay away from them. Done and done!

But as I got older and I started to rethink that thinking. A friend of mine in college was a herpetologist, a snake guy, and he said to me once, "If you fear snakes, that means everything you know about snakes is wrong."

Rational thinking to an emotionally charged fear, that was true. And, I have to say, I tried. He taught me about the good they did for the environment and their place in the ecosystem. He even got me to hold one, a harmless, four-foot-long bullsnake. (Harmless!). All well and good, but I was unprepared for the thousands (at least) of the withering writhing snakelets (or whatever they were called) that my son was so proudly showing me.

As a mature adult and a father who wanted to set a good example for the younger generation, I tried to rally. "Those are nice, son," I said, trying to keep the quivering quaver out of my voice.

"I know, Dad. They are so cool." He wrapped his arms around my waist and hugged me. "This is the best birthday present ever."

I cleared my throat. "You know we can't keep them."

"Oh, I know." He grinned at me. "I just like knowing they're here. I can study them."

Wow. And here I thought the book I got him about strange Grimm Fairy Tales would be a hit. (It actually was.) But I have to admit, it was wonderful to see him so excited.

I hugged him, steering clear of the snakes. "Well, I'm glad you like them," I said. Your mom and I had nothing to do with it, but I'm glad you're happy."

"Oh, I am, Dad. I really am."

I hugged him some more. He really was a great kid. "I'm glad."

I left then and went to work. Later that afternoon, we had a great Mother's Day/Andy's Birthday and everyone had a super good time. Andy enjoyed showing off the den of gardener snakes to Jack and Linn and Arnie and Amber and Sam and Willow. The common consensus was that they were "Awesome!" I was the only one who had the willies over them, but I did my best to hide it. After all, not only was it Andy's birthday, but, as my rationally minded son keeps telling me, "Dad, don't worry about them. They're completely harmless.'

He's right. They are harmless. And I'm trying my best to get on board and come to grips with the snakes my son so adamantly admires. In fact, he and I go out there every day to check on them. Each day it gets easier, so maybe it's working. It's been over a week now, I haven't even had any nightmares.

June

One Saturday, my friends Jack and Arnie came over to help me set up our garden. While we worked, their kids Sam and Willow played with my kids Andy and Allie, some kind of game that involved trying to find gardener snakes. Andy had found a nest of them the month before on his birthday and had basically adopted them. The fact that there had to have been hundreds of them didn't seem to bother the kids at all. On the other hand, I had a fear of snakes that I was trying to deal with and had drawn the line at Andy bringing any (or even one) inside our cabin. He was fine with that, pointing out, "Dad, don't be silly. They don't belong indoors." He good-naturedly shook his head sadly at his reptile-challenged father.

It was the third week in June and close to the summer solstice and the longest day of the year. While the kids searched the yard and the collapsed garage in back for signs of snakes, Jack and Arnie and I worked on the garden.

Due to the poor soil, it was going to be a raised bed. We'd purchased the wood earlier in the week from the lumber yard in Park Rapids and hauled it up to my place. Now Jack was using his drill to secure the boards together to build a ten-foot by twenty-foot by twelve-inch-deep frame. The boards were an inch thick, and they were sturdy, not to mention heavy.

With the last screw in place, Jack stood up. "Okay, that'll do it."

Arnie and I looked over his work. "Looks great," I said. "Thank you."

Arnie looked closely at the corners and gave them a pull. "We should put some braces on these corners, Jack. Give them more stability."

"Not a bad idea." He looked around. "Got any scraps around here?"

Now, I'll be the first to admit that I know absolutely nothing about carpentry. Wood was wood as far as I was concerned. "Um." I pointed to the fallen-down garage where Andy had discovered the nest of gardener snakes. "How about over there?"

Jack glanced at Arnie who grinned. "What Jack means is decent wood, amigo." He pointed. "That stuff's probably rotten."

"Not to mention a home for Andy's snakes," Jack added, laughing. Then he said, "Hold on. I've got something in my truck I think I can use."

Jack's F-350 could not only drive through three feet of snow, but I swear he had every tool known to man in the toolbox behind the cab. He also had a bunch of scrap lumber. In a minute he'd selected the pieces he wanted to use and set out his circular saw on the tailgate. He gave me a hundred-foot-long extension cord. "Go plug this in," he said pointing to the outlet on the side of the cabin.

I did, and in a minute the saw was singing. In another minute, the wood was cut. Ten minutes later the corners were secure and the frame was completed.

"Okay," said Arnie, now taking over. "Time to fill 'er up!"

Jack laughed. "Now the fun begins."

Arnie had suggested that I fill the frame with a mixture of black dirt and ground-up horse manure. Not knowing a thing about gardening, at least subsistence gardening like what Arnie and Jack and their families did, I was all ears.

"Black dirt gives the roots stability," he told me when we talked about it earlier that spring. "The manure gives it nutrients."

Who was I to argue with the experts? "Sounds good to me," I said.

When it came time to build the frame, I called down to Park Rapids to order some, and a few days later watched a dump truck from the Park Rapids Garden Center dump a full load where my wood pile used to be. Seemed like a lot of soil, which I learned is what we were getting. When I had inadvertently called it "dirt" Arnie admonished me. "Dirt is what you sweep off the floor, my friend." He grinned, grabbed a handful of the rich, black mixture, held it to his nose, and drew in a deep breath. "This," he said, almost reverently, "this is the good stuff. This is Soil!"

And now it had to be transferred from the huge pile to the garden frame. We used shovels and wheelbarrows. With three men working, it took a lot less time than I thought it'd take. An hour later, hot and sweating, we were done.

Meg must have been watching from the kitchen, because she came out and joined us with a big pitcher of iced tea. "How about a break?" She set the pitcher down on our nearby picnic table and poured glasses for each of us. Then she pointed to the garden frame. "All done?"

"Yeah," Arnie said, whipping his brow with a red handkerchief. He took a glass from Meg and toasted her. "Thanks." He drank thirstily and then asked, "Got your list?"

"Yeah," she said. "I've been talking to Amber."

"Good." He set down his empty glass and grinned. "Thanks for the iced tea. It hit the spot." Then he picked up the heavy wheel barrel like it was a toy and tossed it in the back of his truck. "You should be good to go then." He turned to Jack. "Ready?"

Jack finished his tea. "Thanks, Meg." And then made sure all of his tools were loaded and secure in his truck. "Yep. All set."

I put up my hand to stop them. "Wait. Do you guys want to stay and have some lunch or something? Something to eat?"

"Thanks, but no," Jack said. "We've got to get set up for tomorrow."

"Yeah," Arnie added. "We've got a permit to cut on the other side of Aspen Lake." He pointed south. "We'll get the truck into the forest there today and start cutting tomorrow."

"So, the ground's not too soft?" I asked. Soft ground was the bane of a wood cutter's existence. Trucks could get stuck in the mud and if that happened no wood was getting cut anytime soon. And cutting wood was what it was all about for Jack and Arnie.

"Nope. Hard as a rock." Arnie said.

"Okay." I waved my hand at the garden frame now filled with rich dark soil. "Thank you so much for all of this."

"No problem." Jack shook my hand, something he did every time he left. "Now you just have to plant your veggies." He grinned. "Have fun." He waved to Meg. "Bye."

Jack got in his pickup and Arnie got in the big wood-hauling truck with the crane. They both tooted their horns goodbye and off they went. Meg went inside to work on an editing project and I kept Andy and Allie with me.

"You guys can help me plant the garden," I told them.

"Yea!" Andy was excited.

So was Allie. "Goody!" was her comment.

I had them help me lay out string across-wise to keep the rows straight. We started with beans, green and waxed. The planting went well, probably because the kids could handle the big seeds so easily.

Then we moved to lettuce with a little less success due to the smaller seeds. Andy hung in there but Allie soon lost interest.

She turned to me. "Daddy. Can I go look for Andy's snakes?"

"Sure." I looked at Andy. "You want to go with her?"

He shook his head. "No way. This is fun."

I said to Allie. "You can go, just don't wander off, okay?"

She pointed to the collapsed garage. "I'm just going to be over there."

It was only fifty feet away. "Sounds good," I told her. "Just be careful."

She smiled. "I will."

I watched her skip off. It was a warm afternoon, maybe seventy degrees. Both the kids were wearing shorts and tee-shirts and tennis shoes.

I turned to Andy. "Okay, let's tackle the kale next."

We bent to the task and then moved on to carrots and soon we were immersed in our seed planting.

Then Allie's screams filled the air.

"Daddy!" She yelled. "Daddy!!"

I'd never heard her scream like that. It sounded like someone was sticking hot needles in her.

I jumped to my feet and ran in her direction telling Andy. "Go get your mom."

The screams were coming from behind the garage. I covered the fifty feet in about two seconds, urged on by my daughter's cries. "Daddy! Help me!!"

She was calling out for help and screaming and crying all at the same time. I'd never heard anything like it. Adrenaline kicked in. I had to save her.

I spun around the corner of the garage and took in the scene. Oh, no! It only took a moment to figure out what had happened. My poor little daughter was sitting on the ground slapping at bees swarming all around her from a hole in the foundation of the garage. They were big and black. Wood wasps! And they were attacking poor little Allie with a vengeance.

As I ran toward her, I could see them stinging her exposed skin and stinging her through her tee shirt. They were relentless. Her screams filled the air. I did the only thing I could think of. I picked her up on a dead run and took off for the lake. My thought was to get her in the cold water to help ease the pain from the stings. As we ran, I bushed off the wasps that still clung to her.

"It's okay, sweetheart," I told her, running for all I was worth. "Daddy's got you."

She buried her head in my chest and sobbed. "Daddy. It hurts."

I ran faster.

The lake was only a couple of hundred feet from us. I ran as fast as I could and didn't stop for a moment as I held Allie tight and plunged into the cold water. It was June and the ice had only been out for less than two months. It was pretty cold. Really cold, actually, but cold is what I wanted. And it did the trick.

I waded out so we were both submerged up to our necks. I held Allie and rocked her in my arms and whispered to her. "It'll be okay, Sweetheart. Daddy's got you. I'll keep those bees away. Don't worry." Honestly? I don't know what I said. All I wanted to do was to comfort my poor daughter.

After a few minutes, the pain from the stings started to subside. I knew because I'd been stung a few times too. They had felt like hot needles being stuck into our skin.

By the time Andy and Meg got to the lake, the pain had almost gone away. But the trauma for Allie hadn't. Meg waded out and took our daughter in her arms.

"What happened?"

I explained about the wood wasps behind the garage. Then I said. "I'm sorry. I should have paid better attention."

Meg surprised me by saying. "Well, maybe." She rocked Allie who now had quit crying. She had her eyes closed and seemed to be resting, probably from the shock. "But, it's not like we can watch them every moment of the day."

Which was true. But I still felt bad.

We went back to the cabin and Meg fixed an ice pack that she used to soothe Allie's stings. It helped a lot, and they didn't swell up too much.

"You know," Meg said, laying Allie on the couch and looking closely at the wasp stings. "I think getting her in the lake so fast really helped." She continued to apply the ice pack on some of the bigger red areas. "The cold water helped keep the swelling down." She turned to me. "Good thinking."

I know I make a lot of mistakes. I know that Meg rolls her eyes at stuff I do and say every day. Usually more than once. And I truly felt horrible that the wasp attack that took place on my watch. A father hates to see his kid hurt.

So, thank god the lake was close by. I'm not sure what I would have done if it wasn't. I'd probably still be running with my daughter in my arms and a swarm of angry wood wasps on our tail. I'm glad it didn't come to that.

July

It's funny how things work out, and by funny I mean interesting. Here it is July 2021. The pandemic has been going on for over a year, nearly a year and a half. Somehow, a year ago many of us thought we'd be done with this by now. Not even close. A new variant has raised its ugly head and cases are on the rise. We've had the vaccine available for nearly six months and about half the population has chosen to get vaccinated. Which is good. But the other half have chosen not to, which is bad. Those who have chosen not to receive a shot (or shots) are getting sick. And oftentimes dying. People are wearing masks. Many are not. Kids are planning to go back to school this fall. But maybe not.

People are getting worn out, mentally fried, and sick of the pandemic.

So are we.

But Meg and I continue with our commitment to do whatever we can to keep our kids healthy. We will get our boosters when we can. We will continue to wear masks and practice social distancing. We will try to stay safe. Thank goodness our friends Jack and Linn and Arnie and Amber have decided to do the same. We have our own little Pandemic Family we call ourselves. We are all committed to doing what we can to protect our kids. Knock on wood, no one has gotten sick from the coronavirus yet.

I've been working at the Quik-Stop a couple of blocks down the road from us for nearly two months now and let me tell you, you meet all kinds of people at a gas station. Toss a pandemic into the mix and things get interesting.

First off, in spite of the pandemic showing no signs of letting up, the anti-maskers and anti-vaxxers are stubbornly hanging onto their beliefs like their lives depended on it. Which they do, it turns out. 95% of all new Covid cases are with people who have refused to get vaccinated. Which is their prerogative, but it puts others at risk. At the Quik-Stop I have a clear shield at checkout, which helps. And I wear my mask and clean my hands, but still… It drives me nuts that people come in mask-less and wander around oblivious to others. Meg and I and our friends are vaccinated so we aren't too worried. But it's not about us, it's about our kids, who, of course, are too young for the vaccine. So, we are being careful for them. I wish others were as well. But they aren't.

On the other hand, I kind of like working there. You met some real characters, and, if you take Covid out of the equation, it's kind of interesting. Myrtle Hokinson is a widow who walks into town every day from her home in the woods three miles away. She comes in for a pack of filter-less camel cigarettes and a cold twenty-four-ounce bottle of Budweiser Beer. Able Johnson raises mink. He stops in nearly every day for a lottery ticket. Clarise Yankton is a retired phone company employee who has her daughter and granddaughter living with her. She lives in a double-wide trailer near the station and stops in every day for anything they've run out of. They are on a Food Assist program and I'm glad we can help her out.

I've put a sign on the door that reads *Masks Appreciated.* No one pays it any attention.

I'm working three days a week, from ten to three, Tuesday, Thursday, and Friday. I mainly run the cash register but sometimes do the stocking. My manager, Bob Fischer, is a thin, wiry man about forty-five who I suspect augments his coffee habit with amphetamines. I'm not kidding, and he's not the only one up here. There's a lot pill-taking going on in our county if you know what I mean. It's unfortunate, but it seems the longer the pandemic goes on, the more people are finding strange ways to deal with it, and not with the best outcome either. Drug use is up. Suicides, too. Depression and anxiety are also on the rise. Very challenging times. The few people we are in contact with in Minneapolis (like my brother) tell us the same thing. The country is deep into what is now being called Pandemic Malaise.

Meg and I talk about it a lot. Did we do the right thing in moving up here to little Esker on the shore of Lake Moraine? The answer is still a resounding, yes! When the pandemic is over and life returns to normal, will we move back to our home in Minneapolis? Sure. Anyway, we think we will. We've made the best friends we've ever had in our lives up here with Jack and Linn and Arnie and Amber. So what if I have to work at a gas station run by a coffee-addicted speed freak and get to serve customers who turn up their noses at science, ignore the guidelines, and muscle forward doing whatever they want to? Ain't that America, right? (To paraphrase John Mellencamp.) Land of the free and home of the brave. Right. Tell that to the nearly 600,000 people who have died so far in the United States. And their families. The number keeps rising.

Lately, I've taken to coming home from work, grabbing Andy, and going down to the lake to unwind. We are becoming serious rock skippers, and one day after work, two days before the Fourth of July, that's what we were doing.

"Look at that!" Andy yelled, sailing a nice flat stone out over the calm water. "One. Two. Three. Four. Five. Six. Seven." He counted. "Eight! I did eight, Dad!"

"Good going, son," I told him. It was great to see how well he and his sister Allie were adjusting to life in the Northwoods. Meg was running her daycare (we now called it) for Andy and Allie and Sam and Willow, our friends, Jack and Linn, and Arnie and Amber's kids. And her editing job for *Charlotte's Press* was going well.

I skimmed a rock out over the water and counted to myself. "Looks like five," I told Andy.

He'd been watching and counting. "Yeah, that's what I got." He was silent for a minute, holding his stone, waiting for me to take another turn. Then he asked, "Dad, are we going to do anything for the Fourth of July?"

I threw my stone. Four skips. Hmm. Not my day, I guess. I sat down on the beach and looked out over the water. Andy joined me. It was nice having him next to me. I'd trimmed his hair so it was just above his shoulders. He was wearing cut-off jeans, ripped tennis shoes and a white tee shirt. On his head was his ever-present blue Minnesota Twins baseball cap.

Meg and I had talked about it. The guidelines were that if you were going to be in a crowd, you should wear a mask. But, because you'd be outside, wearing a mask wasn't required. For us, what it came down to was that we just couldn't run the risk of being in a crowd of fireworks display watchers and subjecting the kids to the possibility of getting the Covid virus. Especially not if we could help it. Maybe next year.

"No, I'm afraid not," I told him. "It's too dangerous."

I looked down at him. He had his knees pulled up and he was looking out over the lake. It was nearly three-thirty in the afternoon and getting pretty warm, probably eighty-five degrees. The far side of the lake was about two miles away. It was considered a small to medium-sized lake for the area. There were some sailboats out on it and maybe eight speed boats, a couple of them pulling water skiers. There were three jet-skies buzzing around, and a couple of pontoon boats idling along looking at the scenery. Lots of people sitting quietly in their boats and fishing. It was summer in Minnesota and people were out and about, doing their best to enjoy life and forget the pandemic.

Yet, it still raged on.

"Why not?" Andy asked. "The dang pandemic?"

"Yeah, I'm afraid so," I told him. "Your mom and I talked about it. It's just too dangerous."

He heaved a dramatically heavy sigh. "I hate the pandemic."

I put my arm around him. "Me, too."

He leaned into me. "Are Uncle Jack and Uncle Arnie coming over?" He'd started referring to our friends that way last month when Arnie's wife Amber had announced she was pregnant. I have no idea why. All I know he was especially excited that our friends were going to have a baby.

"Yes, they are. They're bringing Linn and Sam and Amber and Willow. We're going to have a bonfire on the beach." I looked at him. "Right about here."

He brightened up considerably. "Really?"

"Yep. We'll roast hot dogs and make smores. How's that sound?"

"Smores?"

"Yeah, you know. Graham crackers, Heresy's chocolate, and marshmallows."

He smiled, remembering. "Oh, yeah. I love those."

"Me, too."

He got to his feet and started picking up stones. "You know what, Dad?"

"What?"

"If our friends are coming over, I don't think I'll miss the fireworks at all."

I grinned at him. It's a pandemic. We were all doing our best to adjust to it. "I have an idea. When they come over on the Fourth, you want to have a rock skipping contest?" I asked.

"Sure," he grinned. "That'd be great!"

We spent the rest of the afternoon on the shore of the lake skipping stones. It was a little thing, but it was one of those days I'll never forget. In spite of the pandemic, life was going on. And for Meg and me and Andy and Allie and our friends, it was going on pretty well. And that's all we could ask for.

August

Let me tell you, August in the Northwoods is not the most fun time to be there. First off, it's hot. Which is fine. Especially if you live near a lake like we do. Just run down the dirt road behind our cabin to Lake Moraine and jump in and cool off. Right? Sure, go ahead. We tried it once, me and Allie and Andy. We lasted about ten minutes. The water was great, nice and cool, and refreshing. There was light wave action and the lake was pretty was sparkling. Overhead the sky was a deep blue with a few puffy clouds. Perfect, right?

Not quite. To that lovely scene, we must factor in the bugs: the mosquitoes, the gnats (black flies) and deer flies, and horse flies! Oh, and I forgot to mention the hundreds of varieties of ticks (at least). Man, the blood-sucking never ends.

I once read a story entitled *Eaten Alive* about a guy who had nearly lost his mind when he got lost in a dense Northwoods forest and the aforementioned insects attacked him mercilessly and nearly did what the title implied: ate him alive.

And they were bad on that day we went swimming, that was for sure, swarming all over us, getting in our mouths and noses and ears, chewing and biting our arms and legs and shoulders and back. In a word – pure hell. Well, two words, but you get my drift. It was bad. And during the season in August, they're the worst.

So why we decided to go pick blueberries in August is beyond me, but we did.

"Come on with us," Meg said, loading Andy and Allie into the Honda Fit. "It'll be fun."

I pointed down to the lake. "Don't you remember that time I took the kids swimming? We were almost…"

"Yeah, yeah, I know. You were almost eaten alive. I know," she said, chiding me. Like I've said before. I'm not really what you'd consider a woodsman by any stretch of the imagination. Don't get me wrong, I like being up north, especially in the security of our small town, but when it comes to living actually "in the woods" I'll leave that to those better suited for it. Like Jack and Linn and Arnie and Amber. And, now, apparently, my wife. She poked me in the side with her elbow. "Come on, Lee." She turned to the kids. "What do you guys think? Should Daddy go with us?"

Their chorus of resounding "yeses" sealed the deal. I went.

From our cabin, we drove to Arnie and Amber's place on a dirt road for five miles through jack pine forests and bogs, kicking up a plume of dust the entire way. It had been a dry year which knocked back the mosquitoes a little bit, but no matter. The black flies and deer flies and horse flies happily filled the void.

Arnie was with Jack half an hour west cutting wood in the Superior Forest so it was just me and Meg, Amber and Linn, and the kids: Andy, Allie, Sam, and Willow.

As we drove up, Amber came out to greet us, brushing away gnats (black flies) as she approached. We got out of the car and she hugged Meg. "Glad you could make it." She waved at me over the roof of the car. "Nice to see you, too, Lee." She grinned and tossed me a can of Northwoods Off insect repellant. "Meg said the bugs like you a lot. That's too bad. It must be something in your blood."

Was she kidding around? Was I genetically predisposed to be an attractive meal to every single flying, buzzing, and biting insect known to man? "Really?" I asked, buying immediately into her theory. It made sense in a strange, weird way.

She smiled, showing me her white teeth. Into her second month of being pregnant, she looked happy with herself and with life. "Naw. I'm just kidding." She smacked at a particular bothersome horsefly. "They like everyone."

"Great."

"Don't worry about it. Spray yourself down with that Off and you'll be good to go."

So, I did. Liberally. I also sprayed Andy and Allie who covered their eyes and giggled and would barely hold still. They were pretty excited to go berry picking with Aunt Amber which was their new name for her ever since they were told last month she was going to have a baby. Why they chose to call her that I have no idea.

With the kids sprayed, Amber said, "Okay, let's get going."

"Where are we off to?" I asked, brushing away some gnats. The spray worked to keep them off me like the name implied, but they seemed to hover at a point just outside the range of effectiveness of the spray, about a foot. I guess I'd have to learn to live with them and that bothersome fact. At least they weren't landing in mass and feeding on me like a human smorgasbord.

Meg was just grinning at my discomfort. "Come on, Lee. Man up. It'll be fun. A whole new experience."

Meg was taking to Northwoods life in a big way. Not only was she happily running our home daycare for Andy and Allie and Sam and Willow, but she was also forever taking them on field trips out in the woods and fields near us identifying birds, trees, and wildflowers. She had happily assisted me in cutting firewood over the winter, taking over for a few weeks when I'd injured myself with the ax, and Amber was teaching her the basics of home canning. Hence the trip to the woods to collect blueberries. Meg and Amber and Linn were going to make blueberry preserves and blueberry pie. My mouth watered just thinking about eating both of them. So, I was all in, as far as the picking went. Hopefully, the spray would help make keep the swarming hordes at bay.

Amber drove her rusted-out, dust-covered pickup. What it lacked in looks it made up for in serviceability. It ran like a top. (Amber was just as good a mechanic as Arnie, maybe better.) Meg and I and Linn crammed into the front on the bench seat while the kids rode in the open back with the admonishment from Amber to "keep your butts on the floor". Which they did.

We drove deep into the jack pine forest, turning right and left at various intersections until I had no idea where we were. Amber and Meg and Linn chatted away about the kids, her pregnancy, and canning preserves while I looked out the window. There was nothing but pine trees as far as I could see. Not a building in sight, either. We were on state land so it was just going to be us and the forest and the insects. And, hopefully, blueberries.

After about fifteen minutes, Amber leaned over and asked me, "Lee, have you ever picked blueberries?"

I shook my head. "No."

She grinned. "You're in for a treat."

I nodded in agreement. "I hope so." In fact, the further we drove into the forest, the more worried I became. "What about bears?" I asked her. "Don't we have to worry about them? And cougars, I added. I heard someone saw cougar tracks last week."

Amber smiled at me. "Lee, this is their forest. We're the interlopers here. We'll go in, do our thing, pick our berries, and get out. As quick as we can, okay? It should be fine."

Good advice, but why was it the only word that stuck in my mind was "should"?

"You're the boss," I said, trying to lighten the moment.

She grinned. "I am. Stick with me." She pointed to Meg. "Like your wife says, it'll be fun."

Meg looked at me and smiled. "See?"

A few minutes later Amber pulled the truck off the side of the road. "Okay, everybody out." We did as we were told. We were in a clearing in the forest. The ground cover looked to be nothing remarkable, just low-growing grass and fragrant wintergreen, a plant common in the area.

"This is it?" I asked skeptically.

"Yep," Amber said. "Look closely."

I squatted down so I was close to the ground and did as I was told. After a minute my eyes adjusted to what I was seeing. "Oh, wow," I exclaimed. "Incredible." I'd never seen anything like it. We were standing in a blueberry patch that stretched through the clearing as far as I could see. I stood up. "Amber, this is amazing."

She grinned and put on a wide-brimmed straw hat. "It is, isn't it? I've been picking here since I was a girl. Back then, I'd come with my mom and grandmother. It was my great-grandmother who'd discovered it, maybe a hundred years ago."

"Wow," was all I could say.

Next to me, Meg said, "Um, Lee? You might want to close your mouth. The bugs, you know."

"Funny."

"Let's get going," Amber said. She handed out gallon buckets to each of us, kids included. Then she directed us. "We'll just work through the clearing." She looked at the kids. "Pick, don't eat." They nodded solemnly. "And stay together." She looked at Meg and me and Linn. "Everyone."

"Okay," we all said.

Then we got to work.

I have to say, it was fun being in the forest with no one around but us. After the wildlife got used to us we heard birds singing, woodpeckers tapping on trees, and squirrels chattering nearby scolding us. I especially liked hearing the wind blowing through the pines like a loud whisper.

The berries were on low-growing bushes about a foot off the ground. The kids made their way easily through the huge patch, but we adults had to bend over. It was hard work and sweaty work, but Amber kept us entertained with stories of her youth growing up on the Turtle River Reservation. She had a horse named Quicksilver that she rode every day and even entered barrel riding competitions in local rodeos. "I don't ride anymore," she told us when we asked her about it. Not enough time these days. Maybe when the kids are older."

Meg and I glanced at each other. Amber was a good, kind, and caring person, and we were both thinking the same thing: we hoped that dream could eventually come true.

We'd been in the clearing for about an hour and each of our buckets had been emptied once into a larger container. We'd moved away from the road deeper into the pines, staying together and working hard. Now that we had been picking for a time, the rhythm of the task was Zen-like. And, like I'd been told earlier by Amber, it was pretty fun.

But then the bear showed up. Yeah, a bear. A black bear with a cub. It was Willow who saw it first.

"Mom."

"What, honey?" Willow glanced at her daughter.

Willow pointed. "Look."

Amber stood up and followed where her daughter was pointing. "Oh, my god."

Meg and I stood up. "Shit," I said.

"Shush," Amber admonished me. "She doesn't see us. Their eyesight isn't the best. Plus," she tested the breeze with a finger, "the wind is blowing away from her towards us, so she'll have a hard time smelling us."

Meg grabbed my arm and whispered. "Just do what Amber says, okay?"

Which was good advice, because my mind had gone blank for a moment. Meg knew me well enough to know that when it came back, all I would think of doing was grabbing the kids and running for the truck.

Cooler heads prevailed. Amber took over and whispered to the kids. "Andy, Allie, Sam, and Willow, listen up. Walk very slowly to me." Which they did. While they were doing that, Amber turned to us adults and said, "When the kids get here, we will all walk as quickly and as quietly as we can to the truck. Okay?"

"Okay," we whispered.

"The key is not to startle her. Okay?"

"Yes," we whispered again.

And that's what we did. We held our kids' hands and hurried through the woods. I had Andy and Meg had Allie and we all still held onto our buckets, which was pretty amazing when you thought about it.

I glanced over my shoulder once. The momma bear, as Amber called her, and her cub were methodically working their way through the berry patch moving away from us. If they'd seen us, they'd ignored us. Incredible as it may seem, the entire experience, which could have ended horrifically, ended quite well.

Later, back at Amber's, we were sitting around her kitchen table having coffee. The kids were outside looking at the two goats Amber kept for making cheese.

Amber took a sip from her mug. "Well, that was the last thing I expected. I mean there are bears out there for sure, but usually they stay away if they sense humans in the area."

"I'm just glad no one was hurt," I said.

Amber took a bite of her cookie and chewed thoughtfully. "You know, we haven't had much rain. Maybe the momma and the little cub were chowing down on those berries for a little extra moisture or something."

"Do you see many bears?" Meg asked.

"Not really. Like I said, they're around, but they really do stick to themselves." She paused. "As long as they have enough food."

I looked at the gallon buckets of berries lined up on the kitchen counter. And the big container bulging with berries on the floor next to it. "Well, I'm glad we did it. Picked the berries, I mean. It was fun to be in the woods and it was cool to see the bear and her cub."

Amber winked at Meg and said, "We'll make a woodsman out of you yet."

They both laughed. I kind of got it, I think.

Oh, and those blueberry preserves and that blueberry pie? They were the best I'd ever tasted. Meg told me she thought seeing the bear and the cub might have had something to do with it. You know what? I think she might be right.

September

With Andy having turned six a few months ago, he was eligible to go into first grade.

"What do you think?" Meg had asked when we started talking about it, which had been off and on all summer long.

Now, during the first week in September, we were still on the fence.

"I don't know." Which was the answer I'd been giving for months. Meg felt the same way. We'd moved up here to help keep our kids stay safe from the pandemic. Now we were vaccinated, our friends Jack and Linn and Arnie and Amber, though resistant at first, were all vaccinated. We wore our masks in public. We social distanced. We followed the science. And we'd all stayed healthy.

For the kid's education, Meg had begun teaching Andy and Allie at home. That had begun in Minneapolis before we'd moved up here to the Northwoods. Since January, she'd continued their homeschooling, plus she'd taken in Sam and Willow, our friend's kids. But now we were deep into the second year of the pandemic. The children were older, life was moving forward and the big question was this: were we were doing what was best for the kids? Especially, Andy.

Meg posed it this way: "If there was no pandemic, what would we do? Homeschool or send Andy to public school."

I was raised in the public school system. So was Meg. I had no problem answering the question. "I'd vote for public school. Good teachers. A variety of subjects. And…" I held up one finger to make my point. "Socialization. I think it's important for kids to be around other kids."

"I agree," Meg said. "Especially kids from different walks of life and cultures."

In Minneapolis, the public schools were filled with children of different races and cultures, and both Meg and I agreed that it was a good thing for Andy and Allie to be exposed to a diverse mix of kids. However, in Minneapolis as in throughout the state, all of the schools had been locked down for most of 2020 and the first half of 2021. Now, with the new school year approaching and vaccines being available, the restrictions had become less, shall we say, restricted, and schools were opening up again. Though not without some controversy I might add.

"So," I asked Megan again, for what seemed like the hundredth time that summer. "What do you think?"

"Well…" she took a deep breath and let it out. "I think we should let him go. I think we should send Andy to school."

"You sure?"

"Yes," she said. But then she added. "But I'd feel more comfortable if we could talk to his teacher."

I agreed. "That's a great idea." We hugged each other. He was our first born and letting him go wasn't going to be easy. But it was the best thing to do. Even under the specter of the pandemic.

The Park Rapids Elementary School was a single-story, light tan, brick building that housed students in classes one through five. It had been built in the fifties after the original building had been torn down. We found this out when we talked with Mrs. Schaffhausen the week before classes were scheduled to begin.

"Yes, it's a good old building," she said that morning when met in her classroom. "It's seen a lot, that's for sure."

She told us to call her by her first name, Rose. She seemed nice. She was in her fifth year of teaching first graders. She was in her late twenties and had graduated from college north of us at Bemidji State. Her husband was employed by the public works department in town. They were both from the area. And, most importantly, as far as Meg and I were concerned, she wore a mask.

"Oh, yes," she said when we asked her about it. "Definitely I will be wearing a mask. The government is requiring it, and I totally agree with the policy."

Meg smiled behind her own mask. "That's great to hear."

"I'd wear it anyway," she added. "It's the right thing to do."

I was itching to ask if she'd been vaccinated but caught a glance from Meg. The kind of "keep your mouth shut" look she gave me so well. And so often.

Turns out I didn't need to ask.

"If you're wondering if I've had my shots, you can rest assured that I have," she told us. "I want to do everything I can to be safe. Especially…" she waved her hand around, "with the kids."

"Do all the teachers feel like you do?" I asked, looking at Meg. She nodded in agreement with my question.

"Oh, yes," Rose answered. "Our principal, John Lipton, requires it."

I looked at Meg. I could see her smiling. "That's great," she said. "And I'm assuming the kids wear masks, too."

"Yes. Masks for the kids." She pointed around the room. "I've got the desks spread out so we can social distance as much as we can. Same with lunchtime. And recess."

The more she talked with us, the more comfortable we felt. This was going to work out pretty well.

We were getting ready to leave when Rose asked, "If I may, what has Andy been doing for learning in the last year?"

"I've been teaching him at home," Meg said. She pointed north. "We live in Esker."

"So, homeschooling?"

"Yes. It's been working out pretty well. I've had Andy and his sister. Allie turns four next month. Plus, two children of friends of ours."

Rose gave Meg a serious look and asked, "Would you be willing to help out here in the classroom? We're always looking for volunteers."

Meg shook her head. "No, I'm sorry. I've also got a job. I'm an editor for an independent publishing company."

I have to give it to Rose, she actually looked sad. "I'm so sorry to hear that. But..." she brightened up, "at least you've got a job."

Then she looked at me. "How about you? Would you be willing to volunteer?"

I glanced at Meg and she raised her eyebrows. I could her mind working: You? A teacher's aide? In her mind, I'm sure she was thinking that I wasn't the most qualified for the position. I didn't have a lot of disciplinary skills and tended to enjoy playing with the kids rather than teaching them anything. Still... I was interested.

"What would it require?" I asked.

"You just need to be here with me. Help out. Make sure they're working on their assignments. Monitor that they are social distancing. Read to them."

I have to say, it sounded like something I could handle. I look at Meg. "What do you think?"

She grinned. I could tell she thought it was a good idea. "If you want, go for it."

"How often do I need to be here?"

"As often as you want. But usually just one day a week."

It was September. I still had wood to get in for the winter, which Jack and Arnie were going to help me with. I still worked at the gas station. But I could do it. The more I thought about it, the more I wanted to do it. I could be with Andy. I could be part of helping everyone get through the pandemic. Yeah, this could work. I'd make it work.

"I'll do it," I told her.

"Great." She smiled. We bumped elbows. "Welcome aboard."

After our meeting, Meg and I picked up some groceries and drove home. The kids were staying with Amber, and on our way there Meg turned from staring out the passenger's window and said to me, "So, what do you think?"

"About Andy and school? I think it's going to work out just fine. Rose seems nice. I think this'll be a good thing for him."

"Actually, I was thinking about you assisting. How's that going to go?"

"I think good." I glanced at her. "Why?" We had turned off the highway and were heading down the first of many dirt roads on the way to Amber's.

She shrugged her shoulders as the car bumped along. "I don't know. You've always been a loner. You prefer your own company to that of other people. You'll be around kids all day long. And they'll be a lot of teachers around." She looked at me and added, to make her point. "You know, they'll be lots of people there."

Well, she did have a point, but I did, too. I said, "You know, living up here has taught me a lot. I've learned to cut wood, plant a garden, and can blueberries, among other things. I worked in a lab by myself for ten years. Now, I'm working at a gas station waiting on people three days a week for five hours a day."

"So, what are you getting at?"

"My point is that I'm different, Meg." I took my eyes off the road and glanced at her. "I'm not the same as I used to be back in the city." I turned to refocus on driving and steering around potholes. It wasn't the best road. "Living up here, I feel that we are part of our little community, and I want to give something back. Helping out down at the school is the least I can do." I turned to her and grinned. "I sound like I'm giving some kind of a speech for the chamber of commerce, don't I?"

Meg leaned over and kissed me. "Yeah, you do, but that's okay." She paused and then said. "I only hope Andy doesn't mind."

We stopped at Amber's and picked up the kids and

headed home. Meg told Andy about Mrs. Schaffhausen and he was ecstatic.

"I get to be with other kids? Yippee!"

"And…" his mom said. "Your dad is going to help out one day a week. How do you feel about that?"

Andy looked at Meg. Then he looked at me. Then he said, "Awesome."

I smiled. I had a feeling I'd made the right decision.

October

October was a busy month.

We put the garden to bed which meant we dug out our potatoes and harvested our herbs and turned over the soil and got it ready for next year. Our lettuce and kale and cabbage we had harvested and eaten as the season progressed so there was none of that to store. All in all, the garden had been a moderate success.

"It's all about the soil," Arnie kept telling Meg and me throughout the short summer growing season. "We had good soil in there. Next year it'll be even better."

"Thanks so much for helping us with it," I told him time and time again that summer. The day he and Jack had helped build the garden frame and we'd put in the rich, black soil mixed with horse manure stood out in my mind. It'd been great to work with them.

Our cabin had a root cellar and that's where we put the potatoes and the herbs were hung in the kitchen. The effect was to make our little cabin smell fragrant and homey.

School was going well for Andy. He loved being around the other kids and made friends easily. It was good to see him learning to get along with other kids his age, not just his sister and their friends Sam and Willow.

My day for assisting was Monday, so we drove down

together and I helped out and we drove home together. Volunteering was a decision I never regrated. It was fun working with the kids, twenty-four first graders in all. Mrs. Schaffhausen (I never could get used to calling her "Rose" like she wanted me) ran a tight ship. We had learning activities all day long: word study (reading), math (learning "our numbers"), technology (using school-issued iPads for learning activities and even some games), along with art, music, storytime, recess, and lunch. The class was from 9:30 am to 3:30 pm and the time went by fast.

Meg continued working with Allie who was now four years old and Sam who was also four and Willow who was now five and could have gone to kindergarten but Amber wanted her to be homeschooled by Meg and that was fine with her. And us.

Meg also continued editing for Charlotte's Press and I continued working three days a week at the gas station. In the back of our minds was the as-yet unanswered question: What were we going to do when our lease ran out at the end of December? Our landlady had intimated that we could continue renting if we wanted to. "I've had no takers on selling the damn thing," was the way she put it, referring to our cabin. But Meg and I still didn't know what we were going to do. We still had a couple of months to decide so we put the decision on the back burner.

Until then, the one thing we did decide, because we knew we'd have to, anyway, was that we'd have to have firewood wood for heat. So that's what I did. With the help of Jack and Arnie. They set aside some time from their busy schedule and met me at 7:00 am at the cabin the first week of October.

"Okay, buddy. Let's get you set for the winter," Jack said pulling up with his pickup. The morning was crisp and cool, in the high thirties. He wore Carhart overall over an insulated undershirt that poked up from his red and black checked wore shirt. He wore knee-high leather boots and a black wool watch cap. I had on jeans, hunting boots, long underwear shirt, flannel shirt, hooded sweatshirt and an insulated vest. On my head, I wore a stocking hat like Jack's.

He gave me the once-over.

"All set?"

"All set."

"Good. It's a good day to cut wood. Nice and cool. Believe me, you'll work up a sweat in no time."

I grinned. "Sounds good to me."

He pointed. "Arnie's driving the big truck."

The big truck was the loading truck with the claw crane on it that they used in their pulp wood business. Arnie tooted the horn and stuck his head out the window. "All set?" he waved.

I waved back. "I am."

Jack climbed in the big pickup. "You can ride shotgun with me. Let's go."

I climbed into the warm cab and off we went.

Their permit to cut was in the Chippewa Forest about ten miles north and west of Esker. They worked with the Department of Natural Resources to do what was called selective cutting. The DNR would identify areas in the forest that needed to be thinned out and Jack and Arnie did the rest. The idea was to manage the forest for sustained growth and not clear-cut the timber like happened with many other pulp woodcutters.

As we drove, Jack pointed to a cup holder between us. "There's coffee if you want." There were two large coffees from down the road at the gas station where I worked. I gratefully took a sip.

“Thanks.”

“No problem.” Jack turned onto the highway and we were off. “So what are you going to do?” He asked coming up to speed, the truck humming along.

I’d been looking out the window, sipping my coffee, and watching the forest speed by. “What do you mean?”

“About staying up here. Linn told me you and Meg’s lease was up at the end of December.”

“It is.”

“Well, what are you going to do.”

The thing I liked about Jack, and Arnie, too, for that matter is that there were no-nonsense guys. If something needed to be done, say build a garden frame for our garden last summer, they just did it. They’d talk about it, sure, but it got done. Same with their business. If they had a stand of trees to thin, they’d work long hours to get the job completed. Only when the last tree was cut, hauled out of the forest, loaded onto the truck, and driven to the pulp mill would they consider sitting back and resting. I admired that in them.

“Meg and I are talking about it.”

He glanced at me, turning off the highway and onto a dirt road, one of the hundreds if not thousands in the country. “December is only a couple of months away.”

Looking at it from Jack’s perspective, he and Linn would have already decided what to do. Probably months ago. I had an idea. “What would you do,” I asked. “If you were Meg and me?”

He slowed the pickup and pointed the big truck straight down the road and was quiet for a minute, sipping his coffee and thinking. Finally, he said, “Well, it’s your decision you know.”

“Of course. I know that. I’m just wondering what you and Linn would do.”

"You moved up here to get away from the pandemic, right?"

"Yeah."

"But the pandemic is still here." He waved his hand. "It's all over."

He was right. As many people had died in 2021 as in 2020. "Yeah, I know."

He glanced at me again. "So, from my perspective, living up here can't be about the pandemic anymore."

I recently read an article about people like us. The article poked fun at what they called "The Escapees" – people who moved away from the city to get away from the pandemic leaving home and friends behind. People like us.

"I hear you," I said. I did, too. It was what Meg and I were grappling with.

Jack waved his arm. "I love it up here. So does Linn. So does Sam. It's our home. I could never leave it. We were born and raised up here." He turned to me. "Our friends are here."

I had to ask. "Do you think we did a wrong thing by moving up here?"

He sipped his coffee and slowed the truck to turn to the right. He drove another hundred yards and took a left. We were deep in the pine forest now. The sun was coming up over the trees and the sky was clear blue, not a cloud in it.

"Do I think you made a mistake?"

He looked at me. "No, I don't. You did what you thought you needed to do. What was best for your family, especially Andy and Allie." I liked Jack a lot. I admired his confident way about how he lived his life. Linn, too. They were what I used to call the "Salt of the Earth" people. People close to the land. People who were independent-minded and could fend for themselves. Way different than me.

"I appreciate that."

He turned again onto another dirt road. "That being said," he grinned at me. "I'm not you. And you still have to decide what to do." He paused and turned onto a two-track road that led deeper into the forest. The trees were close to us on each side. I turned. Arnie's big truck barely fit. But it did. I had to admit, the guys knew what they were doing.

We drove another quarter of a mile to a clearing. Jack parked the pickup and got out and joined Arnie. I stood next to them and listened to them strategize what they called "The Cut". Then, off we went. We drove the pickup about another quarter mile into the woods. We got out and the guys pointed out the trees they were going to cut and they cut them down. My job was to use my chainsaw and trim the branches of the downed trees. We were cutting birch because it was the best wood to heat our stove with.

When the trees were cut and trimmed, we hauled them to the pickup and loaded them in the back. Then we drove the pickup to the big truck and Arnie used the crane to load the logs onto the flatbed. We stopped occasionally for water and once for a big lunch that Linn had fixed of fried chicken, ham sandwiches on her homemade bread, and blueberry muffins made with the blueberries we'd picked last month with Amber. By the end of the day, the big truck was fully loaded.

We took a minute to catch our breath and check out our work.

"There are about ten cords of wood there, Lee," Arnie said, pointing to the big truck. The arm of the crane was resting over the top of it to hold it in place.

"Should last you all winter," Jack added, giving me a knowing smile. The implication was clear, the words unspoken. *If you're still here.*

We had all stripped down to just our undershirts, and

even they were soaked in sweat. But we'd worked as a team, and we'd gotten the job done.

"Thanks so much, you guys," I said, pulling my flannel shirt on. Now that we had stopped working, we were cooling off. It was about forty-five degrees and the forecast was for frost overnight. I was glad to get the wood. We'd unload it tomorrow and I'd start cutting it up and getting ready for winter.

I wasn't sure what we were going to be doing about moving up north for good, or moving back to the city, but I did know one thing. We'd need firewood soon for heat. I had to get busy.

November

We got our booster shots earlier this month. Yea! And Andy got his first Covid shot. Double, yea! But people are still dying, and the pandemic is still raging on.

Amber, who was a vehement non-mask-wearing anti-vaxxer when we'd first met her in the early part of the year, has become a huge advocate of following "The Science". It's good to see.

"I just don't get it," she said recently when she and Arnie and Linn and Jack and Meg and I were doing something we'd never done before – having a meal together in a restaurant. Yeah, in a restaurant.

I guess I should explain.

The place is called Margie's. Margie is an old hippie who went to college at Bemidji State back in the 60s and fell in love with a local woodworker. So she stayed. Born and raised in Atlanta, she also fell in love with the Northwoods and the pretty college town situated on the shore of Lake Bemidji. She loved to cook and opened a restaurant in an old brick building downtown and slowly built a loyal clientele of customers who liked her hearty food, cooked with an eye for detail and a touch of whimsy. Her sweet potato fries are still a huge local favorite. And she still works there, as do her two daughters and two sons.

We three couples had decided to treat ourselves to a meal out just for the fun of it. Meg had made reservations we'd all driven up Saturday afternoon in mid-November. We were now chatting, sitting around a scarred, wooden table with Native American flute music playing through speakers hung in the corners. The place had an aroma of herbs and grains and natural ingredients that was mouth-watering. It was like stepping back in time.

It was also one of the few places around that required masks for its employees and customers. At least until we were seated. That was a big reason why we'd made the choice. That and the chance to get out and sample some different food other than our own cooking. That didn't hurt either.

We all leaned in as Amber continued talking. "It's obvious that without the vaccine your chances of dying are like ten times greater. Plus…" she pointed to our four kids who were ignoring us and playing a game of Candy Land on the floor in a specially designated Kids Section of the restaurant. "What about them?" she asked, rhetorically.

"I know," Linn added. She, like Amber, had been on the anti-mask, anti-vaccine bandwagon until she and Meg had talked. Now, she was all about being safe and doing what could be done to keep the kids safe. She, too, looked at the four kids. "It just makes sense." She then turned to her husband. "Right, Jack?"

Jack nodded and sipped on his glass of water. Normally extremely talkative if it was just me and him, he took a back seat whenever we six adults were together. So did Arnie, Amber's husband, both of them being content to let the

239

conversation flow around them. "Absolutely," he said. He looked at Arnie. "Right?"

Arnie nodded. "Right." Then he bit into his black bean burger. "Oh, man. This is the best," he said, chewing ecstatically. Then he looked at Amber. "Almost as good as yours." He winked at her.

Amber playfully slugged him in the arm. Three months pregnant, she was starting to show. "You better believe it."

We all laughed.

Meg interjected. "Down at Lee's school, they wear masks all the time. Not all the parents like it, but they comply for the good of the kids. No one wants to go back to distance learning if they can help it. That was a disaster."

I jumped in. "Most of the parents see the value of having their kids with other kids. That socialization is really important. Studies show it."

Linn asked, "What about the parents who don't comply?"

"That's up to them," I said, holding off on shoveling some sweet potato hash into my mouth. "They know the rules." I shoveled it in and chewed, like Arnie, ecstatically. We were loving having some different food for a change.

Meg added. "That's what I like about the school district down there. They set the rules and enforce them. It's not about the politics of masking and vaccinating, it's about what's doing what's best for the kids." She took a bit of her soybean burger and chewed, having made her point.

"Here! Here!" Jack finally spoke up and raised his glass of water. "I'll drink to that." We all laughed and raised our water glasses and toasted with him.

The meal went on like that, good friends just chatting. The kids wandered over and munched on some of what their parents were having, plus a big plateful of onion rings and one of sweet potato fries. It was a fun time.

Before we ordered dessert, I looked at Meg. She smiled at me and then turned to our friends. "Okay, while we're all together, Lee and I have something we'd like to say to you all." I looked at Jack. He returned the look, thinking back, I'm sure to our conversation the month before when we were cutting wood. About whether or not Meg and I would stay up north or move back to the city at the end of December.

Meg continued. "You know that our lease is up next month."

Linn interrupted. "So, have you decided what you're going to do?"

Meg, who never blushes, blushed, turning beet red. "Well…"

Amber excitedly jumped in. "What? Meg. What are you going to do?"

Meg turned to me. "Lee, you tell them."

I looked at Jack and Arnie. They were both grinning at me like they knew. No need to beat around the bush with them. I grinned back at them and spread my arms wide, encompassing the entire table. "We're staying."

Just as the words came out of my mouth, I had a horrible thought. My thought was this: what if they aren't happy that we're staying? Meg and I had talked about it a lot, especially during the last month, about what we wanted to do. When we decided to stay, sell our house in Minneapolis and move to Esker permanently, we thought our friends would be happy for us. But… what if they weren't?

I needn't have worried. As soon as I spoke the words, "We're staying" their cheers told me otherwise. They were happy. Ecstatic, actually. For us and for themselves. It was a great feeling.

For Meg and me, it all came down to this: Friendship. Sure, we'd first moved up north to get away from the pandemic. We figured if we moved to a less populated place, the chances were minimized of us getting Covid and getting sick, especially our kids. We masked up and social distanced ourselves in the city. What was the difference in doing that in the little town of Esker? Frankly, not much. In fact, in many ways, it was worse. Even though there were fewer people up north, those fewer people were independent-minded and didn't like people or the government telling them what to do. Like Jack and Linn and Arnie and Amber. But we'd become friends because of our kids and, because of their kids, Meg was able to convince them that the scientific evidence for the best way to deal with Covid was sound. They turned around in their thinking and the more time we spent with them the better friends we became.

So, when it came time to consider going back to Minneapolis next year at the beginning of 2022 it all boiled down to this: did we want to leave our friends behind?

Meg and Linn and Amber were very close. Meg took care of Sam and Willow five days a week while their mothers worked at their jobs. Jack and Arnie and I spent a lot of time together and though I wasn't as close to them as Meg and Linn and Amber, we still got along well and enjoyed each other's company. I was a loner by nature but was becoming less so the more time I spend with the two of them.

So, yes, that's what it came down to – leave our friends behind and move back to Minneapolis, or stay in Esker and keep building our new life in Northern Minnesota.

As Meg put it, "When all is said and done, the pandemic eventually will go away. Friendships, though, can be forever."

Which is what I said to the table that Saturday afternoon.

Jack laughed. "That's kind of poetic, Lee."

I pointed to Meg. "It's Meg's line."

Jack said, giving me a hard time. "I thought so."

Arnie leaned over and shook my hand. An unexpected, but nevertheless, much-appreciated gesture. "That's great news, Lee. I'm glad."

I don't know why, but knowing Jack and Arnie, two guys I admired greatly, were glad about our decision, really made me happy. I looked at Meg. She wiped a tear from her eye just before both Linn and Amber stood up and hugged her.

Jack shook my hand like Arnie had and said, "We'll make a woodman out of you yet."

All three of us laughed. It was a good feeling.

December

"Well, that's it," I said to Meg. "Done deal."

She looked over my shoulder. "The purchase agreement?"

"Yep, signed, sealed, and delivered."

She hugged me. "Great!

And with that, the circle had been completed. Our home in Minneapolis had been sold. Pretty easy all the way around.

My brother had been watching the house while we'd been renting our cabin in the small town of Esker. Every now and then a realtor would leave a card on the door asking him (or someone) to connect them. Just for fun, he started doing it. In September, I got a call from him.

"Lee. I've got to tell you. If you are thinking of selling, now's the time."

So, Meg and I talked about it. We'd already decided to stay in Esker. Now the decision even made more sense. Why rent for another year when we could use the proceeds from the sale and buy the cabin? The conversation didn't take long. The Minneapolis house went on the market on November first, and five days later it sold for ten percent above the asking price. The realtor was happy. The new owners were happy. We, of course, we ecstatic.

"What's next? Meg asked, referring to the sale. We were working together in the kitchen making dinner. I was doing the spaghetti and Meg was putting together a salad.

"Nothing, really. The paperwork is all done. We just need to go down to Minneapolis and pack up everything."

Meg paused in cutting up some carrots. "What do we need?"

"What do mean?"

"From the house. What do we need?"

"Well…" I started to say, but then I thought about it. She had a point.

"We've been living here for nearly a year. We've got everything that's necessary, right? Even our photos and keepsakes and things like that."

I thought about it some more. She was correct. Everything we needed was right with us. "You're right," I said dumping the noodles into a colander in the sink. "What are you thinking?"

"I've looked into it online. We could hire a company to sell everything in the house and donate the rest. They can even clean it out for the new owners."

"Wouldn't that be expensive?"

"Sort of. But we can pay for it with the proceeds of the sale. Plus," she added. "It might be hard. You know, emotionally, to go back."

She had a good point. We hadn't been to Minneapolis and our old house since we'd moved out last January. The longer we were away, the more our roots were spreading in the north county. Honestly, I felt the same way as Meg did.

The more we talked about it, the more it made sense to make a clean break. "Do you have a number to call?"

"Yep."

"Let's do it."

Now, it really was a done deal.

Our landlady Gladys Hawkinson was as happy to sell the cabin as we were to buy. It'd been on the market when we contacted her last December in 2020 about renting, and it was still on the market now. I gave her a call once we'd decided to sell just to make sure she was still keen to sell the cabin. She was. We put earnest money down and went ahead with the sale of the Minneapolis house. With that done and with the house taken care of the final step was to contact her and finalize the sale. I called her that night to set up a meeting.

"Okay," I said, hanging up the phone. "All set."

"When?"

"Tomorrow. Wednesday."

"Great."

The next morning we loaded the kids in the car and left our little cabin. We followed a well-known (to us, anyway) gravel road through the woods and dropped our daughter Allie off with our good friend Amber. "Good luck," she said, coming out to meet us when we pulled up. She was showing even more with the new baby. She gave us each a hug. "Take your time." We waved her hand. "I'll be right here. Good luck with the closing."

Allie ran off to play with Willow who was building a snow fort near their barn. Over the year they'd become fast friends and it was good to see them getting along so well. We'd been getting snow off and on since before Thanksgiving and there was at least a foot of it on the ground. All the locals were saying it was not only going to be a white Christmas but one with a higher-than-average amount of snow.

"Thanks again," Meg said. "We'll be back as soon as we can."

It started snowing as soon as we left Amber. Her and Arnie's place was deep in the pine forest northwest of our cabin. I drove us five miles through the woods and out to the highway where I pointed us south to Park Rapids. By the time we dropped Andy off at school and made it to the office of Northwoods Reality where Gladys was meeting us, the roads were covered with an inch of snow and it was coming fast.

The wind was picking up, too, and we fought it getting from the Honda across the parking lot to the office. Sandy Bergeson, who was doing the closing met us.

"Cold out," she said, holding the door for us. She'd been waiting. "Let's get this deal done and then all of us should head home. The forecast is for a blizzard."

Our first thought was Andy. "What about school?" Meg asked.

Sandy glanced at the clock on the wall. It was 9:45 am. "I heard they were going to be closing by noon."

I looked at Meg. "Let's get the papers signed and pick him up on the way home."

"Absolutely."

Gladys walked up and joined us from Sandy's office in the back. She lived in Park Rapids and didn't have far to drive. Still, she'd lived in the north country all her life and she knew a bad storm when she saw one.

"Let's get going," was all she said. "I want to get home."

We sat around a conference table and got the papers signed and notarized (by Sandy) and in fifteen minutes we had ourselves our own new home.

"Congratulations," Sandy said after the last of the documents had been signed. She shook Meg's hand and then mine. "Welcome to the northland."

I have to say, it felt really good to hear her say that.

Gladys spoke up. "Okay, if that's it, I'm going to get going." She looked at Meg and me. "You two should, too."

"That's right," Sandy said, organizing the papers. She

put ours in a large envelope and gave it to us. "These are for you."

Meg took the envelope and put it in her oversized shoulder bag. "That's it?"

"Yep," Sandy said. "That's it." Then she looked out through the front window of the office. "You guys better hit the road."

I followed her sightline. The snow was falling so fast, I couldn't see the car. "Come on, Meg." I grabbed her hand. "Let's get going."

After one more round of quick handshakes, we left the office to get Andy. Or tried to. The school was only a few blocks from us but it took fifteen minutes. The snow was blowing so hard that it was impossible to see more than twenty feet. I drove slowly, the heater and defroster on full blast. It worked to melt the snow on the windshield but the temperature was dropping and some of the melted snow turned to ice making it hard to keep the windshield clear. Which, of course, made it hard to drive.

We picked up Andy and carefully drove through town back out to the highway and turned north. The snow was falling so fast and the wind was blowing so hard that traffic was crawling along at only about 30 miles per hour. Which was good, because I had no desire to drive faster. The road was icy, and the Honda even with front-wheel drive lost traction occasionally and slipped close to the shoulder. I tried not to think about what would happen if we spun off the road and ended up in the ditch. It could be hours before anyone found us.

Fortunately, there were also some cars and trucks out, probably heading home to beat the storm like we were, and there were a set of tire tracks in front of me that I could follow. Thank, god. It was slow going, but we eventually made it to Amber's. It was what we call a *white knuckle drive* all the way, and my whole body was one tightly wound bundle of nerves when we got there.

Arnie's truck was in the driveway. He'd been out already and plowed out a large parking area and that's where we parked. Meg had texted Amber when we were close to their home and she and Arnie and Willow ran out to greet us when we pulled in.

"Thank goodness you're safe," Amber exclaimed, embracing Meg and Andy. Arnie came up and put his arm around me in a rare form of affection. "You okay?" he asked.

"Yeah," I said, taking Andy by the hand and stomping through at least 12 inches of snow to go inside and warm up. "It's good to be here."

Arnie brushed snow off the shoulders of his coat and grinned. "It's good to have you."

Half an hour later, after warming up, we secured Allie and Andy in the back seat, left our friends, and drove to our cabin. The snow was falling straight down but one of the county plows had been out and we made it home in good shape. I was able to park the Honda fairly close to the cabin and we tramped through the snow to the back door. I used a shovel to move the snow away and we went inside. "Our new home!" Andy called out as we all struggled out of our snowy clothes.

We all smiled. In spite of the drive through the blizzard, we'd made it safely. That was the main thing. The only thing, frankly.

After dinner, we play *Candyland* and *Shoots and Ladders* with the kids and got them to bed. We tidied up the living room and stoked the fire in the stove and then sat on the couch to relax. Meg sipped her nightly glass of red wine and I had a cup of chamomile tea.

She turned to me. "Well, Lee. What do you think?"

I was still thinking about driving through the blizzard.

I'd never experienced anything like that before in my life. I blinked to focus on what she was saying. "What do you mean?"

She set her glass down. "I mean about moving here. For good. You think we made the right decision?"

I thought about it. We'd moved up here to get away from the pandemic and give our kids a chance at not getting infected. Which had worked. They still hadn't gotten Covid and that was a good thing. Andy was vaccinated and maybe next year Allie would be, too. But now there was a new variant in the mix, Omicron. People were still dying, mostly unvaccinated, but the point was that the pandemic was still with us. Probably for a long time. So moving north to escape the pandemic hadn't worked. When all was said and done, we'd been incredibly naïve.

But we'd done what we thought was the best move at the time and that was the important thing. I'd lost my job and we'd taken our best shot, (sorry for the bad pun) and something wonderful had happened. Our lives had changed for the better. Andy was in school and was making friends. Allie and Willow and Sam were the best friends one could ever imagine. Meg's daycare was going well and her job as an editor for Charlotte's Press was going great. I was making some money for us at the gas station, and I loved volunteering at Andy's school. So that was all well and good.

But the main thing was our newly formed relationships. In the city, neither Meg nor I had many friends. We were the kind of people who enjoyed time alone or with our little family; it was all we needed. But things had changed since we moved north. In a big way. We'd found friendship in the unlikeliest way, with Jack and Linn and Arnie and Amber, four amazingly wonderful people. People who became our friends. People who, in the end, were the real reason we'd decided to stay.

I turned to Meg and said, "What do I think?" I grinned and hugged her. "I think it's the best thing we've ever done."

She smiled. "Well, maybe not the best thing. But right up there."

Surprised, I looked at her. "What do mean? I thought you liked it here. You're still on board with the move and everything? Right?"

She laughed. "Oh, I am. I definitely am."

"What then?" In response, she took my hand and put it on her stomach. My eyes went wide. "Really? You're pregnant?"

"Yep. I just found out. Baby's due in August."

I hugged her and we embraced for a long time. Our little family was getting bigger. I couldn't think of a better place for that to happen.

"I'm super glad," I told her.

She kissed me. "Me, too." Then she looked at me. "Next year is going to be a great year."

I hugged her. "It really is," I said.

Then we kissed some more.

About the Author

Jim lives in the small town of Long Lake twenty miles west of Minneapolis, Minnesota. He has held many jobs in his life, the longest being twenty years as a course developer and training instructor for a large manufacturing company. After he retired, he worked in a garden center and then became part owner of a small gift shop. In 2015, he made the commitment to follow his dream of becoming a writer and started to seriously write fiction. Since then, his stories and poems have appeared in nearly 500 online and print publications. He was nominated for the 2021 Pushcart Prize by *The Zodiac Review* for his flash fiction story *Aliens.* His first collection of short stories *Resilience* was published in February 2021, by Bridge House Publishing. In August 2021, *Short Stuff* a collection of drabbles and flash fiction was published by Chapeltown Books. Since then his publications include five collections of short stories, two novellas, two novels, one collection of poetry, and one collection of haiku. His books are all available on Amazon as well as through independent publishers. You can check out his blog to read more of his stories and to learn more about him at: www.theviewfromlonglake.wordpress.com.

Like to Read More Work Like This?

Then sign up to our mailing list and download our free collection of short stories, *Magnetism*. Sign up now to receive this free e-book and also to find out about all of our new publications and offers.

Sign up here:
  http://eepurl.com/gbpdVz

Please Leave a Review

Reviews are so important to writers. Please take the time to review this book. A couple of lines is fine.

Reviews help the book to become more visible to buyers. Retailers will promote books with multiple reviews.

This in turn helps us to sell more books… And then we can afford to publish more books like this one.

Leaving a review is very easy.

Go to https://amzn.to/3OxRHto, scroll down the left-hand side of the Amazon page and click on the "Write a customer review" button.

Other Writing by Jim Bates

Resilience

Published by Bridge House

Remembrance Day is special for one grandfather. Which story of him and his brother at the lake will John remember today? Blake loves his garden but he's not so sure about the rabbit. Tyler stands up to his dad while hunting crows. What really did happen in the room at the Inn on the Lake? Why doesn't Quinn run away anymore?

"Resilience is an absolute gem. A collection of twenty-seven beautifully written short stories that deal with the central theme of its title." (Amazon)

Order from Amazon:

ISBN: 978-1-914199-00-4 (paperback)
978-1-914199-01-1 (ebook)

Short Stuff
Published by Chapeltown

This is a short sharp collection of well-told stories by Jim Bates who once again brings us some evocative writing with a strong literary voice. We meet a plethora of characters, each with their own concerns and triumphs. They face life's challenges and often have to turn situations around. Will they succeed? Will they make life good again?

In this collections of flash fiction, Jim Bates packs a lot of story into a few words.

"You will not want to put this gem down." (Amazon)

Order from Amazon:

ISBN: 978-1-910542-78-1 (paperback)
978-1-910542-79-8 (ebook)

Chapeltown Books

Praise for Resilience

"Reading the 27 stories in *Resilience*, the collection of short stories by Jim Bates, is like listening to one heartfelt tune after another being sung by 27 singers and never hearing an off-note. This is writing at its finest, where fiction is so well hidden in the life-affirming stories – a hallmark that almost defines Jim's writing – that it's easy to forget that the plots and characters aren't real. In *Resilience* relationships aren't merely vehicles for moving a story forward; they are the raison d'être. These are stories about husbands and wives, parents and children, grandparents and their grandchildren, brothers, and friends, both young and old, and even a few animals. Not one of them in the entire collection feels fake or contrived, which is incredible. It's hard not to think that each character isn't someone Jim knew or knows. There's no exaggerated soap opera or melodrama between the characters or in the stories. People live, die, are loved, missed and mourned, as if they stepped out of the photographs and obituaries in real family scrap books and photo albums. The tension and conflict in many of the stories hums just beneath the surface, but the focus is on the small moments in the lives of the characters, which perfectly mirrors our own lives. The drama and tragedies that exist in some of the stories never overwhelms the plot and never wanders into unrealistic territory.

"*Resilience* is a mix of Thorton Wilder's *Our Town*, Edgar Lee Masters' *Spoonriver Anthology*, with just a touch of a subdued J.D. Salinger thrown in. I didn't do a word count, of course, but I think there are at least three novelette-length stories included in the collection, the quasi-crime story *Sugarfoot* being my favorite among them. I can easily see Norman Rockwell doing the illustrations to Jim's stories, which is particularly true of his stories about boys coming-of-age, especially in this collection as a companion to *The Last Time I Ran Away.* Jim knows the landscapes that serve both as backdrops and center pieces to his stories; his descriptions of places in Minnesota and North Dakota are written art pieces all their own. I highly recommend Jim's collection."

> *Brilliant author Steven Lester Carr had many books published in his sadly shortened lifetime. He was also an incredible mentor to many aspiring writers, myself included. He left us in 2022. May you forever rest in peace, Steve.*

Praise for Short Stuff

"*Short Stuff* by Jim Bates is a book of wonderfully heart-warming short stories. Jim's words will touch you with joy, sorrow, love, loss, and every emotion there is. Each story will introduce you to characters that will become your friends, neighbors, and family. I loved each and every story in this book. I could not pick a favorite, but will mention a few. In *Soap Bubbles* the warmth of a loving family allows an aging grandfather feel youthful and happy again. In Pancakes a young lad tries to make breakfast for his mother, who is going through a hard time. The story is so real-to-life, that you will believe it is happening to someone you know. Fear of Snakes shows the almost-humorous side of relationships, as one person tries their best to accept the quirkiness of another.

"Each short read in this book is a look into the wonderfully creative mind of Jim Bates, and how he treasures stories surrounding human relationships. Since the stories are all between one and four pages long, you can pick the book up and put it down as you need to. But, believe me, you will not want to put this little gem down."

Acclaimed poet Ann Christine Tabaka has published 18 collections of poetry. Her most recent is entitled Children of the Storm.

"Jim Bates does it again with a truly delightful little book of flash fiction and drabbles. From the cheerful cover to the end, this book is chock full of short stories and drabbles, all of them thought-provoking and entertaining. Some stories are gentle and soothing, like a cup of tea on a cold afternoon. Others pack a punch, showing the darker side of life, but always with a dash of kindness. One of my favorites was *The Magic Of Butterflies*. It is touching and dreamy, and the concept of coming back after death into the form of a butterfly to see one's loved ones, is a desire held by all. Jim weaves stories of redemption, hope and love throughout this book, just the right size to tuck in one's purse or back pack – sweet, short reminders of life that you will want to thumb through over and over again. I highly recommend this book!"

Award winning author Sharon Frame Gay's most recent publication is a collection of western themed short stories entitled The Wrong End of the Bullet.